LCG Worldwide, LLC
Copyright © 2023 by Koby L. Bowie
Originally produced in the United States of America

Originally published on May 6th, 2023
Paperback ISBN: 979-8-9877748-3-0
Library of Congress Control Number: 2023904616

1842
Koby L. Bowie

For my parents.

A note from the author

My goal in creating this book is to inspire people to exceed expectations and rise from failure. Often times, people try to tell us who we are, which can either be right on the money or very inaccurate. But regardless, we all have the job of figuring out who we are for ourselves. In several ways, writing this book was a way that I figured out more of who *I* am. I have not read a great number of books, nor have I ever had the desire to do such a thing. Back in elementary school, I actually had to take special reading classes to get on track with the reading levels of my peers. In class, whenever I would read aloud, you could audibly detect the level of anxiety within me as I tried my best to read sentences with proper enunciation and tone. But *writing* is a different story. I have written very many papers over my academic lifetime (and still am writing them, at this point). Many teachers would give me praise on the way I put words together in my papers. Perhaps, that was me putting on paper what I failed to spew out in words. I always saw math as my best subject in school, but writing was always the most natural. Rarely did I ever stumble over different verb and noun forms, or how to detect differences in the various dialects of English. It all seemed simple to me. Even so, writing to beat out strict deadlines is entirely different from creating an entire novel. The level of thought, time, and effort it took was something I never thought I could accomplish. But now that it's done, I can whole-heartedly say that I love writing stories. I'm excited for you to see the raw enthusiasm and progression of my work. If you pay attention, you'll see the art of writing gradually become more apparent as you continue through the chapters. I'm sure that I'll be more polished cover to cover in my future pieces, but I'm so grateful for the sincerity of this one. Hopefully, it'll be a book that I look back on and appreciate the amount of courage and zeal I had while creating it.

Throughout the story, you will closely witness how these youthful characters process the labels and expectations that are projected upon them. Being a black man raised in Oklahoma City, I chose to create characters from a similar community that I was brought up in. But I understand that the issues they face are not things that other communities are immune to. The black experience is one thing – well, really, a spectrum. Yet, the *human* experience is of a much larger scale. It is my hope that people, from all places, will enjoy the story and process/apply the lessons within it in their own way. Several depictions will be things that are not necessarily the norm, and that, friends, is on purpose. I want to spark the creativity of minds, both young and old, to believe in accomplishing unbelievable feats and having a harmonious rhythm to life. I must add, however, that none of it is possible if you are not committed to putting in the necessary work and making consistent, healthy decisions. At many times, we are our best helper. In other moments, we are our worst enemy. Hopefully you purchased this book in route to figuring out how to be more of your helper than enemy. And if not, well then, I hope this story can help convince you to start doing so. Thank you for supporting me at this part of my life's journey. Enjoy the story, guys.

With gratitude, *Koby L. Bowie.*

CHAPTER 1: WHO IS SHAWN?

March 22nd, 2018 (present day)

"Failure is relative. Success is, too. All in all, it depends on your perspective in life and what you truly want for yourself. Vision, along with the courage to act it out, is all it takes." Lisa concluded.

"Well done, Lisa," said Mrs. Gates, the 10th-12th grade English teacher at Love High School. "Now, who would like to go next?"

Shawn Clement sunk into his seat. He hated giving speeches. It was not like talking to his friends at the mall or video chatting with a girl he asked out to dinner. In fact, he had asked Lisa out the week before, and she turned him down. It was not through direct message on social media, either. No, she turned him down in the middle of the commons during lunch period. Everyone knew about it. Lisa Webb, the smartest girl at Love High School and also, to many, the most drop-dead gorgeous, had turned down Shawn Clement, the number one baseball player in the country. Though still a junior, national sports media already rated him the favorite to be the number one pick of the 2019 professional draft. So yeah, Shawn could get any girl he wanted. At least, any girl not named Lisa Webb.

"Shawn, how about you?" Mrs. Gates asked.

"No, ma'am." He answered in embarrassment.

"Fine, but you *will* present today. I want the class to hear your brilliant work. Don't expect to be saved by the bell, sir."

After four other students presented, Shawn was finally forced against the ropes. He was the last one left to go. Wishing she had been wrong about the clock not saving him, he looked at the time. It read one o'clock – class ended at 1:15. There was no more evading it, and, thus, he went up to the podium. While up there, Shawn did all he could to avoid looking at Lisa, who had given the best presentation out of everyone who had gone. Her topic was The

Relativity of Success, and the entire class was moved by her words. Okay, everybody except Shawn. While she talked, all he could think about was the moment she rejected him. Plus, the fact that she was so beautiful made it worse. Her saying no made him want her even more, but he did his best to hide it.

Shawn's speech was entitled Facing Fear. It took him three hours to finish a five-page paper on the topic. While the rest of the class had bright-colored index cards to present with, Shawn had traditional white cards with blue lines. Only, instead of a blank back side, the backs were filled with baseballs. He loved the game. Incorporating it into his school efforts helped lessen his anxiety about executing various academic skills (public speaking, of course, in this case). Contemplating his decision to present, a spiral of nervousness ensued. Then, his eyes could not help but find Lisa Webb. When he beheld her, all he thought was, "Man, that girl is fine." Lisa grinned back at him as if she had heard him say it out loud. She then looked back at her desk, pretending that she was reading her notes. Immediately after, he thought, "Get yourself together, Shawn!" He took a deep breath. He closed his eyes for three seconds and then opened them up again. Finally, he began his speech.

"The fear of failure is a fact of life. Left unattended, it keeps us in the state of familiarity and comfortability. It is the toxin that restrains hopes and dreams from blossoming into something beautiful and great. No one is immune to this fear. I think it is fair to say that all of us here want to experience success of some sort. With that, I know we all have some level of fear about falling short of that success. Yeah, I get it. To most, I am the number one player in America, and it looks like I have it all together. But does that automatically make me a success? Do I not have more work to do? Am I like a superhero all of a sudden, completely desensitized to my own human soul? No. I still fear failure sometimes. Because, along with that failure, comes the one thing that no one welcomes. Rejection."

Hearing him, Lisa then looked down at the floor. Part of her was embarrassed for rejecting him, but she was more so concerned because someone else's speech had finally surpassed hers in terms of depth. Nonetheless, she was impressed. She and her classmates were witnessing a side of him that had never been seen before.

For the following five minutes, Shawn gave the best speech of his academic lifetime. After his final remarks, the class applauded him as he walked back to his desk in triumph. He knew that it was his speech – not Lisa's – that was the best of all. When the bell finally rang, Shawn, feeling scholarly, headed straight to his next class. He usually went to his locker or to the bathroom (or did anything else to take up the eight minutes of break time). Not in this moment, though. He was now eager to seize the rest of his school day. But little did he know that, during that same break time, Lisa had gone by his locker and waited for him. She wanted to congratulate him for delivering such a powerful piece. Though extremely respected for her academics, she was humble enough to give honor and credit where it was due. Yet, Shawn was no pushover. He knew when to withdraw his attention from a girl, even one as stunning as Lisa. He was secure enough to do so.

Shawn grew up in a town right on the northern side of Oklahoma City, named The Village. Love High School was only seven minutes southeast of where he lived. His dad, Marvin Clement, was one of the top financial advisors in the entire Bible Belt. A strict father, he always pushed Shawn to be the best at everything he did. Marvin's goal was to raise a future Ivy League valedictorian, a feat he himself had almost accomplished at Yale (he finished fourth, Economics major). Shawn was no super student, but he did well each year. And though he had a good feel for business and economy concepts, it was not the same as his father. In fact, the main thing that energized and inspired him to conquer academic challenges was baseball. He had been in love with the game for as long as he could remember. And contrary to those conventional stories you hear about baseball players wanting to please their dads through the game, Shawn drew his inspiration from a *different* well.

It was spring break of the 1999 school year. Marvin was just getting ready to catch his flight back to Connecticut, but his two best friends, Lewis Johnson and Quentin Carter, urged him to go catch a new comedy movie that had just dropped. Like Marvin, they were premier scholars from the OKC metro area. Quentin was going to Oklahoma State, while Lewis attended Wichita State. Even so, they all hung out for much of the break, discussing their first-year experiences at their respective schools. Both Quentin and Lewis long desired to go to Yale, but when Marvin got accepted in their stead, they were genuinely happy for him. Rarely did the three of them ever have a serious dispute. And if they did, they would resolve the conflict within the next day or so. They might as well have been blood brothers. Anyhow, going to see a show culminated their week together and, also, gave them something to piggyback on once the summer hit. They went to the theater that had just opened, right off the corner of MLK and I-44. Upon purchasing tickets, Marvin headed to the concessions desk to buy a pack of chocolate covered almonds and a strawberry soda. He had previously told himself he was done drinking pop, but his feelings of the occasion convinced him that it wouldn't hurt much. He was gonna have to wait a while, though, as the line was very full. Noticing this, Quentin, mild-mannered and gentle, immediately went and sat on the bench near the rooms entrance to wait for him. Meanwhile, Lewis, who was the opposite of Quentin attitude-wise, grew frustrated with Marvin. He did not like the fact that Marvin still wanted to wait in a line that seemed, in his mind, endless.

"Marvin, you could have brought snacks on the way. Let's go, I'm trying to actually see the movie before it ends. What are ya doin'?"

"Well, you're real funny. The line is moving quick, bro, just relax. Besides, I'm not holding you back with a rope and duct tape, keeping you away from the entrance. Go wait in there if it hurts too bad." Marvin answered.

"Whatever, guy." Lewis said, with an attitude.

Marvin smirked at him as he walked over to the bench and sat next to Quentin. Lewis hated being alone, and the fact that the three of them were so inseparable was therapeutic for him. Marvin and Quentin were the brothers he always wanted. Though he was quite impatient, being there with his best friends counteracted his restlessness.

Even so, Marvin stood in line for a good seventeen minutes – he was not a man who often went without what he desired. At the eighteenth minute, he finally made it to the line's front. He then walked up to the counter. Behind it was a young girl making popcorn for the next line over (to Marvin's right). She blended in well with the medium-lit space, as she was wearing a black long sleeve polo and black pants (she also wore a black visor hat). In waiting, Marvin glimpsed at her from behind – the *way* that most men typically do – but thought nothing more. A guy, wearing a nametag that read "SCORE," finally greeted him.

"What's up man, what can I get you?" The boy asked him.

"Hey, my man, I need a box of chocolate-covered almonds and a medium strawberry soda. Oh, is your name really Score?" Marvin replied.

"Gotcha, comin' right up. And yeah, it *really* is." Score answered.

"That is so cool." Marvin said, fascinated.

As Marvin watched him make his drink, the girl making popcorn finally turned around and returned to the desk. She stood about 5'8", with black hair that was short and curly. Skin as beautiful and vibrant as a L'Oréal model, mocha brown complexioned. Though she wore a visor, her eyes sparkled hazel everywhere she looked. And her shape was one akin to that of a world-class sprinter. Marvin had a thing for "thick" girls anyway, but he was blown away by her overall appearance. He looked at her with more focus to ensure he was seeing correctly. And he was. She felt him staring but never looked back at him. For about five seconds, Marvin felt as if the earth had stopped its movement. Nothing else mattered during this time. Not Yale, not the movie or his snacks, not even his very own breath or pulse. All that mattered was one person. It was like his pause was paying respects to God, the Creator of pure romance and Master of spontaneity. As he looked at her, only one word came to his mind: "Wow." He had seen many girls that were very good looking, and several, especially at Yale, just as much intelligent. To him, she eclipsed them all. He felt as if his future, bundled up into a single human, was standing right before him. But soon, Score brought his snacks to him, and he finally snapped out of it. He remembered that it was still spring break of '99, and he was at the brand-new theater in Oklahoma City at 1:56 in the afternoon. He paid for his items but stayed near the counter.

"Excuse me, man, who is that girl?" Marvin asked, pointing.

"That there, dear brother, is Claire Hollins. Don't worry, you're only about the *thirtieth* guy to ask about her today. She's pretty, huh?" Score answered.

"Yeah." Marvin said, in total admiration.

He wanted to approach her but was never one accustomed to forcing things. His two friends, who were still waiting for him on the bench, steadily grew worried that they would miss the movie's beginning. Plus, the lines were growing even more chaotic. It was a tough environment for any man trying to step to a young lady, let alone one who was working in its midst. Hence, he made his way towards the entrance without having said anything. Claire was not unaware of him, though. As he was walking away, she took a look at him. She hoped he would look back at her once more, but he didn't. So, she kept working.

After about an hour into the movie, Marvin got up from his seat to go to the restroom. At least, that is what he told his friends. In actuality, he went back to the concessions counter, looking for Claire. He found her there talking with Score and two other male workers. They were no longer dealing with the heavy traffic that had hit them between 1:00 and 2:30. Thus, the coast was finally clear. Before getting all the way up there, Marvin paused. His anxiety made an attempt to overcome him, but it failed. The man knew what he was after and that nothing in the world was going to stop him. He took a couple more steps forward and got their attention.

Score, knowing he was back for Claire, asked him, "What's up, man, what can I getcha?" He was really helping Marvin, for had he thought of speaking to Claire first, he might have stumbled over the words of his greeting or mispronounced a one-syllable word or something. Marvin was a guy who was extremely obvious. Many women from his past claimed that he was too basic and that he did not have enough mystery about him. In fairness to Marvin, he was simply being a genuine person. He was never one to operate with an agenda. Always clear and honest, because that is how he wanted others to be with him. Claire could sense this in his energy. She thought it was both commendable and cute.

"Umm, I'm actually here to ask for the young lady over there. *Claire*, you said?"

"Oh!" Score replied. He moved closer to Marvin over the counter and whispered, "Relax, bro. She's cool. Just be yourself. And it's 1999, chill out with the whole chivalry thing."

He went back over to Claire and pointed to Marvin. "That *guy* wants to know if he can talk to you."

Claire looked at Marvin. She thought he was very handsome and admired his 6'2" frame and toned physique. He also had a crisp and fresh haircut, along with a nice white t-shirt and black shorts. Many guys had approached her that day, but he was the one who actually drew her interest. Her heart began beating slightly quicker. Still, she walked up to him.

"Hey. You're looking for me?" She asked him.

"Hi, my name is Marvin Clement. I was just talking to your guy Score about how pretty you are. Just wanted to tell you directly. You are *so* pretty."

"Thank you so much!" Claire responded kindly.

"Oh, can I get your name?" He asked, even though he already knew it. He was respectful.

"I'm Claire Hollins." They shook hands.

"It's great to meet you, Claire. So, where are you from, if you don't mind me asking?"

"I'm from Shawnee, actually. Sophomore at Clear High School. Where you from?" She asked, smiling at him.

"Here in OKC. What are you doing all the way up here?"

"I work here a lot during the summer. Since it's spring break, I decided to make some extra cash. Nothing wrong with that, is it?"

He was impressed.

"No, nothing at all. I was just wondering, since it's a good drive from here. How you like the city?"

"It's cool. Shawnee's better, but I like it here."

Marvin smiled at her. "I only been to Shawnee once – for a debate competition my junior year. Y'all beat us."

"Cause we're the best, didn't you know?" She said jokingly. "Where do you go to school?"

"Yale. I went to Springs, though, right around the corner from here. Class of '98."

Claire was also impressed. She almost thought that he was lying to her. A black boy making it to Yale, out of OKC, was not common news. Even so, she knew he was very intellectual based on the way he pronounced his words. He was proper and eloquent. Yet, she managed to maneuver her emotional intelligence and refrain from directly complimenting his academic achievements.

"Yale? What, are you there on basketball scholarship?" Claire cleverly asked.

"No, actually. I'm there on academic scholarship, studying economics. I do not play sports. *I mean*, I work out and stuff, but only to stay healthy. Most of my time goes towards studying. I wish I could hoop, though. Basketball is fun. You hoop?"

"Nah, I play softball." Claire stated.

"Really? What position?"

"Center field and pitcher."

"*Impressive.*"

"Well, thank you."

Impressive was an understatement. Sixteen-year-old Claire Hollins was the best softball player in the state, and she knew it. Many girls that played against her claimed that she was the best they had ever witnessed. Bragging was never her thing, though. She was always humble about everything she did, as her folks had raised her right. Yet, since Marvin had been out of the state for nearly a year, he had not heard anything surrounding the Oklahoma athletic scene. He rarely kept up with sports anyway.

After a little more small talk, they had a short and awkward pause. Then, Marvin cut to the chase.

"Listen, I'm gonna be heading back north pretty soon, but I'd like to get to know you more. Hopefully, I can school you as to why Oklahoma City is so much better than Shawnee. Can I give you my number?"

She laughed. "Yeah, I'd like that."

He wrote his number down on a white napkin he pulled from the dispenser. She put it in her pants pocket and then on her dresser when she got home. Two weeks later, she called him. They talked every weekend after that. Eventually, they made plans to see each other once it was summer break. Lewis and Quentin took exception to it but were eventually respectful and understanding. They knew Marvin would still make time for them, just not as much as they initially hoped. This was the beginning of their natural development as men. All of them knew that they would stay tight, but they also understood that they had to grow in their own separate ways. It was a challenging thing for them, as they were still very young. Even so, Quentin and Lewis both knew that Marvin would be the first one to evolve in this way. And that was something that they were okay with.

That summer, Marvin must have taken Claire on a walk in every park in Oklahoma City. It became their go-to thing because they just loved talking to each other. It was like talking on the phone, except, on steroids. And every time they went out, it felt like the very first time. They would walk together in matching strides, without even realizing it. Time would seem to go by at a very fast rate, but the freshness never wavered. While with him, Claire would tell Marvin about all of her years playing sports and working on her family's ranch (she was raised by a cattleman; her mom was a teacher). He, in turn, would talk about his experiences traveling to business seminars, leadership conferences, and job fairs (he was raised by *two* doctors). He impressed her with his level of energy and drive. The boy was not even 20 at that point. But one thing they connected on most was their love for Christ, and it was evident in how they operated with each other. Always pure. Always respectful. As the summer went on, too, their chemistry and connection advanced to new levels. Despite being from very different backgrounds, and having many unrelated interests, they committed to learning more about their different worlds. For them, it was the *person* that was the center draw, and everything attached with the person was extremely cool to get to know. It gave each of them a warm, comforting feeling inside. Claire *really* felt this, though, as time passed. Marvin was the most incredible person she had ever known, and it wasn't even close. She felt lucky. And as you know, Marvin discerned Claire's uncommon glow from jump. Something inside of him said, "There she is. She's yours." And that something turned out to actually be the voice of *God*.

Later into the summer, Marvin got more creative in his dealings with his new companion. Whenever Claire would be working, he would surprise her at the theater desks and wait for her to go on her next fifteen-minute break. Once she would join him, they would sit outside on one of the sidewalk benches, facing all of the cars in the parking lot, seeing all of the people coming and going. Their conversation would always be a continuation of whatever they last talked about on the phone. Sports. Movies and TV shows. Dream cars and traveling trips. Home ideas. *Dating histories.* Music. Fashion. Racial climates. They drew from so many wells. Outside the theater, they would often get so deep into it that Claire would lose track of time and spend 25-to-35 minutes with Marvin. Score always covered for her, though, as he knew what she was up to. Marvin was extremely grateful for the guy and thanked him whenever he saw him. But Claire loved the thoughtfulness that Marvin had. Think of it like this: if Marvin was a terrific student, then he was one of the greatest of all time at the art of romance. It was just natural for him, and Claire was his perfect inspiration. Still, though, she was protective of her peace. When she would travel back home to Shawnee, she never extended an invitation to Marvin. To her, OKC was a safer place for their stage of dating. It had many public and open spaces that created an optimal environment for socializing. Shawnee, on the other hand, was more secluded. It was her shield of privacy. She needed to give their relationship more time before she could grant him that level of access. In addition, patience was never a skill she lacked. Marvin did not see this as a red flag, even though his impulses informed him otherwise at first. That initial feeling had just been his heart's condition after previously dealing with girls who were no good for him. But he had become wise enough to tell what Claire was doing, and that made her even more desirable. Having her in his presence elevated his life experience, and he was willing to follow the necessary instructions to keep her nearby. She made him feel like he could accomplish anything he sought out to do. Unlike the ones before her, she never drained the energy out of Marvin, and that was a sign that he did not miss. Anyhow, they ended up spending the fourth of July together at a festival in downtown OKC. On that day, everything was confirmed in Marvin's mind. Later that night in his home, he wrote a vision down in his journal. Here is what it said.

I'm about to be 20 years old in September, and I have already met the love of my life. Her name is Claire Hollins. A year ago, I thought I was going to be kicking it with a girl up near Yale. At least maybe in New York, Jersey, or Philly. I did not think I would find someone in my own town, just five minutes away from where I went to high school. Our chemistry is natural. Sex, though mutually desired, is not needed at all. Still, I know that the more I get to know her, the more powerful our interactions will be. She is just a very beautiful person inside and out. I wanna honor that forever. I want to do it the right way. God's way. Once I graduate and find my job, I will ask for her hand in marriage. I hope and pray that she says yes.

Filled with faith and determination, he did exactly what he wrote down. In spring of the next year, he graduated from Yale two years ahead of schedule, as he took on the heaviest workload known to man (in addition to testing out of several of his courses). When he arrived back home, a job was waiting for him at an investment firm in downtown Oklahoma City. He was set to already be making

$250,000 annually. Three weeks after he started his new gig, he asked Claire to talk to her father about marrying her. Even though she was just seventeen and approaching high school graduation, Marvin gave Claire's family his word that he would take care of her. And, unlike most men his age, his present reality, alone, backed up those promises. He was the only 20-year-old in the world that could earn her family's trust so soon. He loved her, and in August of 2000, Claire Hollins became Mrs. Clement.

Marvin had to plan their honeymoon strategically since Claire was entering her senior year at Clear High School, back in Shawnee. In late September, he jokingly asked her if he could have her time during fall break, and she yielded. Weeks later, he took her on a three-day trip in Puerto Rico. It was there where their son, Shawn, was conceived. As a result, she was not able to play ball in the spring. It stung her a little, but she was satisfied with her performance during the fall season. Either way it went, she had nothing else to prove. A season earlier, as a junior, she shattered the *national* high school batting average and strikeout records. Both records had stood for over twenty years. Following her illustrious season, recruitment letters from every major college in the nation perpetually filled her family's mailbox. And when they found out about her pregnancy, only a few of them withdrew interest. In fact, many of the schools wanted to accommodate her, both during and after her process. She was a once-in-a-lifetime talent, and no one wanted to miss out on her. In the end, though, she elected to take two years off to focus on Shawn.

Even so, as Claire approached graduation in the spring of 2001, she began to grow very restless. Her family wanted her to stay in Shawnee for the remainder of her pregnancy, but she insisted on moving in with Marvin as soon as possible. Marvin tried to get her to listen to them, but she, in all her youth, was determined to be with him. If it was up to Claire, she would have commuted from OKC to

Shawnee every school day, like many of Clear's teachers were doing already. She had not dealt with the distance well, especially since his son was growing inside of her for nearly the whole duration of her senior year. She needed him. During that time, Marvin was staying in a two-bedroom apartment about ten minutes north of his place of work. As much as Claire was ready, Marvin was even more anxious for her to join him. Still, he was able to acknowledge boundaries and respect them. Hence, he convinced her to stay with her parents for the rest of her school year.

Claire finally moved in with Marvin in the middle of June, just two weeks after her graduation. Two more weeks later, on July 1st, 2001, she gave birth to their son, Shawn Uriah Clement. His father insisted on the middle name because he loved Uriah the Hittite's integrity. In coincidence, for some reason, Claire had always loved the name 'Riah'. Anyhow, on the day that she was released from the hospital, Marvin took Claire to a particular spot that they had stopped at during a walk they took in the summer of '99. Located in The Village, it featured a beautiful two-story house, with a medium arch attached as its north wing. He remembered Claire's words verbatim. "Marvin, this house is *next level*. It's perfect." Like he often did, he took her words as motivation to manifest something. Only this time, it was her exact word and desire. He bought the house in April and had hired movers to furnish it in late May. It was hard for him not to tell her, but he kept it a secret in plans of a big surprise. And now, the time had finally come. When they pulled up to the estate, Claire asked him, "Babe, what are we doing here?"

"We're about to go in our house." He responded.

Claire looked at the house for about ten seconds. Then, she looked at her husband. She had forgotten about the house for all that time. But now looking at it, everything suddenly came back to her. She immediately recalled the walk they had taken and started to get emotional.

"You didn't." Claire said to him.

"This belongs to us, honey. I got it in April. Right here is where we are going to build our family. I wanted to wait until Shawn was finally here so all three of us could enter in together. Anything you want, you better bet that I'm gonna try to give it to you. You motivate me every single day. You deserve this and so much more. I love you, Claire." Marvin replied.

Holding their son, Claire lightly stepped in front of Marvin and kissed his lips. Starting to cry, she told him she loved him back. She soon put Shawn in his car seat and let her husband take him. Then, they all went inside to look around their new home.

Marvin and Claire possessed something so beautiful and rare that they often looked at each other, saying, "are we really doing this?" They really were. *Undoubtedly* in love and only growing in it more as the days went on. Of course, their marriage was not without its realities. But they were so in tune with each other that they solved disagreements quickly and often forgot about them. They were a perfect match, and everyone knew it. And so Marvin, at the age of 21, had graduated from Yale two years early, met and married the woman God created for him, had a son, earned a position as a top financial advisor, and bought a home. Clearly, he was focused and driven.

Three years later, in August of 2004, the Clement family was firmly established in their place in OKC. Marvin continued to thrive in his job downtown, while Claire took care of Shawn during infancy and toddlerhood. It had been a year past the time she had committed to take off, and schools were beginning to pressure her about playing again. Before Claire had the chance to focus on choosing a college, Marvin asked her if she ever thought about training girls to play softball. He always praised her as "the greatest to ever do it," and knew how much she loved the game. Moreover, he knew her heart and that she was someone who did not hesitate when it came to pouring into others. She thought about it for about two weeks and eventually decided that it was something that she would like to do. Thus, she obtained all her essentials and began looking for an available space. Marvin was able to finance a facility in a spot about a mile east of downtown (he was the definition of 'financially free'). They named it *Claire's Corner* and opened it for business at the midpoint of September. Almost instantaneously, she drew fifty clients in the first month of operation. Business had already become so good that she had to start hiring other trainers to fulfill her clients' needs. Still, she always made a way to help all her students and connect with them personally. So, in what seemed like world-record timing, Claire became the top softball instructor in Oklahoma. Though Marvin was making plenty of money from financial advising, Claire was, what the kids call, *balling*. She was extremely good at softball, but equally adept at training others how to accomplish greatness. It was one of the things her husband admired most about her. Shawn, three at that time, watched from a distance, as she brought him to work every day – Claire made sure that a special, safe area for young children was created and sectioned out in the building. He was fascinated by the players he watched train every day, but nothing amazed him more than his mother. Even he could tell that she was a special gift to the game. He soon wanted to become like all the others and have his mom teach him how to play. So, at home, he began asking her to play catch. She tried showing him how to throw over-handed, but he kept throwing it under-handed. He did it because that was the way he had seen her instruct young pitchers. He had never seen men and boys playing baseball, so he did not know that a difference existed. Claire thought it was cute. Thus, she allowed him to continue the motion but gradually taught him the over-hand throw. And from that point on, playing ball was all Shawn ever wanted to do.

On December 11th of that same year, Claire decided to buy Shawn his very first glove. She went to the local sporting goods store and bought him both a right-handed and left-handed glove. Her intention was to guide him into throwing lefty, but she had noticed him throwing the ball right-handed more and more. Both gloves were blue, Shawn's favorite color and, also, first word. But upon leaving the store, she noticed that her car's gas hand was very low. She then proceeded to go to a nearby gas station. When she got out of the car, she looked back as if she had forgotten something. Quickly, she remembered that Marvin had the day off and that Shawn was at home with him. She was so used to having her son with her everywhere she went. Yet, when she confirmed that he was safe with his father, she was able to relax again.

Before Claire walked through the store's entrance, she saw a man going in before her. He was wearing all black, with a dark grey baseball cap that covered his face. When she went in and waited in line, there was an uneasy feeling that stirred within her again. Even though she had navigated through her initial withdrawal-like reaction, she still knew something was off. There were three people in line ahead of her. At this point, she was ready to pay for her gas, quickly pump it, and then get the hell out of there.

Three minutes passed. Just as the last person in front of her walked up to the counter, the man in black took everyone by surprise.

"This is a stick-up! Everybody on the ground!"

Claire and the other shoppers immediately obeyed. The clerk stood frozen with both of her hands raised in the air.

He swiftly pulled out a silver revolver and pointed it in the face of the clerk. When he did, Claire flinched. When she moved, though, her hands were near the pockets of her pants, and the gunman noticed it out of the corner of his eye. So, his focus shifted towards Claire. He then pointed the gun in her direction, warning her to stay still. She remained as frozen as she possibly could. On the ground, looking directly at back at him, tears began rolling down her face. Fear was not what caused her move of emotions. Claire was as fierce as anyone. Rather, it was thought of her husband and son losing her at such an early point in their family journey. Few people have that type of selflessness, and she managed to have it in all her years. She had experienced so much success in every area of her life. So much good had happened for her. She knew that high crime was present in OKC, but never did she actually think she'd be in a situation like this. Her bold, hazel eyes pierced through the eyes of the robber.

"Don't shoot!" Claire commanded him.

The man did not expect to confront a woman that showed no fear of him sticking up the joint. In truth, he was the one that was actually afraid. Afraid of Claire reporting his description to law enforcement. Afraid that he would be found guilty in court and locked away for years – hell, maybe even life. Afraid that he had run out of any extra margin for error. Thus, in that fear, he pulled the trigger. When the gun shot, its bullet traveled into Claire's neck and blood immediately began pouring onto the checkered floor. Seconds after, the man fled the scene. Then, one customer quickly got off the ground and called the local ambulance. All of the other ones sprinted outside to their cars and left. Meanwhile, the clerk ran over and put multiple t-shirts on Claire's wound to try and stop the bleeding. Emergency personnel arrived seven minutes after receiving the call. At that point, she had already died. Too much blood had been lost. Claire Hollins-Clement was only 21 years old. A wife. A mother. Softball legend. Trainer. Christian. Gone. The man who killed her was never found.

About an hour later, two policemen arrived at the front door of the Clement estate and knocked on the door. Marvin, thinking that it was the mailman, came and opened the door. When he saw it was the police instead, he grew nervous.

"What's up, guys?" Marvin asked them.

With sorrow, the officers gave Marvin the news. The devastation that came over him was beyond description. He had lost his rib. His partner. His best friend. His everything. Shawn was sleeping at the time of his dad receiving word. About ten minutes after the police departed, Marvin went and picked him up. Knocked out cold, he momentarily opened his eyes, saying, "Hi, Daddy," and then immediately fell back asleep on Marvin's shoulder. He carried him to his car, becoming more heartbroken with every step he took. He went to the coroner to confirm that it was her. Afterwards, he and his son made the fifty-minute drive to Shawnee to inform Claire's family. When he arrived and told her folks, they wept with a noise that could have been heard all the way from the state's eastern borders. What started out as a normal day in Oklahoma, turned into one of the darkest ones that anyone could remember. The sun still shone as daylight, but it might as well have been absent. The *entire* state was in mourning.

For a long time, Claire's parents, out of raw emotion and anger, blamed Marvin for their daughter's passing. She would have never been in Oklahoma City that day if she had not met Marvin, they once figured. She would have been somewhere playing ball and attaining a degree. They never said the words out loud to him, but he could sense it in the way they would look him in the eye. What pain for a man to bear. And on top of that, what grief for two parents who had done excellent work in raising a beautiful, successful daughter. Clear High School, and the rest of Shawnee, lost a literal hometown hero. She was such a graceful person. Everyone was inspired by her. Claire's Corner was flooded with flowers and signs from people from all over the state, honoring Claire's joyful and success-filled life. Out of everyone, though, Shawn took it the hardest. He cried for his mother day and night. Marvin never got annoyed with any of those cries, either. He felt and understood them. He wanted to cry right along with him, but he had cried *so* much within the first week of her passing that his muscle memory made him stop the tears from flowing so often. Every now and then he would cry alone in bed, though. Like Claire, he never pictured anything like this happening. He had big plans for his family, and another man stole them away. Partnered with the grief, anger steadily built itself from the deepest part of Marvin's soul. Day by day, he had to restrain himself from seeking vengeance. He often did this through prayer in Christ's name. Other times, he did it by simply looking at his son. In truth, the reason keeping him from finding the killer, and then returning the favor, was the thought of his son living without both of his parents. While sleeping, he would often have dreams of him and Claire going on walks. At the end of them, every time, she would tell him, "Marvin, I love you. Give Shawn a kiss for me." Marvin was a man of his word, but with a loss that affected him so deeply, he had to rise against an unprecedented challenge. Never backing down, though, he made it his mission to continue his wife's legacy through their son.

Claire's belongings were retrieved out of her car, which was kept longer for forensic purposes. But among her possessions was a letter Marvin had written her while he was finishing his degree at Yale. They also found some perfume, a blue jean jacket, and the pink softball bat that she had used her during junior year. Lastly, they found the two blue gloves that she had purchased for her son. When they took the items to the Clement residence, Marvin brought them all into the living room and sat down. He picked up the letter and began reading what he wrote to her. When he finished, he noticed the bottom of the page had a red lipstick stain near his postscript. She had kissed the paper in pure love and excitement, as she was missing him during their time apart. Marvin pulled the paper to his lips and kissed her back. *This* time, he stood no chance in holding back his emotions. He cried one of deepest cries of his young life. Ironically, Shawn was doing much better that day and came up to comfort him.

"What's wrong, Daddy?" Shawn asked him.

Marvin always tried to be strong for his son, but he could not stop his tears. For ten minutes, Marvin cried on the floor, with his three-year-old son in his lap. Shawn laid his head on Marvin's chest, sensing that his sadness was about his mom. Beginning to tear up himself, he said to his father, "It's okay, Daddy."

Even so, once Marvin was able to muster up the strength, he presented the gloves to his son.

"Here, son. Your mom got these for you."

Shawn, excited and smiling, tried on both gloves. Realizing he needed to have one hand free to throw, he removed the glove that was on his left hand. It was as if Claire was right there with him, guiding his choice as she had done so many times before. When he fitted it, he happily ran circles around his dad. Urging Marvin to look at him, he began doing throwing motions. Standing with his hands and feet together, Shawn focused in on his imaginary battery mate (catcher). Then, he initiated his pitching movement. Marvin was unaware of what Shawn was really doing. To him it just looked like he was trying to throw under-handed. But in actuality, Shawn was, out of honor, performing Claire's pitching windup. He learned to do it by intensely watching several sessions she had with catchers, where she would throw a ten-pitch bullpen (pitch practice) to them. This was her way of helping them get familiar with pitches that have good movement. One thing was for certain: everything that Claire did, especially concerning softball, made a permanent stamp in Shawn's mind. Realizing his son loved softball/baseball with just as much passion as his wife, Marvin signed him up for tee ball the following year.

Since the day he first stepped onto a tee ball field at four years old, Shawn and baseball were a perfect match. He was a natural ballplayer. Years later, in kid pitch, he hit a ball so hard one day that the other team threatened to forfeit the game if he was allowed to bat again. Marvin took exception to it, for his son was one of the youngest boys in his grade. Hence, he was usually the youngest on any field he stepped on. Age was no factor, though. Shawn was a supreme talent, just like his mother was. His dad wanted to make sure that he always had somewhere to practice, so he decided to keep Claire's Corner open for business. Too, Shawn ended up being a source of healing for Claire's parents, particularly concerning their attitude towards Marvin. They made sure to always support Shawn in school and athletics, as they could not help but love him and see so much of Claire in him. But just as much so, they saw some of the things in Marvin that Claire loved so much – the most notable thing of all, how good of a father he was. Once Shawn was about nine years old, all the resentment they had against his father was gone.

Even so, when Shawn reached middle school, his dad finally began dating again. Now, it was *his* turn to develop resentment towards him, as he thought it was still too early. He thought that, by bringing another woman into the picture, his mom would be forgotten. Marvin had to explain to him several times that his mother was forever his greatest love, and that he would have never traded her for the world, especially since she was his mom. Shawn still did not understand him. In reality, though, Marvin was in his mid-thirties. When they lost Claire, he was barely 25. Thus, he was presented with the formidable task of navigating through his twenties with one of life's most unwanted griefs attached to him. At the same time, he had to push through and resist the natural urges occurring within him. He was still a very handsome, wealthy man. Women were always drawn to him whenever he stepped out. And when he became a millionaire in 2007, women eyed him even more, as his status quickly became public knowledge. Everywhere he went, he saw a gorgeous woman seeking his attention. Marvin, in all his greatness, was still made of flesh. That same year, he slept with a woman he had met at a business conference in New Jersey. It happened on three different occasions. His initial goal was to abstain until he finally healed and married again, but he met the lady at one of his greatest moments of weakness. His body had been chemically primed for it. Who can blame him, though? If anyone seemingly had room for error, it had to be him. Though he fell, he refused to completely forfeit his nobility. After the third and final time with the woman, he apologized to her, left, and never came back. To keep himself from backsliding, he deleted her number from his phone, and, furthermore, changed his own to ensure she could not call him. Soon after, he recommitted to sexual purity, deciding that thoughtless fornication was not worth his time and energy. Besides, he still missed Claire and had more healing to do. She was the only woman he had ever loved beyond just the physical. He loved the person she was. Yet, by Shawn's seventh grade year, Marvin was finally ready to get back out there in a healthy state of mind.

Marvin met a woman named Alicia Harris in March of 2014, right when American school calendars were beginning to read 'Spring Break'. At first, anxiety arose in him, as he remembered it being spring break when he and Claire kindled their romance. Even so, he had done a lot of work on himself. Plus, Alicia was a true catch. Born in Barcelona, Spain, she was the youngest of four children to Alec and Sophia Harris. Alec was a former big-league ballplayer. He was playing overseas in Spain when he met Sophia, and they got married a year later. When Alicia was four, her dad decided to bring the family back to the United States – New York City, New York, to be exact. There, Alicia quickly learned to speak English. It also helped that there were already so many people there that were fluent in Spanish. It helped her become more comfortable. As she grew older, she developed a passion for art and became very skilled in multiple disciplines of painting. When she was just sixteen, she won a national award for a painting she drew of a city skyline. Instead of letting the award get to her head, she became an even better artist. So much so, that she went on to travel across the globe, making several millions of dollars from her pieces.

Through early adulthood, Alicia never settled down and got married. She had too often come across men who had nothing to offer her except sex – and most were not very great at that, either. But realizing that those sexual encounters created insecurity in her, she, like Marvin, decided to abstain from sexual relations. Also like him, she made that decision at the age of 29 (Marvin in 2009, Alicia in 2011). Immediately, their decisions brought loneliness and jealous inclinations. Over time, though, they each became more excellent and self-aware. They grew to hold dear to their devotions, which ended up paying a rewarding dividend.

It all started when Lewis, Quentin, and Marvin decided to travel up to New York together. Throughout the years, they remained in touch as much as their lives allowed. Lewis became a professional photographer and moved to San Francisco. Quentin had become a lawyer, and Philadelphia was the place he lived and did his work. Yet, they would often fly back home and spend weeks with Marvin and his son. Shawn grew close to them as well, referring to them as his uncles. Anyhow, while they were in New York, Lewis had the idea of going to an art exhibit in Brooklyn. Marvin and Quentin wanted, instead, to go watch the Knicks play the Cavs, but Lewis hated Madison Square Garden. The reason was that five years earlier, he had gotten into a fight outside of the arena, after watching a pro boxing match. Both he and the other guy had downed one too many drinks. On top of that, the fighter Lewis was rooting for lost via 12th round knockout. Nothing went right for him that night. After having such a horrible experience, he vowed to never step foot near

MSG again. So, Marvin and Quentin yielded and gave Lewis his wish. When they got to the exhibit, they were greeted by two very attractive women. Lewis talked to one, and Quentin talked to the other. But Marvin continued to go inside. Upon entering, he saw all of the breathtaking sculptures and paintings that comprised the entrance display. He stayed there and studied the pieces for about seven minutes. Then, he made his way into another area of paintings. When viewing, *one* caught his attention more than any other piece in the section. He had locked eyes on a painting of a softball player running around the bases with her arm raised in the air. It was yet another reminder of his beloved Claire. Determined to push through, he took in the painting for three good minutes, inhaling and exhaling deeply. It was therapeutic. Right when he became more well, he started to hear the sound of heels approaching from behind him.

"Well, what do you think?" The voice uttered.

Marvin turned around and beheld a light-skinned woman wearing a brown dress, accented with bright white heels. He was amazed at her figure and appearance, for she literally looked like she was just coming from a cover shoot for a beauty magazine. Like the kids also say, she was *bad*. Marvin slightly grinned back at her.

"I think it's pretty good." He looked at the title that read: *Por la Victoria*. "What's the title mean?" He added.

"You're the first person to ask me that tonight. It means, 'for the victory.' It's Spanish." Alicia responded.

"I see. Yeah, I don't know a lick of Spanish, as you can tell. But I think it's a beautiful language. Not as beautiful as this painting, though."

Alicia starting blushing. She was attracted to Marvin, and his compliment made her wonder more about him. Still, she kept things professional.

"I appreciate that, sir. Well, let me give you some background on this painting. Randomly scrolling through some newspaper archives, I read up on this girl who broke national high school records a couple years back. She was only a junior in high school when she did it. I, *myself*, was a junior when I won my national award for art. I kind of related to her in that way, and that fueled the inspiration of this piece."

Marvin paused and stared down at the floor. He did not know whether to ask more about the specifics or to let it rest. Any other person in the room would have complimented her and continued looking at other artworks. Most would have not even thought of purchasing it, as softball and baseball were not your typical art themes. In a subtle way, he knew that the painting was made exclusively for him. He finally figured that asking her would not hurt anything. "Surely, someone could have broken the records by now," he thought. He looked back at her.

"If you don't mind me asking, do you remember the name of that girl you read about?" Marvin replied.

"If I remember correctly, *Claire*. Yeah, Claire Collins."

Marvin's jaw hit the floor in amazement. Once again, he was at the perfect place at the perfect time.

"Hollins."

"I'm sorry?"

"Claire Hollins. She died four years after she broke those records. Also, I was married to her. She's the mother of my son."

Alicia was stunned.

"You know what? This is so full circle. I'm gonna give you this painting, free of charge –"

"Don't even think about it. You did fine work. It deserves every penny. I'm sorry, I didn't get your name?"

"Alicia. And yours?"

"Marvin."

"Well, Marvin, I *am* going to have this painting sent to you personally. I refuse to take any money from this painting after meeting the man who had a key role in Claire's life. I did not even know she passed away, and for that, I am sorry. I am giving you this painting, sir. And even though we just met, I am not taking no for answer. You and your son deserve this."

For Marvin, the moment felt surreal. Deep down, he thought it as a sign from Heaven. He envisioned Claire saying, "it's okay, Marvin. She's good for you." And anyway, Marvin never hesitated to make up his mind. Most importantly, he felt peace about it. After giving her his information to send the painting, he asked Alicia for her number in return. She gladly gave it to him.

A month later, he flew her down to Oklahoma for their first date. From jump, they found each other extremely compatible. Yet, Marvin knew better than to make this process any faster than it needed to be. Shawn still struggled with him moving forward in his relationships. He missed his mom and needed the feminine nurturing she had provided for him as a baby. Somehow, however, he found a way to accept Alicia. After all those years of deep sadness, which seemed like they were gonna last forever, his dad was happy again. Though it was not easy, Shawn finally gave his dad the green light, and both of them became better because of it. Consequently, in December of 2016, Alicia and Marvin got married. The Clement household was finally complete again.

That catches you all the way back up to present day (Thursday, March 22nd, 2018). Shawn had just given his speech in Mrs. Gates' class and was feeling like a million bucks. When school let out, Lisa continued searching for him, but Shawn had already taken off for practice. When he got to the locker room, though, his phone buzzed. It was a notification from the local news that read, "Happs HS player shatters Shawn Clement's sophomore record for doubleheader." The year prior, Shawn had hit four triples in a doubleheader against

Clear, the high school his mother attended. The previous mark was three, set in 1986 by a center fielder from Locust Grove. He just knew that the record was safe for at least twice the time of the one before his. Instead, it didn't last a whole season. Shawn could not tell if he was more amused at his failed prediction or more shocked that someone had managed to hit *seven* triples in a day's work. Happs High School was located on the northeastern side of OKC, in a town called Spencer. Shawn could not help but wonder, "who in the world are they talking about?" Happs had not had a winning team in nine years. If he hadn't had to get to the field, he would have read and found out who. Instead, he would have to just wait a while.

CHAPTER 2: WHAT OTHERS THINK ABOUT BOBBY

Three days earlier.

"Baby, I can't come over tonight. I have so much homework to do, and if I fail this chemistry test tomorrow, I can't play Thursday. What I look like being known as the player who became ineligible the week after hitting a game-winning grand slam? C'mon, babe, cut me some slack. I promise to make it up to you. You believe me, right?"

"Whatever, Bobby Ray. I just feel like you been having a whole lot more to do lately. First, it's baseball. Then it's a dinner with the guys. Now, it's studying. You have been making time for everything and everyone except me. I thought you cared about me, but I guess I was wrong. Call me back whenever you get free. I mean, *if* you ever get free."

"That's unfair. JoJo, don't do me like that –"

The phone was disconnected.

Bobby Raymond Bowen, a fifteen-year-old sophomore student at Happs High School, was going through it with his girlfriend, Joleen "JoJo" Gonzalez (sixteen, sophomore - Happs). He hated being called Bobby Ray, but whenever JoJo said it, he could not help but soften up to her. There was something about the rhythm and tone of her words. Her Mexican accent was very unique and flavorful. Anything she said to Bobby had the capability of persuading him whichever way. But he especially liked the sound of her voice when she was mad at him, for her accent would grow in potency. JoJo was frustrated because she had been trying to hang out with him for three weekends straight, but during such time, Bobby was out of town playing baseball. Finally, she grew tired of it and began distancing herself to get his attention.

Bobby was the catcher for his high school team. The year prior (Bobby's freshman year), Happs had a senior catcher named Gary Thompson, who ended up signing a contract to play ball in Australia after graduation. He was the real deal. Still, the Happs Chargers had a miserable season, winning only two out of twenty-five total games. This year, though, they actually started off decent. Bobby, a right-handed batter, took a slow start out the gate but began catching fire during the fourth game of the season. His teammate and fellow sophomore, Ryan Martin, had also been a force in left field and in both batter's boxes (switch hitter). Together, they led their team to a 3-4 start. The Happs Chargers' next two games were scheduled against Creek High School in Muskogee, Oklahoma. Luckily, Bobby had passed his chemistry test Wednesday and avoided making the ineligible players' list. The pressure of having a big game the next day had heightened his focus and determination. The next morning, he and the rest of the team made the trip to "the Gee."

Bobby's swing was feeling better than any point of his young baseball life. When Gary Thompson left, no one expected Bobby to have a chance at the level of greatness Gary accomplished. He had left giant shoes to fill. Bobby didn't look at it that way, though. In fact, he always thought of himself as the best player on the field, no matter where he was. Though he had no gaudy numbers or awards to his credit, he was supremely confident in his abilities. Like Shawn Clement, he loved everything about baseball and worked hard at the craft. In contrast to Shawn, however, Bobby had quite the temper and was easily distracted by people who attempted to get under his skin. The fight he had with JoJo just so happened to be his most recent distraction. On the way up to Creek, he tried to forget her hanging up in his face. Since that phone call, he had sent her several long text messages telling her how much he loved and appreciated her. She read through the messages but did not respond. At school, during lunch period, the couple usually met at the door of the janitor's closet to share a passionate kiss. It was one of the few places that did not have a camera pointed in its direction, so no one ever caught them. Yet, for two days straight, Bobby stood at the door by himself. Out of the five months they had been dating, this was the very first time she did not show up, and it bothered Bobby tremendously. Laying against the window with his legs across his seat, he closed his eyes. Then, he put in his earphones and played smooth jazz music from his cell phone. It immediately calmed his anxiety, which helped him fall asleep for majority of the ride.

Creek's mascot was the Warriors, affectionately imaged after a Native American fighting chief. Their Muskogee ballfield was one of the very best in the state. When the bus finally arrived, Bobby was fully awake and rejuvenated. He was among the first players to step off the stairs and process the view of the Warriors' park. To take it in even more, he paused, took out his earphones, and listened. The field's speakers were blasting country music (it is *Oklahoma* we're talking about). Bobby had never played there before, nor had he played at any of the other nice fields in OK. It was only his fourth competitive season of baseball, so his travel experience was still limited. That actually played to Bobby's advantage on this day, though, as he was a lot calmer than the other players on his team. Everyone else, including Ryan, were nervous as all get out. Creek had made it to the State finals in the year prior but lost to Shawn and the Love HS Bulldogs (11-to-9 in ten innings). But they had all their best players back for their junior and senior years, and all of those boys were hungry for revenge. Coming into the new spring, Oklahoma sports media rated Creek the number four team in the state. Happs, on the other hand, was ranked near the bottom. Aware of the projections, most of the Happs players counted themselves out before they even stepped on the field. As they entered the entrance gates, Bobby overheard them praising Creek in a fearful, intimidated tone. He didn't like it one bit. Walking into the dugout, Bobby boldly threw his bags down and commanded his team to gather around him.

"I know y'all not walking in here scared like a bunch of babies. We can beat them. They bleed just like we bleed. They imperfect just like we are. No team is unbeatable, and I hope y'all know that. Let's keep playing the good ball we been playing. We gon' be fine, y'all, trust." Bobby told them.

He said those words as if he knew something that they didn't. Bobby was always a source of positivity whenever the team needed it. But as inspiring as he was, this time, none of his teammates took his speech to heart. They were already mentally defeated. A doubleheader against the fourth team in the state only meant bearing the misery of getting pounded on, they thought. Ryan had played against several of Creek's players during summer ball the previous year. His talent was right along with the best on their squad, and he had proved it. Even so, Ryan had a tendency to cave under the pressure of situations that stretched him. Whenever things were going good, he could do no wrong. Yet, when things got hard, he became a shell of himself. He would often complain about other people's mistakes and blame all factors outside of himself. This got under Bobby's skin because he saw the greatness that Ryan possessed. No one in Happs' dugout knew it, but leading up to gameday, Creek was *actually* becoming nervous about facing them. It was primarily because they had swept in their previous series (culminating in Bobby's game-winning grand slam). Yet, when Creek's players studied the Chargers' body language coming in, all their nervousness quickly turned into unblemished focus and confidence.

So, the only Happs player to walk onto Creek's field ready to play was Bobby. He saw it as a chance to prove his own greatness in the face of high competition. Yes, he was great in the previous two weeks, but none of those teams were anywhere near Creek's level. Still, Bobby loved challenges. During warm-ups, he made sure to stretch every part of his body, especially his right arm. He ran two laps across the outfield fence (foul pole to foul pole). Finally, he went to Creek's away bullpen to warm up Happs' game one starter, Kyle Fields. Soon after their session, the head coaches met with the umpires at home plate. Then, Bobby quickly ran back in to get ready to bat, as he was the leadoff hitter.

On the very first pitch of the game, Bobby crushed a fastball down the left field line. The ball ricocheted off the corner of the fence, and the left fielder played it poorly. As a result, Bobby made it to third standing up. During his next at-bat, he hit another ball down the left field line. Though firm, it was not hit as hard as the first. Yet, it bounced on the grass long enough to earn him another triple. On defense, Bobby was a nightmare for Creek's runners. Before the game had reached the fifth, Bobby had already thrown out four of them – all of which had struck doubles to the outfield fence. He was not done, though. In the bottom of the sixth inning, two more attempted to steal second. Both were gunned down. That made *six*. As a result, Creek's coach forbade stealing for the rest of the day.

During Bobby's third and final time at the plate, he lined a curveball down the right field line. The right fielder got to the ball very quickly, but Bobby still rounded second with no intentions on slowing down. He gained speed with each stride. When the relay throw came in, Bobby slid into third with his arms in the air. Creek's third baseman received the ball and then tagged him at, what looked like, the exact moment his foot touched the base. Looking in from behind the play, the umpire called Bobby safe. Creek's coach became irate. Though he knew that the play was bang-bang and could have gone either way, he was mad at the fact that Bobby Bowen, a sophomore no one had ever even heard of, was torching his team full of juniors and seniors (several of which were ranked in the state's Top 200 List). Even so, as great as Bobby performed, the rest of his teammates were completely ineffective. The pitchers constantly gave up extra base hits and walks, and all batters hit either weak grounders or flew out. Surprisingly, however, Happs batters ended the game with less strikeouts than Creek's players (2 compared to 5). But that was about the only thing the Chargers had an advantage in. Bobby, who had hit three consecutive triples, never scored from third base. No other Happs batter reached past first. And in the end, the Warriors destroyed the Chargers, 9-0.

Prior to the second game, Bobby, frustrated that he had no help in the opener, ran to the corner in right field. When got there, he laid down on the grass and took several deep breaths to calm himself. Bobby's teammates were very embarrassed at how they played. All of them leaned on the dugout rests and gazed at him resting. They felt guilty for leaving him as the only player that had any energy and enthusiasm. Despite their embarrassment, though, they were amazed at how great Bobby's performance really was. None of them had ever seen someone on their team play so well. Shoot, even Gary Thompson, in all his four years, never had a game as good as Bobby's. Realizing that they had to rise up and support their leader, the Chargers finally got pumped up for the opportunity to play some ball. Ryan, who had just popped out twice and made two errors in left, fought off his immaturity and locked in on the next game. The sudden energy shift within the Happs dugout was palpable. Creek was now about to face a *completely* different team.

In the second game, Bobby led off the top of the first with, you guessed it, another triple. This time, he lined a first-pitch fastball into the gap in left-center. While standing on third, he thought to himself, "wow, they're gonna keep throwing me fastballs. So dumb. I'll take it, though." It was like he was going on a fast. No meat. No soda. No bread. No sweets. Just triples, off of Creek pitchers. Ryan batted right behind him and hit yet another pop fly. This time, however, it was hit to deep center field. The defender caught the ball with his feet on the warning track, and Bobby tagged up and scored with ease. Happs was finally on the board for the day, and just like that, the ice was broken. All three batters behind Ryan hit hard singles to center field. With the bases loaded, their six-hole hitter, Marco Santiago (senior, third baseman R/R) hit a double over the left fielder's head. All three runners scored standing up. Out of nowhere, Happs was winning four-to-nothing.

Creek's coach could not believe what he was watching. Prior to the bottom half of the first, he yelled at his players at the top of his lungs, urging them to get their act together. As a result, all of them started pressing in the batter's box, swinging as hard as they could in effort to hit home runs. But instead, they struck high fly balls to the Happs defense. Bobby was already proud of his teammates for responding the way they did. At this point, he did not care anymore about winning. All he sought out to do was empower them. He realized that the best way for him to do so was to lead by example, and he did just that. When it was his turn to hit again, in the top of the third, Bobby hit a ball so far past the outfield fence that it hit the building just north of it (on one hop). Only the biggest sluggers in the state ever hit 'em there. Still, the ball was foul. The next pitch, he quieted his swing and hit *another* triple down the left field line. On the pitch afterwards, Ryan hit a two-run homer to dead center, which put them up 6-0. The following batters managed to capitalize on the momentum and made the score 9-0. And for the first time all season, the Happs Chargers batted all the way around in one inning. Then, with two outs, Bobby came back to the plate to give it another go.

Creek's left-handed pitcher looked into his catcher's fingers, desperately trying to figure out how to get Bobby Bowen off balance. The catcher put down the sign for slider, but the lefty shook him off. Instead, he chose knuckleball, for that was the only pitch Bobby had not yet seen. Out of the stretch, he gave quick looks at Happs' runners on first and second. Then, he looked back at the plate. After finding the proper grip, he came set and then threw the pitch. Recognizing that the pitch was a knuckler, Bobby kept his weight back and stayed light on his stride foot. As the ball entered the hitting zone, he took one of the most beautiful, fluid swings anyone had ever seen. The ball connected with the sweet spot of Bobby's bat with a noise that could have been heard from a mile away. On a line, it traveled to right field and stayed in the air for what seemed like forever. Finally, the ball struck the very top of the fence, just about three inches left of the yellow line. Gravity then completed its work, as the baseball bounced back onto the outfield grass and then into the glove of Creek's right fielder. The two runners on base scored, and Bobby gracefully slid into third base, even though there was no play. It was a slide that Bobby performed just for emphasis, with the goal of making his journey from the batter's box that much more dramatic. And, God, did he do it beautifully. Bobby had hit his fifth triple of the day, which broke the previous doubleheader mark set by Shawn Clement (Love HS). His team was now winning 11-0.

Creek's players, coaches, and spectators had no words. They were *literally* speechless. None of the Happs fans or parents made the trip up to Muskogee, so there were no Charger supporters in the seats. But none of their players cared about any of that now. Bobby had been the spark, and they found a way to add fuel to his fire. Their coach, Lonnie Dillon, urged them to stay focused and not let up. And they listened. Though Creek had responded in the fifth, scoring five runs to stave off the run-rule (+10 runs after 5), the Warriors never made a full comeback. Bobby saw the plate two more times and hit two more triples, putting an exclamation mark on his new record. Ryan nearly made history that game, too, almost hitting for the school's first-ever cycle. All he lacked was a single.

Happs defeated the number four team in the state by a score of 16-to-5. They now had a record of four wins and five losses. Yet, it was this fourth victory that was the greatest triumph by far. On the bus ride back to Spencer, the players laughed and rooted "BOBBY! BOBBY! BOBBY!" Marco Santiago even had a bottle of sparkling grape juice in his school bag. He had been saving it for a big moment but did not think it would happen so early in the season. But it more than pleased him to break it out. So, he shook up the bottle and then splashed juice all over everyone and everything. They were happy and proud of one another. Even the bus driver was proud of them and grateful for witnessing their epic feat. Not only did the Chargers accomplish something great together, but their leader had entered the state's record books. It was the greatest day of baseball for each and every one of them.

When the bus arrived back in Spencer, a crowd of people in Chargers' gear was waiting in the parking lot. Truth is, many of those people had never been out to see any of the Happs baseball games before. Usually, the family members of players, and maybe a couple of their girlfriends, were the only ones cheering them on. Not this time. When news arrived of their enormous victory over Creek, hundreds of Happs fans rushed to the school's campus. They made signs that said, "WE ARE PROUD OF YOU," and "NEXT STOP: STATE." The players were aware that majority of them had never supported the team. Nonetheless, they welcomed the praise, receiving the fans just as a pro team received its loyal supporters at the post-championship parade. Each player was greeted with high fives, front-camera selfies, and autograph requests. It was as if they had each been drafted to the major leagues, boosting the name of their hometown to new levels. Bobby was satisfied with sharing the spotlight, even though he was the one carrying the load. He understood that this endearment would potentially play a key role in other players gaining confidence. Not everyone had the inner security to call themselves the best player in the world. Some people have to hear it from others in order to further develop their sense of competency. Bobby was very smart.

Unlike Shawn, Bobby did not pick up a baseball bat until the age of eleven. Football was his favorite sport growing up. During the collegiate season, he would watch the top schools battle against each other on national television. He loved watching it so much that he would draw pictures of player statistic graphics that would show on the bottom of the screen. Instead of an actual player's name, he would write, "Bobby Bowen, Junior QB. Yards AVG 300.4 Comp. % 72.8 TDs 29." Seeing his enthusiasm about the game, his mom, Shelby Bowen, then placed him in little league football when he was just six years old. Bobby initially played cornerback exclusively, but he made the transition to quarterback in his third year of playing. He had no other reason for choosing the position other than the fact that he was tired of playing corner (it became boring to him). His coaches helped him transition in practice, and he held his own pretty well. Throwing a football so early, and so often, was the source of his arm strength development. As he grew older, he just became better and better at slinging the pigskin. In middle school, he earned the starting spot of his sixth-grade football team and played very well. That same fall, however, during the last game of the season, Bobby suffered an injury. During the third quarter, a boy from the other team sacked him pretty good on a play action pass attempt. When Bobby went to the ground, his head struck the turf with a force that resulted in a concussion. After that, his mom, fearful of her son having brain injuries later in life, forbade him from ever stepping onto a football field again. Bobby was resentful toward his mother for the rest of the semester. He, in his youthful ambitions, could not understand why she took his injury so serious. Yet, Shelby had raised him up as a single mom and was always very protective of him.

"Son, I know you wanna play football, but it's not worth your life. There is so much more to life than sports. You're not gonna challenge me on this. I'm sorry, baby."

"You are being so unfair to me. Concussions happen all the time, Ma! I can get a concussion at the skating rink if I fell the wrong way. You gon' stop me from skating, too?" Bobby replied.

"ENOUGH OF THAT," She yelled. "We're done talking about this! Go in your room if you know what's good for you."

Bobby went into his room as his mom commanded. When he did, he tore down all of the pro football posters that she had bought for him. *She* was the reason he had started football in the first place, he thought. Now, after a subtle health scare, she was taking it away from him. In a superficial way, Bobby's complaints were justified. He was truly on his way to becoming one of the premier football players in the district. In fact, he was causing such a stir that the Happs HS football coach had begun watching him from a distance. Bobby never even knew about it. That probably was for the best, too, as he would have used anything he could to try and convince his mother that he should keep playing. Nothing of that sort ever came about, though.

Once the spring semester started, Bobby was looking for a new extracurricular activity to take the place of football. He thought about playing tennis, for he had always had very good hand-eye coordination. Track and field also had his attention because he saw himself as a potential 400m runner – football had kept him well winded. One day, though, as he was walking to his algebra class, he saw a bright blue flyer that read, "BASEBALL TRYOUTS – SIGN UP BEFORE JANUARY 22nd." He never saw baseball as something he wanted to do. To him, it was tedious and boring, especially when it was on television. Something inside of him was curious about it, though. He somehow knew that the experience of playing baseball would be vastly different from spectating it. It made him develop a genuine interest. Thus, he signed his name on the flyer and went out for practice the next week.

From that point on, Bobby's attitude about baseball changed. He started to fall in love with it. From the grass, to the foul line chalk, to the sound of the bat-to-ball impact. He even loved seeing umpires call runners out or safe. It was poetry in motion to him. Bobby played third initially, but eventually became a catcher, which is a position very similar to the quarterback position in football. Most captains in baseball are catchers. No play, pitch, or sequence happens without the catcher's influence. Hence, it is like no other spot on the diamond. Bobby understood this from jump and worked his absolute best to become better day in and day out.

One other thing that Bobby grew fond of was the attention baseball brought him. And not just *any* attention. This attention drove his natural body hormone levels and affected the way he operated on the daily. Yes, you guessed it, again. Girls. Coming up, Bobby had deep insecurities that were created by having no father to guide and affirm him. When Shelby placed him in sports, he began viewing his coaches in a very favorable light, praising everything that they did, and unintentionally copying their mechanisms. Many of those men noticed this and withdrew from him. And Bobby, though young, sensed what they were doing and was broken whenever it happened. So when girls started noticing him for his efforts in baseball, it didn't take him long to experience the validation that was eluding him for so long. Many of the girls chasing Bobby were already sexually active, at just the tender ages of twelve, thirteen, and fourteen. He tried to stay away from that aspect for as long as he could. Just the topic of sex, alone, made him nervous. But when he started growing more into himself, he could not resist.

During his freshman year at Happs, he and a couple of his buddies went to the football team's home opener. While they sat in the bleachers, he noticed a beautiful, chocolate girl, with straight black hair that went past just past her shoulder blades. It was almost the exact way Marvin had looked at Claire that one day in the theatre. The only difference in this situation was Bobby's burning lust, which grew worse every time he saw a shapely girl or woman. Anyhow, the girl was walking across the stands, about four rows in front of Bobby and his friends. Bobby quickly made up his mind to approach her and soon began his journey down the steps. She was only about twenty feet away in distance, but as Bobby walked, it seemed like a mile. Half the way down, he paused in contemplation, as his insides were beginning to flare uncomfortably. *Still*, he was determined. He then continued and made it to the bleacher level she was on. He maneuvered his way around all the other students and, finally, stood right next to her. Then, he lightly tapped the girl's shoulder.

"Hey, darlin', my name is Bobby. What's your name?"

"Hi, I'm Veronica Redding. What are you doing so close to me?" She replied.

In slight panic, he slid a couple of steps away from her.

"Umm, well I saw you from across the way, and I think you pretty fly. Really, my friends thought I was too scared to approach you, but I wanted to prove them wrong. They're up a couple of rows behind us."

Bobby knew that his two friends had not said a single word about the girl. Instead of being focused on all the different sweeties present, they were actually locked in on the game. He lied to her out of desperation. She looked back to locate his friends.

"So what, y'all made a bet or something?" Veronica asked.

"Well, not necessarily. I just wanted to show them I'm man enough to step to a girl like you. Just wanted to tell you that I think you're really pretty."

Veronica welcomed the energy he was beginning to exude. When she looked at him while he talked, she could see clearly into his soul. If only Bobby understood what depths certain girls could take him to.

"Well, Bobby, I appreciate the compliment. You seem really nice. Do you have a pen?" Veronica asked.

"Umm, yeah, I do actually." Bobby said, pulling out a dark blue pen from his pocket. He handed it to her.

Veronica then grabbed Bobby's hand and began writing on his palm. "Here is my cell phone number. Call me tomorrow, okay?"

"Sounds good!" Bobby responded.

"Enjoy the rest of the game, *darlin'*."

Bobby wanted to stay there longer to get to know her, but he obliged. He had got the number, though, and that was better than nothing.

"Bet. Nice to meet you, Veronica."

She grinned back at him. "The pleasure is all mine."

Bobby walked back up to the row where his friends were. He kept looking at Veronica's handwriting on his palm. The feeling he had was similar to the very first touchdown he ever scored in football: though he was aware that he had scored for his team, a big part of him was in disbelief that he actually did it. From time to time, he looked at his hand to make sure the blue ink was still there. It had faded in the slightest bit, but it was still clear enough to read. Veronica had also written, "don't forget," under her telephone number. Every time he looked down and read her handwriting, he grew more excited. And for the rest of the night, he walked on air. Oh, and in the end, Happs football won its first home game 45-17.

The next day, around about 5 p.m., Bobby gave Veronica a call. She was waiting for him to call and was surprised he had not done it a little earlier. Still, though, she picked up for him. They ended up talking for about two hours. Right before they were about to say bye, she asked him if it was okay to come over. Bobby, excited to have a girl over for the first time, gave her the green light. Through text, he sent his address to her, attached with the phrase, "see you at 8." Bobby quickly hopped in for a quick shower and then put on one of the coolest shirts he could find. Veronica was only about three and a half miles north of the Bowen residence. She had been driving for a full year, and her dad had bought her a 2014 sky blue Chevy Camaro for her sixteenth birthday. In addition, Bobby's mom was a dedicated nurse for a hospital twenty-five minutes west of Spencer. On weekends, she usually worked later than she did during weekdays. She trusted Bobby to be responsible, as he was fourteen years of age at this point. Though, for the very first time, he was about to take full advantage of her weekend absence. Knowing that she would be gone till at least 11:50, Bobby was super confident that he was in the clear.

When 8 o'clock hit, Bobby went to the window, searching for Veronica's Camaro. He saw nothing and walked back into the living room and sat down. He waited. Fifteen minutes passed by, which seemed like forty-five to Bobby. Nervousness was building up in him, and he started to doubt that she would even show. Yet, at the time of 8:18, he heard the sound of a vehicle pulling into their driveway. Veronica had finally made it. She stepped out of her sportscar wearing blue short shorts that matched her sexy ride. In addition, her shoes were also that same color. Up top, she wore a white tank that fitted as a premium crop top. Across her perky breasts read the word "babygirl" in a sparkled cursive font. Her exposed skin looked absolutely amazing. Dark brown. Soft. Moisturized. Appealing. Goodness, gracious. As he watched her from the window, Bobby was frozen. It was as if each one of her movements was in slow motion. When she finally reached the door, she looked at him looking at her through the front window.

"Umm. Are you gonna let me in, Bobby? Or should I go back home? What are you doing in the window, man?" She said to him.

Bobby snapped out of it and hurried over to let her in. When she entered, Bobby now had to deal with her extremely attractive scent. The fragrance she wore was a toilette that smelled like the mix of a cinnamon apple and all-natural honey. With it, though, was a clean and clear scent, like something you would smell walking near a waterfall or fresh-water lake. Everything about her completely stimulated him, especially her stare when their eyes met. He was starting to drown in the ocean of her femininity. Even so, Bobby did his best to keep his head above water. As he welcomed her in, he guided her to the couch in the front room.

"I know we been talking on the phone for a couple of hours, but what you been doing all day?" He smoothly asked her.

Laughing on the couch, she answered. "Well, really, I just been chilling with my friend Rachel. She goes to Love. You know, over there in the Village?"

"Yeah, I know Love. Their baseball team is fire." Bobby responded.

"Yeah, their tennis team is pretty good, too. Rachel is the sophomore captain. We have been best friends ever since we met in sixth grade."

"That's what's up. You want something to drink?"

"No, I'm good."

They had a couple of awkward moments before Bobby turned on the TV. Out of all the channels he could have chosen, he cut on the hip-hop music channel. Veronica looked at him intensely and started wondering.

"Alright, so tell me. Why did you *really* approach me last night?"

"I told you then. I think you're fly – *I mean*, I find you very beautiful. Any guy with sense would shoot his shot at a girl like you. Just wanted to get to know you more, that's all."

She got up and walked over to the same spot he was sitting. At this point, he could feel the drift of every breath she took. She looked into Bobby's eyes and grabbed his hand.

"How much more?"

Bobby got the hint. Keep in mind that he was still a virgin then and had only kissed a girl once... on the cheek. He had absolute zero feel when it came to actual sex situations. You couldn't tell him that, though. Veronica knew his exact circumstance. In reality, she might as well have been a local thief entering the Bowen home to pilfer its most expensive item – in this case, Bobby's purity. She leaned in and kissed him. Energy exploded through Bobby's body in a way unlike any other time in his life. The kiss lasted for about eight seconds. Pulling away, Bobby stared at Veronica and received zero mixed signals from her. She didn't plan on going any place else, any time soon. Then, they got up and went into his bedroom. It doesn't take a rocket scientist to figure out the rest of what happened.

After his night of euphoria, Bobby woke up the next morning extremely depressed and unmotivated. He had not felt that bad ever since the week of his concussion and departure from football, which was three years earlier. Veronica Redding was the only thing that could make him better. In the span of just 30 hours, he had already turned into a total fiend for her companionship. Later that Sunday, he tried calling her. She did not pick up. He called again. Still, no answer. In Veronica's mind, there was nothing else to discuss with him. Bobby never knew it, but she had been hawking him down ever since the first day of school. She and her friends saw him joyfully walking down the hall and debated if he had ever been with a girl in intimacy. Somehow, they all agreed that he hadn't. Bobby had a glow of energy that was unlike any other freshman boy at Happs. Veronica accepted the challenge of taking his v-card, and she did it masterfully. He texted and called her all throughout the succeeding school week, but she still did not respond. Becoming aggravated, she blocked his number from her phone. Bobby felt like someone had cut his heart out, stomped on it multiple times with all their might, and then, with unlicensed surgeons, put it back inside of his body. He had been played. In that moment, he became more insecure than ever. Now, any girl that showed him attention automatically had an opportunity with him. He was *that* weak.

During the following school year, he went to a Halloween party with Ryan and a couple of other sophomore ballplayers. At said party is where he first met JoJo. She stood a good 5'7" and had the slim-thick build that girls go for nowadays. More than anything, though, she was insanely pretty. Bobby liked what he saw and went after her with no hesitation. She yielded, and they started dating in the middle of November. A month later, on the day before Christmas, JoJo and Bobby had sex for the very first time. It had been a little over a year since either one of them had done anything of that sort – Bobby, of course, with Veronica & JoJo with her previous boyfriend from Yukon. The experience was beyond blissful for both of them, and it created a bond that was deep and strong. Though they connected out of trauma and insecurity, to the rest of the world, they were the cutest thing going. Bobby's social media was constantly full of photos and videos of him and his girlfriend. JoJo would post him as well. They even had a photo that went viral under the #cutestcouples hashtag. It was a picture JoJo posted of them at the Happs winter formal. Thus, they were a very hot topic, both online and in real life.

That catches you up on Bobby Ray.

Bobby had finally got home from his team's doubleheader in Muskogee. Coach Dillon had given him a ride. It was about 8:30 p.m. when Bobby walked through the door of his home. About thirty minutes later, Shelby walked in and immediately embraced her son.

"I'm so proud of you, son! Seven triples? I see your hard work has been paying off! I found out about it while watching the news during my last break. It was on the bottom of the screen. Baby, I'm so sorry that I could not be there."

"It's all good, Ma. I appreciate everything you do for us. I know you just doing what you gotta do. I know you was there with me in spirit." Bobby replied.

"Next weekend, I'm taking a day off to come and see you play, alright? I wanna see you break some more records!" She said, laughing in excitement. "Bobby, I just want to see you happy. Always remember that you should be having fun. It's baseball, okay? It's just a game."

"Yeah, I know. I had so much fun today, Ma. It's crazy cause me and JoJo got into it a couple of nights ago. I was feeling down because she been ignoring me ever since. Despite all that, I was able to unlock something that I had never experienced before. It was like my focus went to a whole 'nother level."

"Baby, that little girl will be okay. Y'all are young. She needs to understand that you have priorities. And, hun, you unlocking your newfound focus, at a time when JoJo is absent, should tell you something. I know you really like her and all that, but I'm just saying. If you really want to be great, you have to figure out how to find the zone you were in today, but with consistency. Unfortunately, that may take some hard sacrifices. Think about it, son."

She walked over to Bobby and kissed him on the forehead.

"Imma go shower up and get my stuff ready for tomorrow. Did you already eat?"

"Yeah, we ate when we got back."

"Okay then. Good night, son. Love you."

"Love you, Ma,"

Their deep talks always made him feel so much better and at peace, even in the midst of him and JoJo's worst moment to date. He thought long and hard about what she told him. Had he not broken Shawn's record earlier that day, he might have not considered her words much. But Shelby had made perfect sense. He was truly on a special level that day, and if he really wanted to take baseball serious, he would find a way to accomplish that consistency. He also knew, though, that scaling down his relationship with JoJo would be extremely hard. They were inseparable. On some days, she even tossed to him in the batting cages and helped him with his catcher fundamentals. She even massaged his body from time to time. Bobby had included JoJo in so many things that it felt awkward doing life without her. In truth, he was missing her company, for he would have celebrated so much more if she was there with him. As soon as he was thinking that, he received a text message. It was JoJo. Her message simply read, "congratulations, love you." Bobby replied, "thanks, baby love you too. miss you." The next day, at lunch, Bobby went to the janitor's closet once again. To his relief, JoJo was right there waiting for him. They kissed. Bobby held on to her with a grasp tighter than normal. JoJo could literally feel that he did not want to let her go anytime soon. And so, in the span of a 45 second embrace, JoJo managed to make Bobby forget everything his mom had said to him the night before. As good as good as it felt to win, and make history in the process, nothing made him feel as good as JoJo did. And it was not even close. He was, as they say, *head over heels* for her.

After school, Bobby and his teammates headed towards the locker room to prepare for practice. Coach Dillon was waiting for them. Before they could get dressed, he told everyone to take a seat at their lockers. As they waited for everyone to arrive, much rambling went on in anticipation of coach giving them the day off. Yet, they still were not sure. Marco, often late anyways, was the last one to get there. Surprised to see everyone silent and still in school clothes, he quickly took his seat. Finally, Coach Dillon began speaking.

"Marco, how nice of you to join us!"

Everyone laughed.

"My bad, coach. I got out of English late." Marco replied.

Everyone else looked at each other, with the look of, "yeah, right!" Marco gave everyone a grin, for, he knew that they knew.

"No worries, son. Hey, guys, listen up. Words cannot describe to you how proud I am of you all for yesterday's performance. Walking into Creek, you had been counted out by many people, and, for a lot of you, even your own selves. All the negative things that were said seemed inevitable at first. You showed up and got hit in the mouth. But you didn't fold. You rose up like champions and proved the entire state wrong. Because of that, I want you all to end your week on it. Remember what it felt like to take down a giant. Remember the moment you all refused to let one loss define you."

Everyone smiled and looked at each other in excitement. It was their first off day all year. Coach continued.

"Go home and get some rest for next week. But don't think we're not getting right back to work on Monday. Pitchers, take care of your arms. Hitters, if you do some swing work, let it be at a minimum. Allow your bodies to recover, gentlemen. Now, enjoy the weekend and don't do nothin' stupid. You all are dismissed."

All the Chargers left the locker room feeling like they had just beaten the Yankees. Many of them developed a little cockiness, but it was warranted. The number four team had been talking trash about them ever since the season started. Several Happs players even received DM's talking about how horrible of a squad they were. Coach Dillon was right. All haters had to eat their words. He knew not to mess up that feeling by making them have a hard practice the next day, or even an easy one for that matter. He wanted them to fully process what it was like to be victorious and respected. And they did.

Even so, Bobby looked at his new availability as another chance to reaffirm his beautiful girlfriend. After leaving the locker room, he immediately gave JoJo a call. She answered right away.

"Whassup, babe! Aren't you at practice?" JoJo said.

"Baby, guess what?"

She got nervous.

"What is it, Bobby?" She said with a slight attitude, expecting something negative.

"Dang, girl, relax. It's good news."

"I *am* relaxed, sir. Tell me."

"Coach Dillon gave us the day off!"

"Oh, word?" She asked.

"Word. He told us we earned it after beatin' up on Creek and stuff yesterday. I was just calling you to see if you had already left. I wanna celebrate with you."

"Yeah, I'm already on the bus. That's good, though. You needed some time off anyway, as busy as you been. Happy for you, babe."

"Well, can we get together later then?" Bobby asked.

"Yeah, sure. Let me knock out my math homework and then I'll text you."

She really didn't have math homework but wanted to make it seem like she was not instantly accessible. She was not all the way over their argument.

"Okay, that'll work. Talk to you shortly, JoJo."

"Bye, babe." JoJo replied and hung up.

About two and a half hours later, JoJo texted Bobby telling him that she was done with her assignments. They ended up deciding to go to the skating rink downtown. The spot was called *Bella's*. It was a great attraction for young teens, bringing in kids from all over the metro area. Also, it was one of the few places downtown that Bobby and JoJo had not been to together. Neither of them were great skaters but decent enough to consistently make it around. Besides, they wanted to hold hands and coast during the "couples' skate" times anyway. They loved displaying their affection in public, but, surprisingly, they were always decent and respectful. They were simply two people who just so enjoyed each other's company. Don't get it twisted, though. In private, they expressed their passions strongly.

JoJo and Bobby rode the bus to Bella's together later that night. They arrived at the downtown stop around 6:55 and walked an additional twelve minutes before getting there. When they walked in, they immediately saw a medium crowd of people. Many of them had on black letterman jackets, accented with gold, that said Worth Baseball (high school in Edmond). In the mix with them were two other boys wearing powder blue jackets that read "Clear Athletics" on the back of them. One of those boys was Leonard Crowell, a junior football player at Clear HS. The other boy was Shawn. He was getting into it with a guy named Terrell Brooks, who was the star player for the Worth baseball team. Terrell had said something about Shawn being overrated, and Shawn tried to play it off. That is, until the ultimate no-no was brought forth.

"Look at this guy. Mr. *Number One Player in the Country*, lookin' ass. Shawn, you barely hit five home runs last year, and the one at State was really a foul ball, if you wanna be real. But look up my numbers, baby. I hit twelve. Twelve to lead the whole state." Terrell said.

"Bro, you got some serious nerve talking to me like that. What you trynna say anyways, you think you better than me? You jealous?" Shawn answered.

"Jealous of you? Nah, never. I don't ever see myself as no singles hitting, weak armed right fielder. You hit like a softball slasher. Oh wait, ain't that what your moms was anyway?"

Immediately angered, Shawn charged at him with all of his might. His friend Leonard quickly intervened and held him back, while Terrell's teammates kept him restrained as well. Bobby and JoJo watched the shocking development from about ten feet away.

"Don't let me catch you over here again, bro!" Shawn shouted at him.

"Bro, you ain't even gotta worry about it. I'll see you in two weeks at our house. We gon' see who the real man is. You better watch your head!"

Love and Worth were scheduled for a ballgame in the beginning of April.

"I DON'T EVER RUN! FROM NOTHING AND NOBODY!" Shawn screamed, as his friend was still holding him.

It was as serious of an altercation you can get without any punches being thrown. Shawn never liked anyone disrespecting his mother. That was the one thing that never failed to piss him off. Early on, Marvin had tried his best to teach Shawn how to be mild-mannered whenever something like that happened. Once Shawn reached puberty, though, it started to go through one ear and out the other. Marvin couldn't blame him. Anyone who ever said a cross word about Claire, in front of Marvin, was asking for a near death experience. Shawn was no better.

When the crowd finally dispersed, Shawn and his friend went someplace else. Seeing them leave, Terrell and his teammates decided to stay a little while longer. Meanwhile, Bobby and JoJo finally made their way to the skates' counter after paying their way in and dodging all the commotion. The worker, wearing a nametag that read *Julio*, came up and greeted them.

"Hey guys, what sizes y'all need?" Julio asked them.

"I need a men's twelve, and she needs a –"

"Ah, I can speak, sir." JoJo said to Bobby, interrupting him. "I will take a ladies' eight, please."

"Gotcha covered." Julio said, as he proceeded to track down their skates.

"My bad." Bobby said to JoJo.

"You're good. So, babe, what do you think that was back there? They looked like they were about to take each other's heads off!"

"I don't know, really. You know how guys sometimes get when the wrong thing is said. We don't always respond the right way when someone challenges us. One of them probably was talking bad about someone's chick or something. That usually does the trick."

They looked on. Soon, Julio was back with their skates.

"Here y'all go! Y'all have fun."

"Thanks, man." Bobby said.

Bobby and JoJo ended up having a great time on the rink. They skated for about two hours, doing the limbo, speed skate, Simon Says, and, of course, the couples' skate. Bobby bought them dinner at one of the dine-in spots near the rink, and then they rode the bus back to Spencer. JoJo did not go over to Bobby's house that night, which was not the usual ending to their dates. Instead, she kissed him at their final stop and headed back to her home. In truth, she really desired sex from him but was still trying to put up a wall to make a point. She hated not having him available upon request, so she returned the favor whenever she saw fit. Bobby was actually okay with it that night, though. He was already tired from his busy week in class and on the field. He remembered Coach Dillon telling everyone to rest up and *knew* that sex would drain out whatever energy that was left in him. Therefore, he didn't put up a fight about it whatsoever. Realizing her game was not working, JoJo walked away bothered that he didn't beg her to come over.

For the next two days, Bobby made an intentional effort to spend more time with his mom. Though she had to work more hours, she had later start times on weekends, which meant she and Bobby could have some time in the morning and early afternoon. Saturday morning, he made his mother breakfast, as well as packed her a lunch to take to work (like she did for him so many times on school and game days). Shelby was surprised to see her son not trying to leave the house, at the earliest opportunity, to be with JoJo. Bobby was fully present, and she enjoyed every second of it. She thought that her message about focus had gotten through to him. Yet, she would soon see that he was merely *behaving* different that day, and that true change was going to take more time.

CHAPTER 3: ATTITUDE ADJUSTMENTS

Right in the center Edmond, Oklahoma, laid E-City Stadium: a beautiful, imposing piece of baseball art. It had been constructed in the early 2000s as part of the city's new millennium planning project. The total cost of the stadium (you might wanna sit down) was $387 million USD, funded 60/40 between the city of Edmond and Worth High School. Built mainly to host summer and winter semi-pro tournaments, which drew millions of dollars for the city each year, it was the home field of the Worth HS baseball team (mascot: Giants). E-City's seating compacity was a jaw-dropping 67,000, which used to be the world-record for non-major-league ballparks. In addition, it was the only baseball field in the state, including college, that featured a retractable dome. Quite frankly, to play at E-City was to play at a place that felt like a world stage. And it had been. In June of 2011, E-City hosted the Semi-Pro National Baseball Championships, a tournament of the best semi-pro clubs from every state. During the opener between Oklahoma and Oregon, the stadium had its very first sell-out crowd. Even so, Kansas ended up winning that year in an epic battle against Texas. The tournament was such a success that Edmond was the host city for the next three years. E-City was a baseball player's dream, and the Worth Baseball Giants got to live it every single day.

Exactly two weeks removed from the incident at Bella's, Shawn and his team made their way north to play Worth. Historically, Shawn had played his worst games at E-City, even going all the way back to state little league tournaments that were held there. It was nothing like when he played at Clear. There, he performed magnificently, imagining his mother clapping for him in the stands. After all, it was the same place where she became one of the greatest players of all time. Clear's fans always cheered for Shawn, even though he was on the opposing team. They were happy to see an extension of their beloved hero. After every game there, Shawn broke down and cried on the way home, wishing his mom was still living. It was both beautiful and heart-wrenching. At E-City, *though*, he had no inspiration of that sort to draw from. Added, he usually played there at nighttime under the lights. The way the lights had been constructed, they gave a slight glare in the eyes of lefty batters (righties had a glare, too, but not nearly as bad). It always made Shawn uncomfortable, which disrupted his timing at the plate (Shawn was a *feel* hitter). As a result, in majority of his E-City at-bats, he hit pop-ups and weak ground balls to the infield. It frustrated him and, thus, directly impacted his defense. Shawn rarely ever took his at-bats to the other side of the ball, but E-City never failed to force it out of him. He hated it and never looked forward to playing there, even as beautiful and pristine as E-City was.

Even so, Shawn's attitude took a turn when he and Terrell got into it. Now, instead of dreading the fact that he had to play at E-City, he focused in on destroying baseballs and playing masterful defense in right field. He was driven by Terrell's comments about him being undeserving of his national #1 ranking. Shawn knew he earned it. That night at the rink, Terrell failed to mention the fact that Shawn batted .589 the previous year, breaking two triples records in the process. First, of course, he broke the record for triples in a doubleheader with four (which Bobby had just shattered). Second, he finished his sophomore campaign with a breathtaking 52 3-baggers. Terrell poked fun at his power because half of those triples would have been home runs if Shawn was stronger – hence, Terrell's "softball slasher" comment. Yet, on top of all of that, Shawn finally had the thing that inspired him to play so well when he was at Clear. Terrell making slick comments about Claire awakened something deep inside of Shawn that energized every part of his being. Since the moment he and Leonard left Bella's, Shawn managed to turn his anger into absolute motivation and positivity. It resulted in him having two *great* weeks of practice. He even finished all of his homework two weeks in advance just so he could be fully locked in when it was time to play Worth. Shawn was determined to silence Terrell, once and for all.

When the Love Bulldogs arrived at E-City, Worth was already on the field taking batting practice. Shawn walked into the park wearing his mom's Clear letterman jacket. On any other day, his coach, Damon Titus, would have forbidden such a thing, but Shawn had explained the story. Coach Titus knew that his star was on a personal mission and did not want to get in his way. In his mind, anything that would make Shawn, the best player in the country, *even better*, was worth allowing. Plus, all of his teammates knew what had happened and were fully behind him. Their senior left fielder, Eddie Ramirez, was also there that night. Only, he was skating on the rink at the time of Terrell and Shawn's confrontation, so he didn't know about it until after Shawn had already left. He, too, was on a mission to "bust their ass," as he told everyone. Eddie, a righty, had been a steady player for the previous three seasons. Yet, in his final year at Love, he was able to put all the pieces together to become a prolific ballplayer. He was actually beating out Shawn in average - .458 to Shawn's .424. Shawn still had him in homers, though, at five-to-four. They were doing almost the exact same thing that Bobby and Ryan were doing for Happs. Only, Love had a full roster of players that could get the job done. In particular, they had a freshman shortstop named Romeo Rodrigo, who was already starting for varsity. He had smooth, quick hands at short, along with a sharp bat from the right side of the batter's box. Romeo's counterpart at second, Oliver Rodrigo (his older brother) was also a special player. Prior to the season, the two of them made a bet on who would end up playing short. Oliver really earned the spot, but

Coach Titus wanted to build Romeo's confidence for the next three years. He had told Oliver that playing second base would still be something he could market in the future. Oliver, though salty at first, went with it, never holding it against his brother. The two of them became a great duo up the middle and, arguably, the best in the state. Love also had solid players elsewhere, and its pitching was top-notch.

After a long walk into E-City, the Bulldogs finally reached the visitors' dugout. All of them were ready to play. Worth, still taking BP, was playing hip-hop music from the stadium's sound system. It was a sort of intimidation tactic. Worth's hitters were very good. Unquestionably, though, Terrell was the best of them, and he was the one in the box when Love walked in. He had just hit four straight balls over the center field fence, which was 411 feet from home plate. All of them were towering blasts. When he swung at the fifth and final pitch of his round, he hit the ball so high over the left field wall that it reached the second deck. It was a gorgeous sight, similar to something you would see at a professional home run derby. Walking out of the box, he looked at the Love players and immediately saw Shawn. Shawn pretended not to notice that it was Terrell who had just hit those moonshots. He was not going to let him get into his head again. So, he ignored him and proceeded to put on his spikes. He and his team then went out to stretch.

Game time was scheduled for 2:30, which Shawn loved because there would be no glare when he was up at bat. Coach Titus had Shawn batting ninth. Yeah, you might be thinking, "how in the world does the number one amateur player in the country bat last in the lineup?" Well, his coach's reason for doing this, aside from the team being loaded with talent, was so that Shawn could face the opposing pitchers after wearing down, however so slightly. Shawn had been a leadoff hitter for the past two years, but his coach wanted to empower all of his players by challenging them (like how he put Romeo at short as a freshman). He knew all of his players and what they were capable of. Frankly, they often exceeded his expectations. It's crazy how hard people will go for you if, in their best interest, you push them.

From first pitch, Shawn and the Bulldogs dominated the Giants. At the top of the lineup, Romeo and Oliver both went 3-for-3 and scored three times. Eddie Ramirez also had a great day at the plate, going 3-4 with a homer. No one dazzled more than Shawn, though. He ended his day going 4-4. Three of those four hits were home runs to right field. The fourth was a one-hopper just past the grasp of Worth's second baseman that resulted in a single. On defense he shined as well. In the bottom of the third, he robbed Terrell of a home run, but that was just the half of it. When Terrell came up to the plate for the final time, he smoked a ball down the right field line that fell in for a hit. Shawn, as quick and agile as they come, took a perfect route to the ball, sliding towards the line to keep it from reaching the fence. He caught it with his glove. Meanwhile, Terrell was about five steps from second and rounding hard to reach third. When Shawn arose from his slide, he took a quick shuffle and threw a missile to third base. The ball went for a distance of nearly 250 feet and got there on one long hop, beating Terrell's slide by about two steps. The third baseman promptly applied the tag, and Terrell was called out by the umpire. As he got back on his feet, he took his helmet off and slammed it onto the dirt, screaming a common four-letter expletive. Yeah, that one. Shawn then casually jogged back to his position, signaling to the rest of his team that there were two outs. Had high-definition cameras been recording the game, they would have zoomed in on him grinning as he watched Terrell throw his fit. Aside from these two brilliant plays, Terrell had a single and a double in his other two times at bat. Had any other outfielder been in right field that day, he would have also had a triple and a homer to complete the cycle. Instead, he finished 2-4. It was the only time in his life that he went home upset about hitting

.500 for the day. Shawn more than accomplished what he set out to do and not once did he say a word to Terrell. He was all business. And so, Terrell had been both out-performed and out-classed by the right fielder opposite of him, after all the shade he was throwing just two weeks prior. Now, the only words he would say to Shawn were, "good game." From that point on, he would think twice before negatively commenting on the great Claire Hollins-Clement. Or, calling Shawn's arm weak, for that matter. In the end, Love won the game at a score of 12-3.

On the bus ride back, Shawn felt the pressure release from his shoulders. He finally had a good game at E-City. He reached into the top pocket of his school bag and pulled out a photo of him and Claire from 2003. He softly kissed it and then laid his head against the window. Looking out of it, he reminisced on all of the bad moments he had at E-City. In particular, he thought of a time he struck out seven times in the three games he had there in a sixth-grade tournament. He had always left thinking that many of his peers and spectators thought he was not a good ballplayer, and, for the most part, he was right. Bad performances often equate to, "he just can't get it done," in the minds of those watching. Especially in the game of baseball. Shawn hated it, because he took pride in being an excellent player. None of them knew that he had been a tournament MVP at a different ballpark. They did not know of the colossal home runs he hit in Verdigris the previous summer. All they knew was that they were watching Claire Hollins' kid, and that he was not looking like he would be as great as his mother. E-City was Shawn's nightmare for all those years. Yet, in one day, Shawn rose up and made it all transform into joy. Usually, as aforementioned, he only cried after playing at Clear. But in this moment, too, he could not help but let out a couple of tears. He finally transcended his shortcomings, and he did it in spectacular fashion. Shawn genuinely loved the game of baseball.

After the team made it back to OKC, Shawn went home to spend the rest of his Friday with Marvin and Alicia. Prior to the couple getting married, Marvin made the decision to rent out the house he initially bought for his family in 2001. He wanted those moments with Claire and Shawn to remain forever engrained in his mind. Strangely, he even wanted to remember the moment OKCPD showed up at the doorstep, informing him of Claire's murder. He really leaned into everything during the healing process, feeling every bit of the pain. He handled it better than many men would have, and it made him an even better person overall. Even so, Claire was the primary inspiration behind him buying the house in the first place. She was the one who was so excited when they first walked in front of it, all the way back in 1999. Therefore, Marvin made an intentional effort to make sure that spot was always dedicated to her. Consequently, all of the rent money went towards keeping Claire's Corner going. Marvin now moved his family to a neighborhood just ten minutes south of the former Clement residence. He had bought the house in August of 2016, four months before his and Alicia's wedding. It, also, was a two-story home, but the backyard was much bigger. Marvin wanted to make sure that there was a party space behind the house, as he was planning on having Shawn's birthday and graduation parties back there. It also featured a large office space. This would be the place where Alicia would continue doing her artwork, as she was still a prominent painter in her late-30s. Shawn never disputed with his father about making the transition, either. He understood his father's reasons and wanted to honor Claire just as much as he did. Aside from friends and family, Marvin never brought another woman inside of that old home, a duration that was twelve years after Claire's death. Now, that truly is something.

Alicia had a very strong influence on Shawn. For all those years, Marvin had been a great father to him. Yet, he was not very good at helping his son process his emotions. He often did not know what to do with him when he was upset about sports, especially after those rough nights at E-City over the years. Remember, Marvin never played sports. He did not know how to relate with his son in that way. Had Claire still been living, she would have helped him tremendously because she knew what it was like to go home 0-for-4 with four strikeouts and an error, or two, on defense. She had been in Shawn's shoes. But moreover, she was his *mother*. His caretaker. For such a long time, Shawn had no motherly nurturing in his life. But when Alicia came into the picture, that all changed.

Later that night, Alicia walked into his room before he went to sleep. Even after such brilliance on the field and overcoming adversity, there was still something bothering Shawn, and Alicia noticed it. Sitting on his bed, he was setting up his alarm for the next morning so he could get an early 2-mile run in. While doing so, he noticed her peeking in from his bedroom door.

"Hey, Alicia. What's up?" Shawn greeted her.

"Oh, I was actually wondering what was up with *you*. Most boys would be feeling on top of the world after doing what you did today. Many would be celebrating with their friends, out bowling or something. I'm glad that you spent the rest of your night with me and your dad, but I couldn't help but notice your awkwardness during dinner. You wanna talk about what's going on?"

He quickly looked away from her. His father had noticed it, too, but he always picked and chose his spots with Shawn. Not intervening was his way of toughening him up. But Alicia was on a different mission, one that would toughen him up as well. She knew that getting him to talk would develop healthier communication habits. Shawn responded.

"No, I'm good. I'm just tired, we had a long day at the park," he said, still avoiding eye contact.

"Boy, I've been around you long enough to tell when something's wrong. It's obviously not about baseball. Is this about that kid Terrell?" Alicia said.

"No, definitely not that dude. I showed him what was up today."

"Okay, so is it about your mother?"

"No." Shawn said.

"Okay, *well did I do something*?" She asked jokingly.

Laughing with her, he responded. "No, ma'am. You didn't do anything and neither did my dad. Y'all are good. Thanks for dinner tonight, by the way."

"Yeah, hun."

There was a pause for about ten seconds. Shawn wanted her to leave after thanking her for the meal, but he could not escape her. Alicia knew that something else was getting at him and was determined to help. She finally walked over to his bed and sat next to him.

"If it's none of that, then this must be about a girl." Alicia stated.

Shawn did not think she would crack the code, but she did. With ease, too.

"Umm. Yes, actually. How'd you know?"

"Just a good guess." Alicia answered. "What's her name?"

"Lisa Webb." Shawn admitted.

"Okay, well don't stop there. Tell me what she's like."

He had another brief pause. Talking about Lisa was hard for him because, out of all of the girls he ever asked on a date, she was the one he revered most. Nonetheless, he tackled the task and started describing her to Alicia.

"Well, she just so happens to be the smartest girl in the district. That's no stretch, either. She's like a genius. And she's a very pretty girl, with one of the prettiest smiles you would ever see. She's probably like 5'7" with long brown hair. Her complexion is like, umm, the color of brown sugar. I normally don't enjoy English class,

but this year, I look forward to it every day because Lisa's in there."
He quickly paused, in slight embarrassment. "I can't believe I just
said all of that to you, don't tell Dad."

"No worries, I won't. I'll leave that up to you. So, what
happened? Did you and Lisa get into an argument or something?"

"Not quite. About a month or so ago, I had asked her to go to
the movies with me. She said no. I, being dumb, did it in the middle
of the hallway, in front of the whole school basically. Everyone was
talking about it, and I guess I got prideful. Here I am, this big
baseball star, and I can't even get a girl from my own school. Well, I
mean *the girl*. I don't know, I guess I felt embarrassed that it didn't
go how I imagined. What can ya do, though. Can't win 'em all." He
said, looking down at his folded arms.

This was Alicia and Shawn's deepest conversation up to date. She
was respectful of his mom's place in his heart and made sure she
stepped in only when it felt natural. This was, without question, one
of those times.

"Shawn, you are one of the best young men out here. The fact
that you are able to respect girls, while making your requests known
to them at the same time, is a testament to how well your father
raised you. You are a good-looking, young black man, who also
happens to be the best baseball player in the nation. But that is not
all that you are. You have so much more to you. Only, Lisa may not
see it yet. If she truly is worth your time, she will see you for your
mind and your heart. But you can't make her do it. She has to want
to *for herself*. Until then, there is nothing you can do except be who
you are, Shawn."

Blown away by how easily Alicia laid out the situation, he looked
at her with gratitude and relief.

"Yeah, I guess I just have to keep focusing on me. I do pretty
good at hiding it, though. My Dad always taught me to never show a
girl that you're sweating her." Shawn replied.

"Yeah, but that shouldn't invalidate your feelings. You're still human, Shawn. You have to process your emotions. Otherwise, they are gonna come out in a way that you don't want them to. How about this. Whenever you wanna talk about Lisa, or anything else for that matter, you just let me know. Of course, you always can talk to your father, too. He always wants to know what's going on with you. But I'm right here whenever you need me. Okay?"

"That works for me. Thank you, Alicia."

"Always. Good night, hun."

"Good night."

And so that entire day was an emotional rollercoaster for Shawn. He did not expect to be thinking about Lisa on the day of one of his greatest baseball moments. After all, he had not really thought about her since the day he and his peers gave their speeches in Mrs. Gates' class. What it was, he was so hyper focused on playing Worth that he suppressed all of his other feelings stirring up inside. In reality, he thought the world of Lisa Webb. Even though he still was a virgin, he often fantasized about intimacy with Lisa, whether it was a daydream or a dream while he was sleeping. She had an aura about her that could stimulate the mind of even the most mature of men. Yet, she had the emotional protection of a great shield or barrier. Lisa understood the potency of her beauty and talent. She knew that, in community with the wrong people, she was bound to be used for someone's motive. So many people had failed her, and it was a lesson she was tired of learning. From that point, she was meticulous about everyone and everything. When viewing Shawn, she thought of him as a school jock who had access to whatever he wanted because of his baseball gifts. In many respects, she was correct. But Shawn was never one to always push that button of instant gratification. His father had raised him right, teaching him to work hard for everything and to never think anything was entitled to him. Lisa did not know that, though. When she rejected him, it was simply because she wanted the record to show that she turned down the guy that every other girl in the school wanted. Deep down, too, she wanted to see how much harder Shawn would try. If he would DM her online or write her a note in class. She wanted to see him beg, like most boys did for her regularly. But Shawn never did. He left it alone.

The following Monday, Shawn went to school holding his head high with his chest out. Though much of it had to do with his game against Worth, the rest of it had everything to do with his newfound self-esteem. Alicia had unlocked something in Shawn. She helped him realize that it was okay to not feel the best when other people did not look at him for who he was. That, it was natural, and he was not alone in that regard. Shawn was very much like his father. It never took him long to put the pieces together. He learned that his breakdowns did not mean that he was weak. Only, they meant that he was hurting from something. Alicia became the catalyst to him getting to the root of the things that damaged him. As a result, he became more aware of himself, which helped him become more confident in his choices. Everyone saw Shawn as confident anyway, but *this* was a new and improved version of that confidence. What they were seeing was the result of a young man finally receiving the motherly guidance that had been absent for most of his life. What they were seeing was an increased sense of security. The opposite thing is usually said about young black boys. Usually, a high percentage of them grow up with their mothers while their fathers live a life elsewhere. As a result, many find their affirmation in the external things provided by the typical American lifestyle. Two of the main avenues of this are romantic relationships and sports. This type of thing usually creates issues that are only resolved once the damage has already been done. Shawn had this in reverse but was met with the same realm of obstacles. Only, he was now blessed enough to have the guiding force that Alicia provided. In other words, Shawn was already secure from his upbringing, but now, as he learned to process things, he could know *why* that was so.

After English class, Shawn went to his locker and was surprised to see someone there waiting for him. You'll never guess who it was (okay, maybe you have a good idea of who). Lisa Webb. Shawn did not know whether to keep walking past his locker or to grab his things and ignore her. But he could feel his father, Marvin, demanding him to be the young man he raised, which was one who was chivalrous, kind, and gentle. He really was just shocked that she popped up just a couple of days after talking about her with Alicia. It was like a magic trick or something, Shawn thought. Even so, he walked up to his locker and greeted her.

"Well, if it isn't Miss Lisa Webb."

"In the flesh," she said, smiling while holding her books. "How are you?" Lisa said.

"I'm well. Just trynna get to my next class, we got a benchmark review in history. Mr. Tyme been on my head about raising my grade." Shawn told her.

"Oh yeah? What you got in there?" Lisa asked.

"I got a 89.2, but he saying I should have a 96 or better. I missed a couple of assignments at the start of the season, so it's the zeroes keepin' my grade down. It is what it is, though. What's been up on your end?"

"Oh, I've just been studying hard. I'll be taking my first SAT on the week before finals. I been feeling that same type of pressure Mr. Tyme been giving you. Only, it's from my parents at home."

"Well, I got no doubts that you'll do your thing and pass with flying colors. You're a great student, Lisa. Trust your work." Shawn said.

Shawn's energy exceeded Lisa's expectations. He was acting as if he had never tried to shoot his shot. She almost didn't walk up to his locker that day, in fear that he would not show up (like before). Something in her, though, told her to try again.

"Thanks for that. I'll do my best. Hey, listen, I know I kinda turned you down awhile back, but I was wondering if I could make it right. I know you and the team gotta work the soccer game Friday. You down to go to Bella's after?"

It was like Alicia had called Lisa herself and told her she was making a huge mistake turning down her son. But, in reality, Lisa was realizing it herself. Just like Alicia predicted the *right girl* would.

"Umm, yeah that sounds nice. I gotta make sure I can, though. I know Romeo and Oliver was thinking about going to Spencer to one of their buddy's house. But I'll confirm with you later tonight, if that's cool?" Shawn replied.

"Yeah, that's great. Let me give you my number. You got a paper and pen?"

Shawn pulled out a black pen and the index cards he had used during his speech (with the baseballs all over the back). She told him her number.

"Got it. I'll text you after I finish my homework. Nice to see you."

"Looking forward to it. See you soon, Shawn." Lisa responded.

Hours later, Shawn had another great showing at practice. Afterwards in the locker room, his teammates gathered around him in sudden excitement. At their game against Worth, someone just so happened to be recording when Shawn robbed Terrell of his home run. Not only that, in anticipation of Shawn doing something amazing again, the guy recorded him on defense for the remainder of the game. Hence, he also captured footage of Shawn throwing Terrell out in the final inning. The anonymous individual proceeded to post it online around 4 p.m. the following Monday, right while Shawn and the Bulldogs were at practice. The video was entitled *Shawn Clement destroys Terrell Brooks at E-City*. It immediately got over 60,000 views within the first hour. Shawn's teammates clowned Terrell in the locker room, calling him Shawn's son and another word that just so happens to rhyme with ditch. Shawn played along with them, for he had a bunch of built-up energy about it all anyways. Though he was usually humble, he could not help but bask in the glory. He was due for it. Whenever he tried to downplay his accomplishments, his teammates were always there to praise him even more. They truly had his back, and he had theirs. Back north in Edmond, Terrell had just got out of practice, too. When he came in the Worth facility and put away his things, he looked at his cell phone. In his messages was the link to the video. After viewing it the first time, he watched it a couple times over again, just to be sure that it was him. Realizing he had been blasted online, he then viciously threw his phone at the wall in anger. Though Terrell lived to see another day, his phone didn't make it.

Shawn's day just kept getting better and better. When he got home from practice, he quickly showered and then knocked out his homework from his history and English classes. He did it in prolific timing, for he had developed strong study habits after finishing his homework two weeks in advance. Therefore, he was able to text Lisa before dinner time. When he did, she did not respond right away. So, in waiting, Shawn went downstairs to get him a quick snack to keep him. And right then, Marvin and Alicia walked through the front door. Shawn greeted them.

"What's up y'all? Where y'all been, I've been home for about two hours now. I already showered, finished my homework, and *everything*."

"Impressive, son." Marvin replied. "But Alicia and I actually have a surprise for you."

"Yeah, hun, we've been noticing your increase in hard work as of late. You have been knocking out your schoolwork just as good as you knock those baseballs out of the park. That is something we hope to see continue. As a reward, we went and got you – well, come and see for yourself." Alicia said, signaling Shawn towards the door.

Shawn, confused and genuinely surprised, walked to where they were standing.

"You ready?" Marvin asked his son.

"Umm, I *think* I am."

"Okay. C'mon, babe, let's show him." Marvin told Alicia.

As they opened the door and walked towards the driveway, there in it sat a 1965 Chevrolet Malibu. Its color was a two-tone blend of baby blue and light green. The chrome-finished rims were perfectly proportionate to the car's frame. On the inside of the car was white leather seating, accented with dark blue suede. Needless to say, it was a breathtaking vehicle. Shawn remembered seeing an old Malibu as a kid and instantly telling his dad that it was his favorite car. Marvin, of course, like he did with Claire and the first house, took it to heart. Keep in mind that he was now a multi-millionaire. He never bought Shawn a car because he wanted him to stay focused on school and baseball. Even more so, though, he wanted Shawn to develop a desire for a car in a healthy, gracious way. Sure, his dad was one of the wealthiest men in the region, but did that mean Shawn automatically deserved a Benz or a McClaren? Marvin didn't think so. But like Alicia mentioned, they wanted Shawn's excellence to continue rising. Staring at the car, he stood in disbelief of what his parents had done for him.

"Are you freakin' serious right now? TELL ME Y'ALL ARE MESSING WITH ME?!" He yelled in excitement.

"Yeah, son. *This* is all you." Marvin replied. "I know you're excited, but before I hand you these keys, we are going to inform you of the conditions."

Alicia interlocked her right arm into Marvin's left, smiling at their son's beaming joy. Shawn looked in his dad's eyes and began closely listening.

"Of course, Daddy. What's the terms?" Shawn replied.

"The very first thing: I don't wanna catch you in this thing with any of those girls at school, unless you run it by me and Alicia first. The moment you sneak around is the moment you lose privileges. Secondly, do not speed in this ride, even on the highway. This is a classic car, and you are a young black boy. You are already a target. Don't give them a reason to mess with you. Finally, you are only to drive the car outside of school. I don't want it sitting in that parking lot for so long. Outside of that time, feel free to do what you want. Got it, kid?" Marvin said.

"Yeah, I got you. I'll drive legal, I promise."

"*Oh*, and you are to keep this car in tip-top shape. That means oil changes, car washes, and detailing on the regular. I know you got ball, but you're going to have to find a way. New toys, unfortunately, are costly. But, if you really want it, you'll do it. We trust you."

Marvin then handed Shawn the keys to the car. Shawn shook his hand and hugged him. He reached over and hugged Alicia right after. Then, he went and sat in the driver's side and rolled down the windows, smiling at his folks as they took photos of him with their smart phones. Shawn was so happy.

When Marvin and Alicia headed back in to give Shawn some alone time with his new car, he stopped them in their tracks. He had remembered something potentially important going on at the end of the week. He did the responsible thing and ran it by them.

"Oh yeah, Daddy, I forgot. This Friday, I may be going on a date at Bella's around *seven-ish*. I haven't confirmed with her yet, but I told her I was going to get back to her. Is it cool if I pick her up in the car?"

"What's this girl's name?" Marvin replied.

"Lisa Webb. She's in my grade. Most likely next year's valedictorian."

Alicia looked at Shawn and winked. He knew the signal was about the dating advice she had just given him.

"Impressive. How long y'all been dating?" Marvin asked.

"Well, this will actually be our first date. She's a good girl, though. Very respectful and everything. Not your average girl, that's for sure."

"I'll tell you what, son. I would rather you not do that, simply because I want you to do things healthy and the right way. Though it would be nice to pick her up, you should tell Lisa to get to Bella's on her own. Once y'all have gone out on several dates and see that it's something there, *then* that's when you ride to spots together. For now, though, this car is strictly *your* space. No one else's. You see what I'm saying, son?"

"I got you. You can trust me, Daddy. Love you."

"Love you, Shawn."

After the conversation about car boundaries, Shawn ignited the engine and took his ride for a spin. He drove south of The Village, eyeing down the sights of Bricktown. Upon making it, he found a 5-level parking garage and drove all the way up to its top. It was about 6:55, and the sun had just begun to set. He parked the car near the boundaries and then stepped out. Then, he walked to the hood of his car and sat on its edge, taking in the overlooking view of downtown Oklahoma City. Processing, he thought about how good he had been playing on the field. How he finally conquered his E-City shortcomings. Then, he thought about how grateful he was to have approved of Alicia, for she had become a true rock for him. Naturally, he then thought about Claire. Shawn had always visualized his mother gifting him with his first car. Shoot, he envisioned her being a part of so many of his firsts. His first home run. His first straight-A semester at school. His first school dance. But she had missed all of those things because a coward, with a gun, took her from him. Shawn didn't cry, but he did have a brief moment of despair. A little bit a rage was in there as well, for, like his father, he wanted revenge on the guy. But Shawn had become much better at breathing deeply, which helped ease the anger out of him and let things go. He knew better than to go off the deep end, especially on such a day like this one. All of it is just to say: he loved and missed his mother. Even so, the last thing Shawn thought about, while atop the parking garage, was Lisa Webb. He was wondering why she, *all of a sudden*, had a change of heart. In the middle of those thoughts, he quickly hopped back into the car and drove home so that he could give her a call.

As Shawn parked his car back into the driveway at his house, he hesitated to go inside. He did not want to have too much more time to question Lisa's motives. So, he stayed inside of his car and dialed her number on his phone. Adjusting his chair, he pressed the green call button and laid his head back on its rest. Mind still racing, he waited as the call dialed. Ten seconds later, Lisa finally picked up.

"Hey, Shawn!" Lisa greeted him. She was in the middle of filing her nails.

"What's up, how are you?" Shawn greeted her back.

"Good, actually! Better, now that you called. How'd your homework go?" She said.

"Oh, I finished it earlier than I thought I would, so I figured it was a good hour to call instead of text."

"Got you, got you. So what's up, you down to go to Bella's Friday? I heard they were doing Glow in the Dark Skate that night. Should be pretty cool, huh?"

"Actually, I wanted to ask you something first." Shawn answered.

Surprised, she stopped doing her nails, wondering what he had to say.

"Umm, sure. What's up?"

"I just need to know why you turned me down last month and then pulled a complete 180. What's different? Why not say yes to when I asked you *then*?"

There was a pause for about eleven seconds. Lisa was not used to boys challenging her motives. It was usually the other way around. She was still able to answer him, though.

"Well, Shawn, I had to check myself. I never stopped to think of you beyond being the number one player in America. To be honest, I try to stay away from athletes because many of them are out of control and only desire one thing from me. I made the mistake of bunching you in that group." Lisa said.

Shawn slightly grew angry.

"So what made everything change?" He asked, with a tone that demanded a crystal-clear answer.

"It was the day you gave your speech in Mrs Gates' class. I felt all high and mighty because I gave this great speech, but then you, as the very last person, proceeded to give one even greater. Shawn, your speech was beautiful. For the first time, I saw you for your mind. And was very pleased. So I guess I just needed a little attitude adjustment. To see that I wrongly judged you and your peers. I wanted to make up for it. Besides, I find you *extremely* handsome."

Shawn's anger disappeared. He understood what she said and chose not to hold it against her.

"Makes sense. I guess it ain't as bad as what I thought."

"So we good?" Lisa asked.

"Yeah, we're good. Okay, how does 7:30 sound for Friday?"

If only Shawn saw the smile Lisa had when he asked her this. It was, perhaps, bigger than the smile he had just an hour prior, when his parents surprised him with a classic, custom Chevy.

"That sounds perfect, Shawn. I'll meet you at the lobby. I guess I'll probably see you at school, but see ya then?"

Shawn laughed. "Yeah, that works. See you then, Lisa."

The two of them were very excited, and Friday came just as quick as they were wanting it to. After working the Love girls' soccer game, which the Lady Bulldogs lost 4-2, Shawn hurried home to eat and freshen up. He decided to wear a grey oversized shirt with light blue jeans. Lisa also chose to wear jeans, but up top, she wore a blue long sleeve that read "LOVE & LITERATURE," across her chest. Anyway, Shawn did as his father asked and went to Bella's alone. Lisa, on the other hand, had taken the bus. She lived on the eastside of OKC, which was about fifteen minutes southeast of where Shawn stayed. Lisa pushed a black convertible Mustang, but it had been in the shop since Wednesday of that week. What solid timing, Lisa thought, for it to start having brake pad issues on the week of her date with Shawn. Still, she did not let it get in the way. She liked walking around the city and using its transportation anyway. It helped stimulate her creative proclivities. She was a true breath of fresh air.

When they met in the lobby, Shawn paid for both of their tickets. They went up and met with Julio, the same guy that had given Bobby and JoJo skates on the night of the Shawn vs. Terrell shouting match. Shawn ordered for a size thirteen, and Lisa ordered a size seven. They put on their skates on a bench about ten feet away from the first rink entryway.

Soon, Lisa and Shawn were cheerfully skating next to each other. Throughout their night, all of their favorite music was constantly playing, hit after hit. Many other high schoolers were there as well and actually, for the first time in a while, outnumbered the middle schoolers. The aura was full of young, passionate energy. Shawn saw several of his friends, including guys that went to Clear and Happs. Lisa saw some of her friends, too. They, all great academics themselves, were eyeing her about being there with a jock. But she ignored them. When it was time for the Couples' Skate, all of the people out on dates went and skated to love songs. That is, everyone except Lisa and Shawn. Instead, they chose to sit down on the bench, right outside of the rink, and talk to one another. They were able to still speak in normal voices, even though the music was playing loudly. The two of them were focused on each other.

"So I heard about what happened a couple weeks ago with that Worth kid. How are you handling that? You all good?"

"Yeah, I'm cool." Shawn replied. "I put all of it to rest last Friday. Honestly, I wasn't expecting for those two plays to go viral like they did. Baseball is hard and will humble you at the drop of a dime. Terrell's embarrassment from that day, alone, would have been enough for me."

"Yeah, I hear you Shawn. But that's not what I heard from Oliver and Romeo at lunch the other day. They said that y'all clowned him pretty hard in the locker room." Lisa said.

Shawn laughed, remembering the moment she was talking about.

"Yeah, we did have a little fun with it. But still, I can't definitively say that, if it were up to me, I would have uploaded the clips. Maybe on the day of our argument, yeah. The guy had dissed me and talked about my mom right over there in front of that lobby," Shawn pointed. "Anyone would have been heated and ready to do whatever. Still though, after the fact and in a rational state of mind, I would not have done *that* to him."

"Shawn, your character is unbelievably noble. I wish we would have done this much sooner than today, if I can be honest."

Shawn grinned and saw an opening for a joke.

"Yeah, we *could* have if you let me take you out the first time. Maybe this would have been date number three or four, instead of just number one," he said, laughing.

"Okay, yeah, I deserve that one." Lisa said, laughing with him. She then stopped and looked into his eyes. "But thank God for first dates, right?"

"Yeah. Thank God."

For the next twenty minutes, they sat there and talked, getting to know more about one another. It was as blissful and pure of a first date that you can imagine. Neither one of them had anything on their mind except being present in the moment. After a while, Shawn bought them food and drinks from concessions. Lisa had a turkey sandwich, ranch tortilla chips, and a lemonade. On the other hand, Shawn ordered two hot dogs (with mustard), fries, and a cup of iced water. When they finally decided to leave, Shawn walked her to her bus stop like a true gentleman. They briefly hugged and then departed for their separate ways. Both of them smiled continuously on the way back home.

CHAPTER 4: GOOD SPORTSMANSHIP

The following Wednesday, Shawn and the Bulldogs made their way to the southside of OKC to play against Martin Luther King High School. In the standings from the prior season, the MLK Tigers were right in the mix. But when their star player, Brooks Lynn, got hurt on the week before the playoffs, the wind was knocked right out of them. Consequently, they ended up losing in the first round of the postseason. Since the start of this new campaign, though, Brooks was a man on a mission. A four-star center fielder, he had been performing on nearly the same level as Shawn. He was leading all of Oklahoma in putouts and assists at his position. And quite frankly, Brooks was better than Shawn on defense. The viral plays that Shawn made on Terrell were the kind of plays Brooks made on an every-game basis. Literally. For example, against Bobby and his Chargers earlier in the season, Brooks made a play at the warning track, where he caught the ball and then collided with the metal outfield fence face-first. After catching it, he then threw an absolute laser to second base to get the guy that was trying to tag up from first. Again, from the *warning track*. Brooks had a black eye for about a week, but when people asked about it, all he said was (about the wall), "you should have seen the other guy." His bat was no slouch, either. Brooks, who batted three-hole most days, rarely ever mis-hit the baseball. His batting style was very cerebral, a lot different from Shawn and Bobby, who both relied more on power. Instead, Brooks was a classic singles hitter who would only hit extra base hits when his team needed them most. By far, he had the best bat control in the entire state.

Shawn and Brooks were good friends. The two met in 2012, at ages eleven and twelve. Shawn, of course, was a year younger.

It was at this time when Brooks' parents began bringing him up to Claire's Corner to receive batting instruction. The facility had previously been exclusive to softball, especially during the immediate years following Claire's death. But as Marvin appointed new trainers over the years, baseball slowly poked its way into the picture. Marvin did not mind it because Shawn was gradually getting more involved with the game. In addition, training at Claire's Corner was a way Shawn stayed closely connected to his mom. Anyway, he and Brooks first met in the batting cages in May of that year. They were being trained by the same instructor, a man named Harold Cupp, who was a semi-pro player at the time. That day, he had scheduled Shawn and Brooks in the same time slot by mistake. When they both showed up, they were confused. For, neither of them had ever done hitting or fielding workouts with another player (sessions were one-on-one). But they were able to make it work, and it actually turned out to be one of the better sessions that either of them had all year. Shawn studied Brooks up-close and liked the way the ball shot off of his bat. As opposed to the classic slight-uppercut hitting style, Brooks hit low line drives to every part of the field. At that particular time, though, he was having trouble with pulling his shoulder, which caused him to roll over a lot. Shawn, on the other hand, was already turning into a hitter that seemingly had no flaws in his swing. It didn't matter if it was a fly ball, line drive, or grounder. Shawn *smoked* the majority of baseballs that were thrown to him. Hence, his bat path was doing just fine. Brooks needed help far more than he did. Their instructor had him do a drill where he could only hit the ball to the opposite field. While it helped, Shawn stepped in and gave Brooks something a little more effective. He told him to adjust the way he was loading his swing. "You're forcing your hands back. Let your body naturally load, and I promise you'll stay through those balls more," Shawn told him. Brooks listened and applied it immediately. The rest of his rounds that day were flawless. Brooks was shocked that he was able to eliminate his habit so quickly, as swing adjustments usually take a while to materialize. He was very appreciative of Shawn's help and also admired that another player was secure enough to offer advice and not expect anything in return. Shawn's demeanor and energy were always genuine, even at that early adolescent stage. Marvin had instilled that in him. But ever since that day, Shawn and Brooks stayed in touch and became good friends and supporters of one another. On the night before their matchup, Brooks gave Shawn a call.

"What's up, my guy! You ready for tomorrow?" Shawn answered the phone and asked.

"Whassup, bro. I think I'm ready, man, I feel pretty good. I was calling to ask you the same thing. I heard you been balling even harder than last year. Of course, you know I ain't surprised. You got every bit of Claire Hollins in you." Brooks responded.

"Thanks, bro, that really means a lot. I just hope she's looking down, smiling at me. But, man, I been hearing the same about you. Bro, you really out here throwing kids out from the warning track?"

Brooks laughed. "Bro, I don't even know how I did it. I busted my face against the wall and somehow still threw the ball on a line to gun him down at second. I can't lie, though. As much as my face hurt, it felt amazing. It was like some Ichiro or Roberto Clemente type stuff. Pretty cool."

"Ain't news to me, bruh. I been knowing you nice with the glove. How the swing been feeling?"

"Man, I started out slower than I wanted to, but I been swinging it a little better the last two weeks. Had some bad habits that I developed during my recovery last summer. It was frustrating, but I got through it." Brooks said.

"I got faith in you that you'll keep it going. Your swing is great."

"Yeah, thanks to you. Ever since the day we met at your mom's facility, my swing has developed into a natural movement. Man, how did you have so much knowledge on swings at just eleven years old? Oh wait – I forgot whose son you were. Never mind." Brooks said, chuckling.

"Yeah, it's gotta be my mom. I got it honest. But, man, I'm gonna be giving you some work out there in center, so you better be ready!" Shawn said jokingly.

"Center is on lock, my guy, just be sure to cut off them balls I hit to you down the right field line. I'm gonna test that arm, too. We gon' see if it's gotten stronger like they been saying."

"That's a bet then! Hey, bro, get you some good rest. I'll see you when we pull up." Shawn said.

"Sounds good, Shawn. See you at the field."

Love and MLK were not evenly matched. Brooks was MLK's only bright spot, while Love had a whole team of guys that were already receiving college recruitment letters. Brooks was a great leader, though. Similar to how Bobby was to Happs, he galvanized other players by setting a great example. Because of it, the Tigers were able to come out hot against the Bulldogs. In top half of the first, their starter pitched a three-up three-down inning, as both Rodrigo brothers flew out and so did the three-hole batter. This created good momentum for MLK going into the bottom half. Both of their first two batters got on with walks. Brooks was next up. But, before he could step in the box, their third base coach signaled a double steal. Thus, as soon as Love's pitcher motioned for the first pitch, both of the runners jetted to their next base. Love's entire defense was surprised at the play, and there was no throw. So, in what seemed like two seconds, two Tiger runners were already in scoring position with no outs. When the second pitch was finally thrown, Brooks poked it down the right field line just like he told Shawn he would. Both runners scored with ease, as Brooks galloped into second base standing up. 2-0. In the next inning, two more Tigers drove in a run. 4-0. The Bulldogs were not expecting to be shook so early in the game. And even though their batters consistently hit balls hard, they were right at the MLK defensive players. For instance, during the top of the third, Shawn smoked a line drive to right-center that would have been a sure double on most days. But Brooks, who was playing over in anticipation for Shawn to pull, tracked it down with no issue. Right after him, both Rodrigo brothers hit line drives directly at the second baseman. Another 1-2-3 inning. In the bottom third, Brooks came back up to bat with one out, runners on second and third. After taking a first pitch fastball for a strike, he swung at a 78-miles-per-hour curveball and connected. After impact, the ball traveled 330 feet in the air and over the left field fence. A three-run shot and just his second home run of the season. 7-0, MLK. But that was as good as it got for him and his team. In the top of the fifth, Coach Titus tore into his Love players, telling them that they were playing like the game was already lost. At one point, he said, "we might as well leave right now, since y'all don't wanna play today." This lit a fire under every player in the Love dugout. They all looked into each other's eyes and gained a collective understanding of what time it was: time to fight back. The kick in the rear was exactly what the Bulldogs needed, as they powered back to score *fourteen* unanswered runs, while also shutting the Tigers out for the remainder of the game. And so, the game ended with a score of 14-7.

Afterwards, Shawn and Brooks took a photo with each other at home plate. It was cool to see that the outcome of the game did not negatively affect their friendship. In fact, it strengthened it. Once everyone, including the OKC sports media, got their photos, the two of them chatted for about five more minutes. Brooks asked Shawn what he had planned for the weekend, and Shawn told him that he was free Saturday night. They proceeded to make plans to catch the local minor league ballgame downtown at 6:30 that evening. In terms of passion for baseball, Brooks and Shawn were identical. Both of them would live at the ballfield if they could.

Whenever their buddies ever asked them to go catch a game, they never hesitated to say yes if they were available. It was rare. Two prominent high school athletes from different schools, and the only ounce of competition they had was the simple fact of them wearing different-colored uniforms. Other than that, they wanted to see each other excel at all things. Healthy relationships are hard to come by that early in life, but they, without question, had one.

Lisa and Shawn had scheduled Saturday morning for a date at Mocha Time, a coffee joint that was just ten minutes south of Love High. Lisa loved the place. Not so much for the coffee, but for the fresh aura it constantly had. It inspired her to be productive, as she and her friends went there a lot to study and work on group projects. She even wrote her first book of poetry there. But when she started dating Shawn, she wanted to go to a place where she knew she would be comfortable and her natural self. Bella's was a cool spot, for sure, but it was very introductory level. Mocha Time was the perfect place for a second date. A place to get a little further beyond the typical, "what's your name, where you from, what's your zodiac sign?" When discussing about it, Shawn agreed to go because he was an occasional coffee drinker. He was not a fan of soda or sugary juices, but a hot latte, with vanilla, would make his entire day. Marvin never forbade him from it because he knew his son only did it in moderation. He figured he'd rather his son catch the occasional caffeine rush than the ever-so-often intoxication of an alcoholic beverage.

Regardless, Shawn arrived at the coffee spot at 10 a.m. on the dot. He was just getting used to pushing his beautiful car around all of OKC. He had even given it a name already: the *Shawn-mobile* (he was not very creative when it came to naming things). But Lisa, contrarily, was running late. Earlier that morning, the work on her Mustang was finally completed. Initially, she had planned to meet Shawn by bus again, but the men who fixed the car called her around 9 o'clock and told her it was ready. The place was in Midwest City, so she took the taxi there, arriving at 9:35. When they gave her the rundown of the car, ten more minutes had passed. She left at 9:51, and heading northwest, she exited Midwest City's city limits around 9:58. Lisa finally made it to Mocha Time at 10:15. Shawn had just pulled out his phone to call her, but she walked through the door right before he could press dial. She rushed up to him at the table, and he got up and hugged her. Shawn then pulled her chair out for her.

"I was getting worried, Lisa. Everything all good?" Shawn asked.

"Well, yeah everything's fine," she said, as she sat down and thanked him for his chivalry. Shawn sat back down in his chair. Lisa then continued. "So, I was gonna take the bus here at first, but they finally finished repairing my car this morning and told me to come get it. I thought I was going to still make it in time driving, but everything took longer than what I thought. Sorry to have kept you waiting, Shawn." Lisa replied.

Shawn looked away for a second. She did not text or call him to let him know that she was going to be late. For a moment, she had thought about doing so, but she let everything play out naturally. As girls do, she wanted to collect more data on her date. Shawn still being there would say a lot about his interest, she thought. But usually, after waiting for that long, he would have left. Shawn had been stood up multiple times before, and it never failed to crush his feelings. So, to prevent it from happening again, he put in a fifteen-minute rule when he was 15. Since doing that, he only had to use it once – on Monica Dominguez, a girl he met at a party at Romeo and Oliver's place (also located in The Village). But this wasn't his first date with Lisa, and he was truly intrigued by her. So, he gave her a pass.

"Ya know, most girls would have been having coffee by theyself after making a brotha wait for so long."

"Well, sir, *I* ain't most girls. And how bout this. Next time, I'll be sure to notify you if I am running a little tardy," Lisa said.

Shawn laughed because she said "tardy," like they were in school or something. She was so charming that even her nerdiness was attractive. He then moved on to the next subject.

"Yeah, that works, Lisa." Shawn said. "Anyway, which one is your car? I feel like I never seen you driving in the school parking lot."

She pointed to her sparkling black Ford Mustang. "That's me right there. It's a 2016."

"Wow, impressive. I thought you would have been in, like, a sedan or SUV. I never would have guessed you for American muscle." Shawn stated.

"Like I said, I ain't most girls. My dad always took me to car shows as a kid. Whenever he would ask which ones I liked, I usually pointed at the current or classic Mustang models. What can I say, I like what I like." Lisa said.

"I feel it, I feel it. Of course, it ain't as cool as Chevy, but it's nice." Shawn replied.

"*Oh*, don't be trying to flex just because your old school ride is Chevy. Fords are great cars and trucks, too. I'll take my Mustang over your Malibu any day, brother." Lisa responded. She was really fronting because she knew that Shawn's whip was very close to the style of the cars she would point out at car shows with her dad. Only, it was more beautiful than any one she had ever seen. But she was never quick to pad the male ego. She was emotionally intelligent.

"Whatever you say, Lisa Webb."

She looked at him and smirked. "*Shawn Clement*, what are you gonna order?"

"I think I'll get a vanilla latte, hot. Probably some scrambled eggs and toast with avocado. What about you?" Shawn said.

"Umm, I'm feeling an espresso today. And I'm thinkin' maybe just a blueberry muffin." Lisa said.

Soon, the waiter came up and got their orders. Lisa and Shawn were turning out to be great friends. Anyone watching them could tell that they had a great connection. Even by the way they looked each other in the eye. It was chemistry. But even more so, it was pure and fun. The only physical thing they had done was hug (and they only did that twice before). They ended up spending an hour and a half in Mocha Time, talking about everything from cars to TV shows, to finances, to school. They even talked about literature, which Lisa said was her favorite thing about Mrs. Gates' class. Shawn was no book-reader, but he listened to her enthusiastic spills on Ellison, Hughes, Shakespeare, and Keats. Her passion for literature mirrored his passion for baseball. When they finished eating, Shawn paid for their breakfast and tipped the waiter. Immediately after, he walked Lisa out to her car. They kept talking on the way.

"Well, at least it's not to the *bus stop* this time." Shawn joked.

Lisa gasped. "Excuse me, sir! Okay, next time, I'll take the bus again just so your walk can be longer!"

They laughed together.

"Okay, kidding, kidding. I'm glad they got you fixed up and that you back rolling again. And hey, I'm happy there will be a 'next time'. I'm having fun doing this." Shawn stated.

Inspired, she looked at him. "Yeah, me too."

Stepping towards him, she saw Shawn stare at her like no other boy had before. It was look of intense appeal but with the graceful touch of safety. One of the rarest things you'd ever see, to be honest. Both of them felt the powerful momentum that usually leads to a kiss, but they hugged each other innocently. The parameters they had firmly in place were very impressive. As a result, they looked forward to their next meeting with *full* clarity and excitement. It was beautiful and refreshing.

Later that day, Shawn met up with Brooks at the downtown ballpark, as scheduled. They had bought seats that were directly behind the first base (visitors) dugout. The OKC Journeymen were hosting a night game against the Brooklyn Storm. Brooks' father had played for Brooklyn during his minor league career. Shawn always thought it was so cool to have a dad who played pro baseball. As a kid, he would envision being inside of the dugout with the players. When dreaming, he would hear the players telling him, "Hey, lil' guy, when are you gonna make it up here with us?" He would visualize all of them taking batting practice, while he helped shag their fly balls. His friend Brooks experienced all of that for most of his life. Shawn was not jealous of him, though. Marvin was an incredible father to him and made baseball provisions the best way he knew how – which, somehow, those provisions were always connected to Claire. So, like Brooks, Shawn had a drive for the game uniquely molded just for him. And God just happened to bring the two boys together in the midst of it all. Man, He really is thoughtful and thorough.

OKC got pounded on by Brooklyn from the very first inning. Brooklyn loaded the bases, and their third baseman drove everyone in with a bases-clearing double. They added on three more runs in the top of the third. OKC did not score until their catcher, a lefty hitter, hit a solo shot in the bottom of the sixth inning. It was no wall scraper, either. He hit the baseball *out of the stadium*, 501 feet over the right field fence and bleacher seats. As the ball was taking flight, Brooks and Shawn stood up and watched it rise through the Oklahoma air. It was one of the coolest things they had ever seen, even in all their baseball years and home runs that they, themselves, hit in ballfields everywhere. Each of them had a grateful attitude about baseball, which helped them easily anticipate special moments and experience them in fullness. To them, the baseball field was a blank canvas, and the players that played on it were the artists who painted the distinct piece of the day – one that would never have a replica. And thank God that baseball has such a capability.

Two other people were at the OKC-Brooklyn game that night, too: JoJo and Bobby. They were sitting on the opposite side of the stadium, behind the left field foul line. They were several rows up. So much so that a shadow, from the deck above their seating, casted over them. Bobby sat with his right arm around JoJo, as her head rested on his shoulder. As you know, JoJo had been on him about spending more time together. "And not just going to Bella's for a quick skate," she had told Bobby. Going to a Journeymen game together was something they had never done before. Plus, most Saturday nights between them were spent in private. Even so, JoJo *loved* when Bobby showed her off in public. To Bobby's credit, he loved it, too. With that, though, he was more concerned with pleasing her, especially after she reprimanded him so hard for his busy schedule. Shelby had taken off that Saturday and wanted to take her son out to see a new-released action movie. But she had surprised Bobby, informing him on that same morning, and he told her that he had already made plans with JoJo. And he never gave anything else, even quality time with his own mom, a thought if it meant cancelling on his girlfriend. During the conversation, his mom questioned him on how much time he was giving JoJo, but Bobby was not trying to hear it. He was determined to come through on his word to her. So, the two of them sat there and watched the game. After the home run was hit, JoJo looked up at Bobby.

"Babe, what's so cool about what he just did? Don't a lot of people hit home runs? Besides, they're still losing. Why is everyone so excited?"

"Yes, honey, home runs *are* hit very often, especially at this level. But did you not see where the ball went? It was completely out of the stadium! That's something that you only see in movies. Even big leaguers rarely ever do that in games. It was impressive, baby." Bobby answered her.

"I guess," she said, still not caring about the home run. "Hey, look at me."

He looked in her eyes in admiration. "*Yes*, JoJo?" He asked, knowing she was about to say something romantic and witty.

"I'm just glad I'm here with you. Right here, right now. This is all I've been asking for."

"*Tú eres hermosa*." Bobby said – the phrase: you are beautiful (in Spanish, JoJo's native tongue).

JoJo smiled and then kissed his lips, lightly biting his bottom one in the process. Then, she put her head back on his shoulder and looked on. The next batter struck out on a 2-2 slider in the dirt, and that was the completion of the bottom of the sixth. Between innings, Bobby got up to go use the men's room nearest to the south entrance. It just so happened that, simultaneously, Brooks and Shawn sought out to get snacks from a concessions stand nearby. As they were waiting in line, Brooks noticed Bobby coming out of the restroom. He had met him just five months prior to date. Tthey were on the same winter team, the OKC Flames, and played in a tournament that was hosted by E-City. Before Bobby could get back to the stairs, Brooks called for him.

"Hey, Bobby!" Brooks shouted.

Surprised, Bobby looked his way and noticed him in line about three seconds later. He smiled and walked over to him. They dapped each other up.

"Yo, Brooks! What's good, bro?" Bobby said.

"Man, *chillin'*. I'm actually up here with my boy Shawn." He looked at Shawn and tapped his chest with his backhand. "Ay, Shawn, this is Bobby. We played winter league together this past season. He go to Happs."

Shawn reached out and shook Bobby's hand.

"Nice to meet you, bro." Shawn said.

"Pleasure's mine. Where you go to school, Shawn?" Bobby replied.

"I go to Love here in OKC. I play right field for them."

"Wait, you Shawn Clement? *The* Shawn Clement?"

"Yeah, that's me." Shawn said, smiling.

"Bro, I'm Bobby Bowen. I just broke your triples record like three weeks ago. I was gonna look for you on socials but never got to it. Man, you been the talk of the entire state the past two years!"

"Yeah, the media can get pretty crazy. I do my best to stay out the way, but they always find a way to get at me. Guess it's just part of it," he said to Bobby. "But, naw, bro, congrats to you on the new record! Seven triples in one day is insane."

"Thank you, man. And congrats to you on the number one ranking." He then looked at Brooks. "And congrats to you, too, bro, for overcoming your injury and becoming an even better player. Both of y'all are headed to big places in this game."

Brooks and Shawn both thanked him.

"Hey, look, I'm gonna go back over here with my girl, but I'll catch y'all." Bobby paused for a quick second and looked back at Shawn. "Actually, I think we play Love this upcoming Friday, ain't that right?"

"Yeah, we got y'all at our place."

"Bet, bro! I'll see you then." He dapped both of them up and started walking away. "Catch y'all later."

The three of them then returned to their respective seats to finish watching the game. OKC never scored again after the big homer, and Brooklyn finished them off, 9-1. But that one home run, alone, kept everyone in the stands filled with energy. You could not tell that their team had lost the game in embarrassing fashion. They rooted for them like loyal, die-hard fans. It was a cool thing to have fans who would support you, regardless of if you won or lost. They didn't care. They were just glad to have a baseball team that they could call their own. But the real story of the night was not that. It was not even the home run ball that left the entire park, even though it made it to the national sports channel later that night. The real story was the fact that three of the state's top baseball players – all from different schools – mingled with each other in the midst of 17,000 people. And all three of them, young black boys.

Six days later, on Friday, it was finally time for Happs to travel to play against Love. For the weeks leading up to the game, Bobby and Ryan continued to lead Happs to victory. They had not lost a game since the first half of their doubleheader versus Creek. Thus, they now had a record of 13-5. But Shawn and the Bulldogs had a record of 18-1. Their only loss came against Lawrence High, which was a school in Tulsa who had the number two player in the state, Daniel Hampton. A tall and lanky right-handed pitcher, he blew away all of the Love hitters that day. The only good contact from Love was a line-drive foul ball hit by Oliver. Hampton was lucky, though. Shawn had a minor hip injury at that time, which directly impacted the path of his swing. On a good day, Shawn would have been the perfect spark for Love. Instead, he rolled over to the infield every time he came to bat. Even so, Happs did not have a pitcher like Hampton or anywhere near the hitters that Love had. But they played hard, made plays on defense, and got hits in crucial situations, which made excitement and new expectations begin forming for them. So much so that Love did not come into the game thinking it would be an easy win like in the seasons before. They were always respectful of their opponents, and that was something that Shawn made sure he emphasized every day at practice. For instance, earlier that week, he told the Rodrigo brothers to get ready to finally face an infielder just as good as them. He was talking about Marco Santiago, Happs' senior third baseman. As Bobby and Ryan led the charge, Marco was right there in the mix, providing the team with insurance in the spots behind them and then playing grade-A defense at the hot corner. Shawn also urged his pitchers to hit their spots, or else, "Bobby Bowen is going to break the record for doubles next." Shawn was right about everything he said to his teammates. The Happs Chargers were for real and only growing more confident as the season went on.

Bobby Bowen came into the game with a ridiculous .677 average. He led off the first inning with a walk, as the Bulldogs' pitchers were being very respectful of him. Right after, Ryan came up (he was batting .430). On the very first pitch, he struck a single up the middle. On the play, Bobby stopped at second base because the ball was hit too hard to try to advance. Then, the next two batters flew out to Shawn in right. Marco Sanitago was the next Charger up. Just as Shawn thought, Marco quickly put his stamp on the game, hitting a three-run bomb to left-center. The following batter grounded out to first. But the score, going into the bottom of the first, was 3-0. For the second week in a row, Love had been hit in the mouth to start the game.

Shawn and the Bulldogs quickly responded, however. Coach Titus still had not wavered in keeping Shawn at nine-hole. At one point, he simply told his guys, "Hey, it's up to y'all if y'all want the number one player in the nation to bat or not." He was the only coach in the state that had guts to do something like that. But it was also because he had players that were competent enough to take on the challenge. Romeo led off with a single to Ryan in left. Oliver came up right after him and doubled to left-center. With the Rodrigo brothers on second and third, the next batter hit a sacrifice fly to put the Bulldogs on the board. Then, they managed to score two more runs through soft singles past Happs' shortstop, making the score 3-3. The inning ended with a groundball hit to Marco at third, which he turned into a 5-4-3 double play. So, they got all the way down to the seventh spot, which meant Shawn would have to wait until in the bottom of the second to bat. Coach Titus was proud of their response and clapped for them as they went back out to defense.

In the top of the second, the Love pitcher struck out the side of Happs batters (7th, 8th, 9th, in the order). This gave the Bulldogs great momentum heading back in. Shawn, knowing he was about to bat, sprinted in, screaming, "LET'S GO, BABY!" He never failed to get hyped up whenever his team did something great. Shawn was a team player, and his energy was infectious. In the bottom half, Love's leadoff hitter hit a looping liner down the left field line that looked to be an easy double. Only, at the last second, Ryan rushed in and caught the ball right before it could touch the turf. Still coming forward, he lightly tossed the ball to Marco, who then tossed it in to the pitcher. It was a dramatic first out that took away a little momentum from Love. But when the next hitter (Shawn) came to the plate, he brought hope right along with him.

Coach Dillon initially thought about intentionally walking Shawn but decided not to. Thus, Shawn dug his spikes into the lefty box for his first at-bat of the game. The first pitch was a high slider that Shawn took, tracking it in perfectly. Ball one. Next was a curveball that caught the bottom of the zone. Strike one. Then, the Happs pitcher decided to be brave and throw a fastball down the middle of the plate. Shawn didn't swing. Strike two. Given Shawn's take, the pitcher now thought that he was surprised and thrown off rhythm by the curveball-fastball sequence. So what does he then throw? You guessed it, another curveball. But this time, it did not catch the low part of the strike zone. Instead, it was a hanger (a breaking ball with ineffective movement) right down the plate's heart. And for the first time in the at-bat, Shawn swung. When he did, he firmly connected with the ball, and it went 400 feet to right-center field. A solo home run to put his team up 4-3. They did not score again that inning, but the momentum from Shawn's majestic blast carried them for a while. *But*, Bobby was due first in the top of the third and had a response to give.

Leading off, Bobby worked the count to full, as Love was still being cautious with him. It didn't make a difference, this go 'round. The 3-2 offering was an inside slider, at about 82 miles per hour. Bobby hit that pitch, on a line, over the left field fence. If you would have looked down at all, you would have missed it because the ball got out of the park in what seemed like a split second. That's how *firm* the baseball was struck. Rounding the bases, even Bobby was surprised at how he did it. Nonetheless, he was classy about it all. And just like that, the score was tied again, 4-4. From that point on, it was a pitching and defensive showcase between both teams. In the top of the fifth, Marco hit a missile to short, but Romeo picked it on one hop and smoothly tossed the ball to first base to get him out. But he had it coming back for him. In the bottom half, he came up to bat with one out. On a 1-1 fastball, he pulled a rocket towards third base. It, too, bounced on one hop. But Marco was playing a couple steps towards the bag. Reacting to the ball, he took one small step to his right, dove for the ball, and backhanded it into his glove. Quickly getting off the dirt, he shuffled once and then threw the ball to first. Romeo was out by half a step. Going back into the dugout, he tipped his helmet to Marco (a signal that meant "nice play"). It was one of those, "you rob me, I rob you back," type instances. Bobby also had a nice catch on a pop fly that was in foul territory and almost out of play, and Shawn had a diving catch out on the right field line. Several other great plays were made by the rest of the players as well. Back on offense, Shawn and Bobby each added a double to their day, but neither was able to score. Pitchers from both teams were grinding it out, getting out of trouble with runners in scoring position. They were playing high quality baseball, and the game's atmosphere just kept growing more playoff-like, with a healthy mix of nostalgia. Everyone in the stands knew that they were witnessing a classic. All the players were locked in, determined to make every play. It was all gonna come down to who wanted it more.

It remained deadlocked for the next *three* innings, and the game was now headed to extras. In the top of the tenth, Happs' 8-hole hitter led things off with a walk. Even so, the ninth batter hit a ground ball to Romeo at short, who turned a double play with his brother, Oliver, 6-4-3. When he tossed it to him, the runner was sliding into Oliver, which forced him to make a gorgeous jump throw that reached the first baseman on a long hop. Now, with two outs and the bases empty, Bobby came back up to the plate. Coach Titus gave his pitcher the green light to compete head-to-head with him.

Bobby saw a first pitch slider that was just off the outside corner. Ball one. The next pitch was a fastball inside. Foul ball, strike one. Next, the righty threw him a disgusting knuckleball out of nowhere, which threw Bobby off completely. He didn't swing. Strike two. But Bobby was geared up for anything after that. So, the pitcher then threw another slider, but this time, it broke down the middle. Bobby swung and hit the ball, but he was a tad early. Foul ball. Next, he tried to get Bobby to chase a curveball in the dirt. Bobby spat on that pitch. Ball two. Running out of options, the pitcher called his catcher up to the mound to meet with him. They discussed for about thirty seconds, and then the umpire called him back to home plate. The battery decided on a surprise fastball, low and outside. When the pitcher threw the ball, he hit his exact location. Had Bobby not swung, it would have been a fantastic pitch. Picturesque, worthy of being framed on the pitcher's bedroom wall. But, Bobby did swing, and the ball went over Shawn's head for a towering opposite-field home run. It broke the tie, 5-4. Ryan came up to the plate after him, batting lefty this time since the pitcher was right-handed. They tried to surprise him, too, with a knuckleball, but he stayed back and hit a sharp liner past Oliver for a single. Happs' third and fourth place hitters both walked. Marco was next. He wasted no time, driving Ryan in with a hard single to right. The runner at second rounded third base with all his might as Shawn charged in and threw a laser to home plate. The energy of the ballpark took a sharp crescendo while the ball was in the air. Somehow, *another* peak moment was accomplished. The runner did his best to make it in, but, ultimately, he failed. Love's catcher caught the ball and tagged him right as he was sliding into the plate. Another assist for the great Shawn Clement, which made for the inning's final out. Fans, from both sides, erupted in the stands. Half agreed with the call, while the other half was disgusted. A typical baseball occurrence. But the score was now 6-4 going into the bottom of the tenth. It was now or never for the Bulldogs.

Shawn was the last Love hitter to have hit in the ninth – he had pulled a smoking line drive down the line, but the first baseman snatched it out of the air for the third out. So, the bottom of the tenth started off with the Rodrigo brothers. Romeo led it off. On first pitch, he fouled a fastball straight back. On the next one, he crushed the ball down the left field line. It took several bounces before finally hitting the corner of the wall and bouncing back towards Ryan. Seeing this, Romeo hurried past first and took a huge round of second. Ryan got to the ball very quickly off the ricochet. Once he fielded it, he took one shuffle and launched the ball to third base. The ball soared in the air for a very long time and ended up being well over the third baseman's head. Only, no one was backing up third base (it should have been the pitcher, but he was caught watching). As the ball landed and rolled toward the backstop, Romeo kept running around third. Bobby, the catcher, was able to get to the ball fast enough to have a play at home, though. Once he got it, he shoveled the ball to the pitcher, who was now covering home, and at that exact moment, Romeo was beginning his slide into home. Catching the ball, the pitcher immediately applied the tag on

Romeo's right leg. It was too late. By a split second, Romeo had made it. The home plate umpire called him safe. 6-5.

After his brother's little league home run, Oliver stepped into the right-handed batter's box to try to do something special himself. The intensity of the game was still peaking, and everyone was on the edge of their seats. On the first pitch, Oliver smoked a line drive to left field. It seemed to be an easy grab for Ryan, but he slipped on his first step reaction. Going into panic mode, he rushed in quickly to make the play. Only, he had misjudged where the ball was going to land, as it ended up going just above his reach as he was attempting to catch it. When Oliver saw Ryan make the error, he quickly headed to second and rounded it hard. Ryan's recovery was not very quick because he was still winded from the previous play. Consequently, Oliver made it into third base standing. So, both Rodrigo brothers positioned Love to, at least, tie the game. The Bulldogs went above and beyond, though. The next batter was their lefty first baseman, who stood about 6'5" and weighed about 230. He had great power and, thus, decided to put it to use. He swung on the first pitch sinker, and the ball was crushed. A 410-foot home run to *dead* center field. And that was all she wrote. The Love Bulldogs were victorious, 7-6 over the Happs Chargers in extras. What a game.

Regardless of the outcome, the efforts that Bobby and Shawn put forth that day were beyond admirable. After the Love celebration had ceased, Shawn made sure to catch Bobby before he and his team left. He approached their dugout as Bobby was finishing collecting his things.

"Hey, Bobby." Shawn said, getting his attention.

"What's up, bro?" Bobby replied.

"Hell of a game, kid. Y'all came to play and gave us our best challenge all year. You looked good out there, man. Keep doing your thing."

"Same to you, brother. Way to come through in those big moments. I see why they say you the best in the country. You deserve it, man. Good game."

"Good game, bro." Shawn said.

Shawn went back to be with his team. As he jogged to the dugout, he noticed Lisa on the front row of the bleachers, holding a notebook in her hand. He winked at her, and she smiled back at him. Holding her phone up and pointing at it, she mouthed to him, "I'll text you." He smiled, gave her the thumbs up, and mouthed back, "okay." Shawn also noticed his folks in the middle row. Alicia and Marvin had made it to the game, as they both took off from work. They did an amazing job at making time to see their son play, even though their busy schedules often made it challenging. On the times they didn't make it, Shawn never questioned them wanting to be there or not. But on a great game like this one, he was overjoyed that they had witnessed him and his teammates rise to the challenge that Happs brought. Marvin and Alicia met Shawn afterwards at a local Chili's to celebrate – that was Shawn's favorite restaurant.

Meanwhile, Bobby and his guys made it back to Spencer around 7:15 that night. Everyone was quiet on the bus ride back. They had given all that they had. No energy was left in any of them. It was a gut-wrenching feeling to lose grasp of a game so suddenly – and dramatically, at that. But there was nothing they could do but learn from it and move forward. Bobby was upset more than anybody, though. When he went into his house, he sat alone in his room for twenty minutes straight, doing nothing but thinking about what had just happened. Finally, his phone buzzed. He thought it was JoJo, but it was someone hitting him up on social media. He opened his app to see who. To his surprise, it was Shawn.

Shawn had sent Bobby a message saying the following:

Bobby, words cannot describe how well you played out there tonight. Quite frankly, I was completely unaware of how great of a team y'all are this year. But I know, for dang sure, that your team benefits from your leadership. I hope that you keep your head up after tonight's game. I know it was crazy how it all went down, but y'all played some great baseball, and no one can take that away. Keep leading your team, bro. As you go, they go. We'll probably be seeing y'all again, come playoff time. Best of luck, my guy. Blessings

Bobby instantly cheered up and went to take a long hot shower. Usually, whenever his team lost, he would go home and either talk to JoJo on the phone for hours or invite her over to spend some quality time. Whichever it was, he just wanted to get his mind off the game. This time was different, though. With his mom still at work and girlfriend unaware of him being by himself, Bobby chose to spend the rest of his night alone. He warmed up the dinner that Shelby had prepared for him before she left for work. Then, he turned on their living room television and watched three episodes of the show Fountain. After watching the sci-fi masterpiece, he brushed his teeth and then went to bed. That night, he slept like a newborn baby, and it was the most peaceful evening that he could remember. When Shelby finally made it back from work, she walked into Bobby's room and saw him passed out under his covers. She then went over and lightly kissed his forehead, telling him, "Good night, son."

Bobby woke up the next morning to the smell of breakfast food being made in the kitchen. Shelby was making French toast, bacon, and scrambled eggs. Ever since he was in elementary, Bobby loved French toast, covered in buttery syrup. Even so, the food and its aroma made him feel like the morning was a continuation of the blissful night he had. Hence, he got out of the bed and made his way towards the kitchen. When he entered, his mother happily greeted him.

"Well, there's my sleepyhead of a son! How are you this morning?" Shelby said.

"Mornin', Ma. I'm good." He hugged her. "How was work last night?"

"Oh, how kind of you. It was alright. Long, as usual. But work is work. Tell me how the game went at Love yesterday."

"It was a good game. We were back and forth the entire time. We took the lead in extra innings, but they hit a walk-off home run right after. It was crazy." Bobby answered.

"Wow! A walk-off, huh? At least they didn't destroy y'all like last year. Man, Bobby, y'all are a lot better this season! I know that has a lot to do with you setting a good example out there. I'm proud of you."

"Thank you, Ma. It's wild, though. One of the guys from their team is, like, the number one player in the whole country."

"Oh yeah?" Shelby asked.

"Yeah, their right fielder. He played pretty great last night, too. I actually met him last week at the ballgame me and JoJo went to together. He's pretty cool. Not at all what I pictured him to be. He even DM'd me after the game and complimented me on how I played." Bobby said.

"What's this boy's name?" His mom asked.

"Shawn Clement."

"Oh! That's Claire Hollins' kid!"

"Who?" Bobby said.

"*Claire Hollins*. She was this great softball player at Clear back in the day. You know, the big high school over there in Shawnee?"

"Yeah, we play them pretty soon. What's the big deal, though? Did she go to the Olympics or something?"

"No, son. She actually became a trainer, instead. You know that facility in OKC named Claire's Corner?"

"Yeah, what about it?"

"That's her place. *Well*, it was. She was shot and killed back in '04."

"Word? That's crazy! I didn't know about that." Bobby exclaimed.

"Yeah, you were only two years old then. Made national news and everything. It was sad, Bobby. But anyway, you ought to stay in touch with her son. Maybe y'all can hangout or something soon." Shelby said.

Bobby paused and thought deeply about it. "Yeah, maybe."

Shelby handed Bobby his plate. For the first time in a while, they spent the morning together and were *actually* present. Bobby was not thinking about JoJo or baseball, and Shelby was not overflowing with anxiety from work. It was her goal for the two of them to spend more quality time, but she allowed him to give JoJo the time she also was requesting from him. When it came to her son's love life, she allowed him to experience girls in full authenticity. Yeah, she would voice her mind about changes she detected in him, as well as possible red flags. But in the end, she knew that he was gonna do what he wanted to do. In Shelby's mind, she would be able to draw him back in due time, whenever it was most crucial. Even with all of that, this particular breakfast was a step in a positive direction. They ate, watched the Saturday morning news, and talked for a good hour or so.

When the clock struck 12:30, Shelby bounced out and headed to work, and Bobby was, once again, left to his lonesome. On the inside, he felt assured that things were lining up perfectly. The fact that Shawn, with all his credentials, praised him for his performance carried significant weight for Bobby. It affirmed him. Even so, Bobby felt hesitant about telling JoJo about all of the events that happened. Everything was going so smoothly, and he did not want to bring JoJo's unpredictable nature into the mix. She already did not care much about baseball and had decided not to travel to Love to see him shine the day before. One part of him wanted to let his newfound harmony continue without any interruption whatsoever.

But he soon concluded that it could not last forever, which was, in other words, an excuse to reach out to his girl. At the end of the day, he loved JoJo and was committed to her. They told each other everything. Keeping something a secret from her almost felt like a cardinal sin. It made him uneasy on the inside. Plus, he had not heard from her since the previous day at school, when she kissed him at the bus and wished the guys good luck before they left. Sights of her eyes and lips, up close to his, invaded his mind. Then, he imagined JoJo's sound. Whenever he would think of her voice, it would sink deeply into his soul, reassuring him that life was better when she was with him. He then closed his eyes and inhaled as if her body was pressed right against the tip of his nose. JoJo always smelled amazing. Seconds later, that was it. Bobby could not delay his hormones and urges any longer. He missed her. Soon, he started wondering what she was doing. He imagined her probably being at the mall or at a clothing store. Yet, he hoped that she was still just chilling at home. So, he called her at about 1:15 in the afternoon. She picked up.

"Hey, baby. What's new?" JoJo said.

"Hi, I was just calling to check on you and see how you were doing. You never responded to the good night text I sent you last night. I didn't know if you didn't get the message or what. I miss you, JoJo." Bobby replied.

"Bobby Ray, I didn't even see your text. Plus, I figured you were tired, so I didn't bother you. I knew you would eventually hit me up and tell me how everything went. But I saw that y'all lost in extra innings. Are you okay, babe?"

"Yeah, I'm good. I was a little upset at first, but I got over it. Actually, their best player hit me up after the game and told me to keep my head up. Babe, the guy is the number one player in the nation. For him to do that was super cool."

JoJo rolled her eyes but pretended to be excited for him.

"Yeah, baby. That really was nice of him. But anyways, I'm glad you called me. Can I come over?"

Bobby knew what that meant, especially since she cut straight to the chase, disregarding what he was telling her about Shawn. It made him forget about it, too. She had a way with him, and her beautiful, distinct accent never failed to make him melt, rather of if it was in person or over the phone. How simple are the mechanisms of males when the opposite sex ignites their core essence! Or maybe, how potent is the female power that causes males to yield so frequently! Without a doubt, it's natural either way it goes. Even so, Bobby went and got freshened up, brushing his teeth and putting on deodorant. Then, he put on a tank top and shorts. Finally, he chewed on a couple of fresh sticks of gum, spraying on some designer cologne in the process. He was ready. The house was all to himself, set for no interruptions anytime soon. A non-school day, too? This meant that he and his girlfriend could spend the entire day bonded together. *Laughing*. Having sex. Binge watching a series online, cuddled under a blanket. Bathing together. Cooking and cleaning together. Just like a married couple, only, without the title and blessing. JoJo got there about ten minutes later, and all of these things are exactly what happened.

CHAPTER 5: CRITICAL LESSONS

It was nearing the first week of May, and the high school regular season was about to close. Shawn and his team were the state's number one seed, at 19-1. They were set to face a team from Guymon: Hamilton High School. Hamilton was a school that no one ever wanted to travel to and play. Oklahoma is known for its wind, but Guymon, and the other areas in the Panhandle, take it to a new level. And baseball is one of those games that is very dependent on weather conditions. You ask any baseball player what to look for first, majority of them will tell you, "Sun and wind." Pitchers love when the wind is blowing towards the infield, for, the baseball will not travel. Hitters, on the other hand, look forward to days where the wind is blowing to the outfield, preferably to dead center (so righty and lefty hitters both have an advantage). The Hamilton Jaguars were not as good as Love, but they were similar in the fact that they had not lost a game at home. It was not because the other teams were worse, either. Rather, it was because they mastered playing the wind. Their outfielders were always perfectly positioned, regardless of which direction it was blowing. Infielders were sure to be quick and controlled when fielding grounders, rarely ever making a throwing error. And lastly, pitchers simply threw strikes and adjusted to all scenarios. In the batter's box, all of their hitters were disciplined enough to bunt the ball on command. This especially helped them on days when the wind gushed in with great speeds. Batters got on base by either bunting or hitting hard singles up the middle. They were one of the few teams who had not hit any home runs that season and had the lowest slugging percentage of all qualifiers. But they were formidable and managed to attain a record of 14-8 (11-0 at home).

Coach Titus was determined to drive his team through a perfect second half after losing to Lawrence in late February. Since then, they had won fifteen straight, making for a record of 19-1 – of course, their most recent victory being over Bobby and the Happs Chargers. Love was as clear-cut of a team that you could get. They hit for power, played great defense, and pitched marvelous innings. But they had not yet been tested by the severe inclinations of mother nature. Most of their wins came in very beautiful weather, averaging out to be 60-72 degrees and sunny. They were able to come back and beat Clear, 7-4, on a day when it was 49 degrees, with clouds and slight sprinkling rain. But that, too, was back in February. All of their players' bodies were conditioned for a pretty day at the yard, which meant that they were in for a rude interruption.

The bus ride up to Guymon was about 4 and a half hours that Monday (the last day of April). The Bulldogs departed from OKC around 10:20 a.m., right after third period had let out. On the way up, Shawn laid his head against the window, putting his puffy pillow in between. Playing through his earphones was a game day playlist that Lisa had sent him. Though she was not into sports, she was very much so into music. She was sure to include songs that gradually grew in intensity so that it would correlate with the trip. It was very thoughtful of her, and Shawn was just as much appreciative. Elsewhere on the bus, the Rodrigo brothers played cards for half of the way, then slept for the latter half. Several others, including the coaches, fell asleep as well. The only one that didn't was Eddie, their star senior in left field. It was starting to become very real for him, as he knew that it would be his last long bus ride with the boys. He wanted to take it all in.

When they made it in, they were greeted by the Hamilton workers at the gate. The clock read 2:41 in the afternoon. On the field, the Jags were already playing catch on the left field line. Also, they had already stretched and took their condensed version of batting practice – one which focused on bunting instead of situation hitting. Hamilton's coach did this to reinforce the fact that a bunt can be just as effective as a base hit. In addition, the wind was playing towards the infield that day, so hitting with power during batting practice would serve little purpose come game time. Coach Titus didn't want his Love players to change anything up, though, especially not Shawn. But one thing he did do was finally move him in the batting order. For this game, Shawn batted in the cleanup spot (fourth). The other Bulldogs felt charged up about it because it seemed like a slight to the players at the top of the lineup, all of whom had been getting the job done all year. "Why change now," they were thinking. But no one ever voiced it to Coach. They had seen his strategic genius play out many times before and, usually, in their favor. Now was not the time to get too much in their feelings. Instead, it was time to take care of business in Guymon and then get ready for the postseason.

Romeo and Oliver both popped out in their first at-bats. Following them at 3-hole was their big first baseman, who somehow hit a triple down the left field line (opposite field). Shawn then singled up the middle to drive him in. 1-0. Eddie followed with a double to left center field, and Shawn scored from first base, sliding. 2-0, Love. But that was the best of what they would do on offense. From that point on, Hamilton's pitchers did nothing but throw slow sliders down the middle of the plate. Love's batters made contact, but it was very soft. The Bulldogs did not score another hit for the rest of the game.

On offense, Hamilton put on an absolute clinic, and it was mostly through the bunt. Love had a righty pitcher throwing on the mound, so the batters bunted the ball to third base, forcing him to cross his body and make a play on the ball. This subtle cross-body movement added seconds to the play, which meant that the batter had more time to reach first base. In the bottom of the first, all of the first five batters got on base in this manner. Coach Titus chose not make the infield adjustment, in anticipation of the batters finally swinging away. And he was right. With the score tied 2-2, Hamilton's six-hole hitter hit a line drive to Shawn in right field. Reacting to the ball's flight, he thought the ball was shooting straight at him, not requiring him to take any steps. But the gushing wind immediately knocked the ball down. Shawn had made the mistake of playing too far back, and the ball ended up dropping into shallow right for a single. Two more runners scored. 4-2, Hamilton. The Jaguars batted all nine batters without getting a single out. When their leadoff came back up, the score was 7-2, with runners on second and third. What does the leadoff hitter then do? Yes, he bunted the ball to third base. Love's third baseman had already made up his mind, though. He was not gonna let his pitcher make another play on a bunt. Seeing the ball roll down the line, he rushed in, barehanded it, and threw the runner out at first. Finally, they had one out, but the runner from third scored. 8-2. Love's pitcher then dug deep to strike out the next two batters.

For the rest of the game, Hamilton destroyed the Bulldogs even more. On one play, a batter would push bunt to Romeo at short. Safe. Then another would bunt it to his brother at second. Safe. Then another Hamilton batter would fake bunt and then swing away at a down-the-pipe fastball, which would drop in for a single. The entire Hamilton squad was an on-base machine, and Love could do nothing to stop the bleeding. Hamilton pushed the score up to 13-2 and, in the end, gave Love just its second loss of the season. Bye-bye, winning streak. Hello, collective doubt.

It was a shocking defeat for the Bulldogs. On the way back to the city, no one said anything to anyone. Even when they stopped to get dinner, no one spoke a word. Most players were not even on their phones. They just looked out of the window for most of the time, occasionally glimpsing at another teammate to see that he was feeling just as bad. But Shawn *did* pick up his phone. Looking through his notifications, he saw that Lisa had sent him a message. It was a word of encouragement (she watched the game through online broadcasts). The message read:

Hey Shawn, I know you guys took a tough loss today. Feel free to call me later if you wanna talk about it. But I know you might want a little space to process everything, and I understand that completely. Just hit me up whenever you're ready. I don't ever wanna be a distraction for you. What I do want for you is to take all of this in and become better. Don't let this loss define who y'all are. Keep pushing towards the ultimate goal. I know y'all are great, but even more so, I know that you, yourself, are great. No doubts in my mind about it. Looking forward to seeing you at school tomorrow. Have a safe trip home, Shawn.

The message made him smile. Lisa had done the very same thing that Shawn had done for Bobby just a week earlier. It amazed him that she had a similar empathetic complex about her, even though she was no sports buff. But she knew that baseball was important to him and wanted to see him do great things. Shoot, even *greater* things. After processing her positive message, Shawn began to re-energize. At first, he was down because he, like everyone else, really wanted to have a perfect second half. But then, Lisa helped him realize something: the loss should only make them better and sharper. They could look back at what went wrong and find a way to prevent it from happening again. Therefore, he sought out a way to help his team see the same thing.

When the bus pulled back in at Love, it was dark outside. The clock read 10:17. Shawn studied his teammates and still saw the looks of defeat. Before anyone could get off, he walked to the front of the bus and confronted the whole team.

"Y'all are Bulldogs, baby. If you ain't motivated by what happened today, then I don't know what you're doing. None of us here are immune to defeat. Yeah, last year we won state. But last year is gone. Yeah, we just lost to an unranked team. But guess what, today's gone, too. The only thing that remains the same is that you still got the L-O-V-E across your chest. Right now, all that matters is us. Not the 19 wins, and, sure as hell, not the 2 losses. But only us, man."

Everyone lifted their faces, steadily feeling better the more Shawn spoke. He continued.

"Even the greatest champions lose. But the reason they are still champs is because they fight back. They never allow adversity to kill their momentum and overall drive. Playoffs are next week, y'all. For everyone that was here last year, forget about the ring you have. Forget about it until you have your second one that you can wear right along with it. For freshmen and new guys, you're about to enter a whole new realm of baseball. Get ready. Pitchers, if y'all think today was tough, then just wait till we get downtown next Friday. Hitters, yeah we ain't gon' have to face that wind again, but how we gonna respond to what just happened? It's time to get back in the lab and make adjustments, however big or small. None of it will be handed to us. We gotta take it, and we will. We will, *together*. Everybody in."

Immediately, they rushed around Shawn, many of them with tears in their eyes. Pumped up, they all piled their fists together.

"BULLDOGS ON ME, BULLDOGS ON THREE. 1-2-3!"

"BULLDOGS!" Everyone shouted.

Later that same week, on Thursday (May 3rd), Happs traveled to Shawnee to take on Clear. Clear was ranked fifth in the state. Like Love had been, the Broncos were on a hot winning streak. Ten straight games, for a record of 17-4. But the Chargers wanted all the smoke. They were on a mission to redeem their heartbreaking loss to Love. No one took it harder than Marco and Ryan. That week during practice, they made every single play with unmatched focus and intensity. Everything they did was crisp. During batting practice, they struck hard line drives to all parts of the field and hit several homers. On defense, they both made every play with ease, hopping right back to their positions to get ready for the next one. These, of course, were things they normally did, but everyone could tell the difference in them. They had fire in their eyes. It was very similar to how Shawn practiced after the incident with Terrell. Completely dialed in and on a mission. Oddly enough, though, Bobby was the least focused Charger. All week at practice, his body language said, "I really don't feel like being here." He was even late to practice on both Monday *and* Tuesday. He told everyone that he was held over time in Chemistry class, but he was really with JoJo. The two of them had a continuation of their Saturday-night session, kissing and fondling each other for ten minutes after the bell rang. They did it inside a secluded space near the school's west wing (complete opposite side of the baseball field). JoJo had done something to him like never before, and he, like an addict, could not get enough of her. She knew it, too. Anyhow, seeing that Bobby was late, Coach Dillon thought about benching him. Yet, the game against Clear, he thought, was too big of a matchup to try and make a statement. Plus, this is the same guy who was carrying the brunt of the load. Surely, he was the one who was allowed to slack a little bit, right? Therefore, Coach Dillon did not penalize him for being late to practice.

From jump, it looked like Happs had a shot. Bobby popped out in his first at-bat, but Ryan and Marco picked him up, each eventually scoring. But Clear had a lineup as good as any team in Oklahoma. In the bottom of the first, the Broncos scored seven runs. Get this, though. All of the runs were driven in on singles. Not one extra base hit that inning. It was like being slain by a thousand cuts. Then, they did a complete 180 in the second, adding five more runs via the long ball – a three run shot and two solo shots. 12-2, Clear. By this point, Happs posed no threat whatsoever, and the Broncos became supremely confident in themselves, managing to assert their dominance even more. In the top of the third, Clear's pitcher, a 5'9" right-hander, pitched an immaculate inning. Yes, that's right. 3 batters up. 3 batters down. Each one struck out on an 0-2 count. 9 total pitches. Flawless. Oh yeah, Bobby was the last batter of those three. Coach Dillon was speechless at how his star player was performing. Bobby showed zero fight in him. Coach figured he would have some moxie about him this late in the season, especially after all of the times he led them through adversity in other matchups (the Creek games, for example). Instead, he was a shell of himself and had nothing to offer. But the Chargers still had Ryan and Marco. In the top of the fourth, each of them came back to the plate and hit doubles. The next batter drove Marco in with a triple and then scored on a throwing error by Clear's shortstop. This short sequence fired the Chargers up, as the score was now 12-5. Despite their leader's shortcomings, there still seemed to be light at the end of the tunnel.

To no one's surprise, the Broncos immediately responded to Happs' big inning, adding three more runs of their own. When they went back out on defense, they made adjustments to the Happs' batters, throwing them mostly offspeed pitches. There was no wind, and the ball was not carrying much. Therefore, the softer velocity, the softer the hit. Most of the Charger batters then hit weak fly balls to the outfield for the rest of the game. Bobby continued to struggle as well. In his third at-bat, he struck out again. Keep in mind that this guy was batting over .670 when the game started. For whatever reason, Bobby went from the team's brightest spot to its worst crutch. Having bad at-bats in the leadoff spot always sucks life out of ball teams. It's just so tough to get that momentum back. The other Chargers tried, but they could not get it done. In the end, they lost 14-to-5, which now made their record 13-7.

Bobby was pissed off afterwards. When he took his seat on the bus, Ryan came up to encourage him.

"It's just one game, bro. You'll get 'em next time. Keep your head up." Ryan told him.

"Preciate you, Ryan. Good game, way to step up and lead the guys." Bobby responded.

This was very much false gratitude, however. Deep down, Bobby was enraged that Ryan even came up to him and spoke on his performance. Most times, athletes don't like reminders of how poorly they played. But baseball, at least in America, is weird. In other sports, whenever a player falls short of a goal, or fouls out or something, that player's teammates usually come up and say, "hey, you're good, man. We got you. Keep working hard." In American baseball, though, players often get so angry at themselves that they don't even allow space for encouragement. It's like a negative sulking. Like, what's the need of a teammate if he or she can't encourage you to do better? Anyway, Bobby did a phenomenal job of hiding this. It was probably because he had been so inspiring, and so consistent for the team, that he did not want to ruin his image as the team leader. But everyone could tell by his actions that he was emotionally bothered and distracted. Coach Dillon especially saw this, and when practice came the next day, he wanted to get to the bottom of it.

After school on Friday, all of the Chargers went and got ready for practice. Bobby was sure to not be late this time around and was the first one in the locker room. When he approached his locker, he saw a white note with dark blue pen markings on it. It read: "Bowen, meet me in the coach's office as soon as you get here. I'll be waiting. – [signed] Coach Dillon." Bobby grew nervous, for, he knew that he had been slacking off. He figured that the meeting would probably be about his recent tardiness and poor performance. As he walked towards the coach's office, his mind raced, seeking to formulate an excuse to tell Coach Dillon. One thought was, "My teacher kept me past the time we were supposed to let out on both Monday and Tuesday, and it not only made me late to practice, but threw off my whole routine." Another thought was, "coach, I had to run off to the nurse's office to get some ibuprofen for my throwing arm." Both were lies. Even so, he respected coach Dillon and never wanted to disappoint him. Bobby finally made it the office. The door was open, and he entered, lightly knocking on it.

"What's up, coach? You wanted to see me?"

"Hey, Bobby. Yeah. Take a seat." Coach Dillon said.

Bobby sat down on a black office chair in front of Coach Dillon's desk. Coach Dillon continued.

"So, I don't have to speak about your performance yesterday. We both know that that wasn't you at all. But what I *do* want to know is, number one, why you were late to two of my practices this week? Number two, and more importantly, what's going on with you, man? You have led this team for the entire season. Yet, all of a sudden, you've become distant. To me and all your teammates. What's the deal?"

"Well, coach. I really don't know. I guess I just haven't been as focused as much as I was last week. To be honest, last week's loss against Love really broke me. I feel like I haven't been the same since." Bobby responded.

This was a lie as well, for Shawn had wiped away all of Bobby's bitterness with the message he sent him post game. But maybe, he thought, Coach Dillon would understand and leave it there. But he was not born yesterday.

"Bobby, you played one of your best games of the year against them. And that's saying a lot because you've played unbelievably great all season. Plus, we lost in extras. You know, just as much as I do, that we had that game won. That's nothing to hang your head about, and I think you know that. So, do you want to try again?"

Bobby was shocked that he immediately cut through all of the nonsense. He really thought Coach was gonna believe him. Even so, he knew he could not lie any longer.

"Okay. I been spending a lot more time with my girlfriend, JoJo. I was with her right before practice when I was late, and I didn't do my regular fundamentals or hitting work because I wanted to get out of practice early – just so I could be with her again. Been kickin' it a lot with her as of late, coach. I'm embarrassed to say so, but you deserve the truth."

Bobby probably should have lied again at this point. For Coach Dillon, molding boys into quality young men came *before* helping them become good ballplayers. In this moment, he knew some intervening force would be necessary. Of course, Coach knew that some of his players were doing their fair share of messing around with girls. These are prime high school athletes we're talking about. But Bobby was, arguably, the brightest star in the metro. You have to remember, Bobby was only a sophomore, and there was no telling how much greater he would become. Coach knew that, if left unattended, Bobby's character holes would come back to bite him and, thus, prevent him from becoming a greater person (both on and off the field). But Coach kept processing.

"Let me get this straight. You are the leader of a team trying to make its first push into the playoffs in almost ten years. Right before we get to where we want to be, you would rather be somewhere else? You just leave your guys out to dry, all for a girl? You're better than that, Bobby." Coach said.

"Yeah, you're right. I am."

Coach Dillon finally made up his mind.

"Here's what's gonna happen. Next week, against Creek for round one, you will not start the game. You might not get to play at all. Maybe you'll get an at-bat if we're killing them, or if they're killing us. But as long as we are in it, you will not play."

Bobby's jaw dropped in pure shock.

"After one game, coach? Really? After everything I've done for this team, you do this to me!" Bobby said, his voice growing louder.

"Mr. Bowen, you did this to yourself. You will not play in the first round of playoffs. Jacobs will start behind the plate instead. Your only job now is to help him get ready for it. Got it?"

"Got you." Bobby said, rolling his eyes.

"Good. You're dismissed."

Bobby walked out of the coach's office with tears streaming down his face. Like a well-known man in biblical history, he had led his group to the promised land and didn't get to enter for himself. Here are some of his stats for the 20 games he played in: .675 avg, 54 RBI, 1.196 OPS. All three led the state of Oklahoma. You must know how insane it is for a leadoff hitter to lead everyone in RBI's and OPS. Bobby had played like it was he, not Shawn, who was the number one player in the country. Shoot, he may have been the best amateur in the entire world, at just fifteen years of age. But all of this was now secondary information. None of it mattered for the Chargers any longer.

At practice, Bobby ran drills with the backup catcher, Nelson Jacobs. He was only a freshman, but he had a good arm from behind the dish. Bobby helped him work on situations and also went over all of the infield signs. He noticed that Nelson had the habit of receiving the ball with his right knee on the ground. Bobby told him to keep both knees off of the dirt so that he could be more true with his reaction time. Also, he told him that it was just lazy to do what he was doing. To Coach Dillon's surprise, Jacobs showed immediate improvement due to Bobby's guidance. And the rest of the guys had a solid practice as well. When they met together at the end, Bobby gathered everyone around to reveal the news. They all sat on the dugout bench, wondering what their leader had to say. Bobby stood in front of them.

"What's up, fellas. First, I want to say that I am super proud of how you all responded after yesterday. You came here and had a great day of practice. Playoffs start next Friday, and we got a good shot at this thing. First playoff game in nine years. That's special. Give yourselves a hand."

Everyone cheered and clapped, for, they knew how special of a season they had. The cheers stopped after about ten seconds, and everyone focused back on Bobby. He continued.

"With that being said, I have something to tell you all. This week, I chose myself over the team. I came to practice late on two consecutive days because I wanted to be someplace else, choosing pleasure instead of hard work with my brothers. It directly led to me being completely ineffective yesterday, leaving all of y'all hanging. Y'all played your hearts out, and I played with no heart at all. As a result of my actions, I have been benched for next week's game. I'm sorry to have let you down, and I hope all of you can forgive me. But I'm going to be right here supporting you. I believe in you." He looked and pointed at Nelson. "Jacobs, I believe in you. It's time to step up, freshman. Take advantage of this opportunity. Lead this team to a first-round victory."

They all bunched around Bobby and encouraged him. None of them were bitter whatsoever. Most of them knew that, if not for Bobby, their record would have not been good enough to even make state. He was the reason they were inspired to rise up and perform beyond expectations. The Chargers' edgy style of play, along with their consistency, was a domino effect of Bobby's stellar performances. As much as it hurt Coach Dillon to not go into state with Bobby playing, he was proud of him for addressing the team how he did. At this point, it was not about baseball. It was about ethics, respect, and brotherhood.

Bobby got home later that day and immediately went into the bathroom. He looked in the mirror at his reflection. One thing was for sure, he was at a crossroads. Most men have trouble with unlatching deep and dear emotional connections. Bobby was still just a boy, so how much more so was this the case for him. As he looked into his own eyes through the mirror, he visualized all of the great things he did on the ball field that season. He was supremely confident, as you know, but he did not think he would perform so wonderfully. Man, it was like he owned the game. There was nothing that he couldn't do out there. Still in front of the mirror, though, he then closed his eyes. He took several deep breaths. Now, thoughts of JoJo took over his imagination. He pictured her beautiful, bright smile and dark brown eyes. Then, tensing up, he thought of her exposed body and all of the times they pleased one another in intimacy. All of the dates they took. Her fragrance. Her touch. Her everything. Deep in his heart, he knew that if he was going to be serious about his future, particularly in baseball, she could no longer be in the picture. But his body could not chemically agree with him. So, he chose not to make a big fuss about it to her.

When Shelby finally made it home, she brought dinner in with her. She walked in and saw Bobby watching TV in their living room.

"Hey, son. How was your day?" Shelby said.

"Hi, Ma. Today was hard, actually."

"Oh really? What happened?" She asked, fumbling through all of their food and other grocery bags.

"Well, coach benched me for the first round of playoffs. I was being stupid this week."

Caught off-guard with the subtle news, she sat everything on the kitchen table.

"What did you do?" She asked.

"I was late for practice two days in a row."

Shelby already knew that JoJo had a role in him being late and was instantly disappointed. She had hoped that Bobby would have listened to her when she initially warned him about spending so much time with her. But he made his decision, and it caught up with him at the worst possible time.

"So you telling me that you gon' ruin your future over a girl. Just forget all the sacrifices I made just so you can play ball. I already told you about bettering your focus and what may be required to do so. Son, you just had one of the greatest seasons anyone in this state has ever seen. You lifted your team up from the bottom of the barrel. And you choose to do this *now*?" Shelby said, growing frustrated with him.

"I'm sorry, Ma."

"Your food is on the table. I'm going to shower and then going to bed." She stormed off, only so she could refrain from saying something extremely harsh. She wanted him to feel every ounce of her disappointment. Sadly, though, it did not affect him like she hoped. Bobby had no interest in getting rid of JoJo any time soon.

After eating dinner, Bobby went into his bedroom and got freshened up. Remember, this was a Friday night. JoJo wanted to meet up with him at her place, as her parents were out of town on business. At first, Bobby had to plan on how to ease on out of the house. But now, he could be as loud and blatant as he wanted to. Shelby left him to himself, never planning on leaving her room for the rest of the night. She didn't even want to look at her son. But if she ever had the thought of confronting him again, it wouldn't have mattered. Bobby was gone, headed to JoJo's house before she could even dry off from her eleven-minute shower. Her son was knee deep.

JoJo was waiting for Bobby in a custom robe, nothing underneath but her bare, almond-colored skin. Like Bobby, she had just freshened up herself. Only, *she* was more thorough. Her hair was wet and curly from washing it. Her entire upper body was wrapped in a $300 dollar perfume named *Intrigue*, and her lower, the smell of cocoa butter. Her thirsty boyfriend hurried over for instant quenching. When he arrived, he knocked on her door harder and quicker than normal, due to the level of stress that had built up in him. JoJo opened up the door and immediately kissed him. Grabbing his hand, she led him into her bedroom. Of course, you know the rest.

A while later, the two of them laid in bed like it was the first time they had done so. JoJo put her head on Bobby's chest and interlocked her fingers with his. Neither of them had any care in the world except for the very moment they were in. She kissed him on his shoulder and then looked up at him.

"How are you, babe?" JoJo asked.

"I'm alright. Today was kinda rough on me." Bobby responded.

"How so?"

"Well, coach benched me for the first game of playoffs because I was late to practice earlier this week."

JoJo looked away in guilt. She then tried to deflect everything, in attempt to keep him from blaming her. After all, he was *already* in her bed. It would not be difficult to persuade him.

"Why would he do that to you? Aren't players late all of the time?"

"Yeah, but it was different. JoJo, I played bad yesterday. Like, *really* bad. For some reason, I just wasn't feeling it. Meanwhile, everyone else was giving it everything they had. I failed the team." Bobby said.

She laid her head back on his chest.

"Bobby Ray, everyone has bad games. It still wasn't right for him to do that to you after all the good you have done for the team. You didn't deserve that."

Bobby looked through JoJo's skylight. The sky was very clear, and the stars sparkled with great brightness. He thought about what would have happened if he had made it to practice on time. How JoJo would have been angry with him if he did not give her what she was asking. How maybe his team would have won if he was his normal, focused self. They were all brief thoughts, though. JoJo still had him.

"Well, it is what it is. I just hope the guys can pull it out next week so that I can play again. I don't wanna finish the year on something negative like this, ya know?" Bobby said.

"Bobby, you are gonna be just fine." JoJo responded. "Let next week take care of itself. Until then, enjoy tonight. Relax, babe."

"I got you."

The two of them recharged for a moment and then had sex once more. Of course, it was a natural thing to be bonded so close. But deep down within both of their hearts laid insecurity and brokenness. JoJo, one of the most beautiful girls in OKC, was always seeking validation from others. Born in New Mexico, she was adopted by Venezuelan immigrants back in September of '03. She was only two years old at that time. But her new parents spoiled her all her life, giving her everything she ever wanted. When she became a middle schooler, she joined the 'pretty girl' crowd and quickly became its mover and shaker. This gave birth to her manipulation complex, which was masqueraded by her beauty and charm. Only those close to her could really see it for what it was. Anyway, her relationship with Bobby was something she used in order to paint a coveted picture to the outside world. It just so happened, though, that Bobby made her feel euphoria for the first time in her life. His energy was unlike all of the boys she had experienced before. He was exactly what she desired. Handsome. Athletic. Caring. Considerate. More than anything, though, impressionable. Whenever Bobby showed signs of switching up on her, she always managed to quickly remind him of how dependent he was on her. Well, really, how much she needed him so that she could uphold her constructed image. Bobby just went along with it because all he cared about was the fact that she was his. Very naïve of him, yes.

Aside from coaches, Bobby never benefited from the leadership of a man. This created a chasm in his heart. Once he started experiencing feminine energy in middle school, he felt the electricity that jolted through his body every time a gorgeous girl interacted with him. It was a new thing, right in line with the pubescent changes he was experiencing. Yet, no man was in his personal corner. No guy ever told him, "Hey, these girls are not always in your best interest. While you are young, many of them will only use you for what they need and then dispose of you with no hesitation. Be careful." Shelby got through to him on so many things, but as far as girls went, Bobby never really paid her any mind. He liked what he liked, and nothing was going to get in his way.

So, JoJo and Bobby spent the night together laid up at her place. When the next morning came, Shelby did not question where her son was. She already knew. Instead of making him breakfast and helping prepare his later meals, she made pancakes and sausage just for her. Then, she got dressed for work and left early to get some coffee from Mocha Time. As she was pulling out of the driveway, she saw her son approaching from down the street. Before putting the car in drive, she looked at him for a good five seconds. It was, undoubtedly, a look of disappointment, with just a *touch* of concern. Bobby knew what she was thinking but had zero remorse for his actions. He stood firm in choosing his girlfriend over everything else in his life. Saying nothing to him, Shelby put the car in drive and left.

Bobby knew that he was on his own for the day, as far as meals were concerned. He had Shelby bent if he thought he had a hot breakfast waiting for him after sneaking out how he did. One thing she did not do was spoil him rotten. As much as she could, she made him deal with the consequences of his decision making. Part of that might have been why JoJo was such a draw. Not only was she spoiled, but she spoiled her boyfriend. She made herself available in any way he wanted, as long as he reciprocated it back to her. Bobby liked being catered to and enjoyed his ego being constantly fed. At home, Shelby *never* made provisions for Bobby's ego. Sure, she spoke positivity into him, but never did she cease in holding him accountable. As much as she was pissed at her son, she knew that he would have to learn for himself. She just hoped and prayed that the damage done would not cost Bobby his future.

When Bobby finally went inside, he took a quick shower. Then, he popped some white bread into the toaster and scrambled up five eggs on the stove. His mom had just purchased some fresh cream cheese, so he pulled it out of the refrigerator to spread on his toast. After fixing up his plate, he poured some orange juice into a small mason jar.

Eating his breakfast, Bobby thought about his mother's recent scolding. He visualized her straight face through the car window. Deep in his gut, he knew he was wrong. At the forefront of his mind, though, was nothing except instant gratification and sensual pleasure. His brain was still in a euphoric state after eleven straight hours cooped up with JoJo. He even dared himself to invite her over while his mom was gone. But he knew that if she were to catch them there, he would be kicked out right along with JoJo. He could already hear Shelby. "You wanna be with her? Then be with her! But I'll be damned if it's under my roof. Go ahead, Bobby!" Trust, Bobby Ray did not want those problems. Instead, he did the rest of his homework and some studying for final exams.

When he finished his chemistry review, he sought to see what was new in the world. He opened his social app and saw that, once again, Shawn was trying to reach him. The message was from the night before, sent at about 7:21 (right when Bobby had left for JoJo). It read as such:

What's up, Bobby! I heard about yesterday's loss man, that's a tough one. But listen, tomorrow, me and some of the guys are going up to Claire's Corner for a pre-playoff training session. It's gonna be mostly Love players and a couple of guys from Clear, but I wanted to extend the invitation to you. We're gonna hit for a while and then do some arm maintenance workouts. We'll get started around 3:30 in the afternoon. Hope you can make it, man.

Bobby had no interest in going. His energy was spent. Plus, he was going to be sitting the bench at the start of playoffs. His ego was jabbing again, refusing to be the one being scoffed at. Yet, he felt something telling him that he probably should go anyways. As his mind probed, he remembered his mom suggesting that he should try to spend some time with Shawn. She had told him a little about Claire's story, and it sparked his curiosity. Added, if he went, he figured, he would have some positive news to break the ice with his mom later. Maybe she would not hammer down on him so hard, seeing that he applied *some* of her recent suggestions.

Around 2:20, Bobby took the bus for downtown OKC. During the week, Claire's Corner consistently stayed busy, but weekends were designated for one-on-one sessions only. Shawn was sure to reserve three batting cages for him and his peers. When Bobby walked in, at 2:54, several players, including Shawn, were already there getting some early work in. Shawn was waiting by one of the cages when he saw Bobby enter. He then walked over and greeted him.

"What's up, Bobby? I'm glad you could make it, man."

"Thanks for the invite, bro. But I thought you said 3:30? It looks like y'all been in here for hours already." Bobby said.

Shawn laughed. "Naw, bro. We all got here about fifteen minutes ago. Just getting our routine work in, is all. Some of the guys are still on the way, anyway, so you're good. Go ahead and get stretched, bro, so you can hop in."

"Got you, bro." Bobby said.

As Bobby got his body loosened up, he watched the other players practice their swings. They were all locked in. He noticed two of the Clear players he had just played against two days earlier. The rest were Shawn's teammates from Love. Between drills, all of them told each other of how excited they were to be approaching the first round of playoffs. Bobby tried his best to tune them out, knowing that his first playoff experience would have to wait. Once he finished stretching, he put his gloves on, grabbed his bat, and went into one of the cages. His warmup consisted of two short rounds of side toss and a short round of front toss. At most, he took 25 swings. Everyone else had already taken over 40 swings during their warmup. Bobby finished before everyone, so he went and waited behind Shawn's cage. Shawn was working off of the tee. After setting it up to hit the ball to the opposite field, he took four beautiful swings. Then, he set it up to hit up the middle. Four more swings. Next, he positioned the tee inside to pull the ball. Just three swings this time. Finally, he put the tee back on the outside corner to finish opposite field again. Four perfect strokes. Bobby watched him closely and was impressed.

When everyone was done warming up, they set each cage up for live arm batting practice. While they were doing so, someone else walked into the facility. It was Brooks. Though he was about ten minutes late, he quickly stretched and hopped right in. Every player that stepped into the cage hit excellent rounds of BP. They were so good that Shawn had an idea to make it more challenging. He told everyone that every round was now a line drive competition. No ground balls and no pop ups. Just liners. Each player would get eight total swings each round. There was a total of twelve guys there, so they broke every cage into four players and two rounds. The winner of each cage would face off at the end. Everyone started to feel the pressure.

Brooks and Bobby were in the same cage, along with the two Clear players. The other two cages had all the Love guys. In the first round, Shawn hit eight line drives for a perfect round. In the cage on the opposite end, a Love player (the big first baseman) hit five to lead his group. But in the middle cage was a battle. The two

Clear players led the round off with five and six liners respectively. Then, Brooks came up and hit seven. Bobby followed him up and hit seven as well. They now had to break the tie. Instead of eight swings, they would get six. Both of them proceeded to go a perfect 6-for-6. Another bonus round. This time, four total swings. Everyone else stood around the cage, hyping up the both of them to stay perfect. Both boys were locked in, ready to battle all day if they had to. This go 'round, still, perfection from both. It was now time to lower the swing total to two. On Brooks' first swing, he crushed a line drive back at the L-screen. 1-for-1. On the next one, he hit a missile to the left corner of the netting. 2-for-2. Now, it was Bobby's turn. On the first offering, he took the pitch, even though it was right down the middle. He didn't get his foot down on time, so he elected to not swing. When the player threw the second pitch, he was ready. He hit a rocket up the middle. 1-for-1. This next pitch was the true test. He had to stay perfect, or else, he would not move on. He started to tense up and lose focus. As the next pitch came in down the middle, he took one of the hardest swings of the day. He struck the ball with great force, but it traveled straight up into the barrier. A pop-up. 1-for-2. Brooks edged him out after *three* bonus rounds. They shook hands, telling each other, "Good work."

Brooks would be eliminated in the final round, though. Guess who beat him? Yeah, that's correct. Shawn. It was crazy because Shawn led off the round and went 8-for-8 again. Love's first baseman then stepped in and only hit six line drives. Eliminated. Brooks was the last one to go. For the first seven swings, he was perfect, hitting beautiful line drives to the middle and opposite fields. But on the eighth and final pitch, he rolled over for a weak ground ball. Shawn messed with him afterwards, but it was all in good fun. Finishing out, the players did some arm maintenance workouts to strengthen their arms in preparation for the postseason.

Shawn was sure to get Bobby's phone number before he left. He wanted to continue getting together once the summer began, and Bobby had no issues with it at all. Still, though, he went home bitter at Shawn and the other players. All of them were about to play in the playoffs, the biggest stage in the game. He hated feeling left out, especially in sports. Baseball had been his one constant. Now, though, it was slipping from his grasp.

JoJo called Bobby later that evening to see if she could come over, but Bobby didn't answer the phone. His phone was actually charging in his room at the time, and he was in the kitchen fixing himself a roast beef sandwich and chips. When he saw that she had called, he texted her back asking what was up. She didn't reply. As you would guess, it infuriated her that he chose to text her back instead of calling. However, Bobby did not pay her any added attention, because he knew that if he didn't keep forcing the issue, she would respond back eventually. Regardless, he had finally found the time to process everything going on in his life. Away from his mom. Away from school. Away from baseball. Away from *JoJo*, especially. He did not know how he got himself into his current situation, for, he and JoJo had been sleeping together for almost six months. During such time, he still was able to play his best baseball season to date. But it was like, all of a sudden, his confidence and ability had abandoned him. Bobby was too young to realize that it was an energy thing. The fact that, coming into high school, he had so much *purity* and *enthusiasm* about him that other people envied his glow. But ever since he became sexually active, all that energy and vibrance slowly started to release from him. In truth, his great season for Happs was just a spillover from what he had originally. But now, at the end of it, the majority of his energy was put forth into JoJo. At this point, he had nothing left to offer to the world.

Bobby could not sleep that night. He figured it was because he had stayed up so late with JoJo the night before. To begin with, it was already a miracle that he was able to do so well at the workout earlier, and he was surprised he was not all the way worn out again. His body remained energetic. But just as much so, he was bothered. It was because something deep in his soul was begging for his attention. Like, one of those feelings you get when you know the right thing to do, but still refuse to do so. Once again, he had pulled up to a crossroads. If he proceeded forward, there was no telling what destruction would be done to his life. But he would still have his dear girlfriend to lean on, making him a happy person. On the other hand, if he turned left or right, JoJo would no longer be part of his life, and that would cause him immense pain and grief. Only, instead of destruction, he could begin rebuilding what he had lost, possibly becoming better than ever before.

CHAPTER 6: HEALTHIER PRACTICES

On the following Friday, Happs lost their playoff opener. They ran into a Creek team that was desperate to get its payback from earlier in the season, especially since they did not have the threat of the backstop catching, triples-fanatic that was Bobby Ray Bowen. Creek obliterated the Chargers, 27-3 (no run rule in playoffs). Bobby was sick to his stomach watching his teammates fall apart. He really thought that they had a chance without him. And theoretically, they did. Aside from the Clear game, they had been hot – seemingly hot enough to bounce right back after a tough defeat. But the loss of Bobby was like blowing out a tire right before reaching final destination. They were done for.

Right after the Creek vs. Happs game, Love lost as well. And once again, they fell at the hands of the Lawrence Lions. It was another classic. Lawrence hitters gave Love pitchers hell all game long. Love's lefty starter could not get the top of the order to bite on his offspeed pitches. This forced him to throw fastballs from behind in the count, and the Lions did not miss when they swung. In fact, they scored five runs in the first inning, nearly batting around in the lineup. For the Bulldogs, it seemed like Deja vu from a week ago at Hamilton. But unlike then, they were now ready for the dogfight. Ready to put everything on the line. Just as they did for most of the year, they responded with powerful offense of their own. Senior Eddie Ramirez hit for the cycle in his last game as a high school baseball player. Shawn was just a double away from doing it also. At the third spot, Love's big lefty first baseman had a homer and two doubles. As far as the Rodrigo brothers, they each had two RBI, but on defense, they were slightly out of sync. It was the magnitude of the moment that was getting to them. Consequently, and in true baseball fashion, balls were hit to them for most of the game, forcing them to perform under the intense pressure. On many of them, they executed beautifully, even having a couple of dazzling double plays (6-4-3 & 4-6-3). But the plays they *didn't* make came at crucial times – with Lions on base and in scoring position. Both infielders had multiple instances where the ball was hit just out of their grasp, clipping the slightest bit of glove leather before proceeding into shallow center field. Even so, on the last play of the game, Oliver had a chance to make everyone forget the shortcomings between him and his younger brother. The score was 10-9, with 2 outs in the bottom of the *fifteenth* inning. Bases loaded for Lawrence. Up at the plate was Lions' best hitter – their lefty left fielder. With the count tied at 2-2, Love's pitcher threw him a slow curveball off the outer edge of the plate. When the player swung, he struck the ball towards the second base bag on a line. It was not nearly the hardest ball of the day, but it was well-hit. Reacting, Oliver ran back and to his right in order to cut the ball off at the lip of the grass. As he got a better read on it, he realized he had a chance to catch it if he laid out. So right when he met the ball, he dove. But when he reached out, with his body in midair, the ball caromed off of his lime green wrist protector and sprung into right field towards Shawn. He had misjudged the ball's flight, and probably would have caught if he had kept his stride instead of diving. As the baseball slowed down and took its final revolutions, Lawrence's winning run scored from second base. Ball game. 11-10 in extra innings. A playoff game for the ages. A game so good that the Lawrence online broadcast was reposted and went viral after about four days. The name of video: *Love Bulldogs vs. Lawrence Lions – The Best High School Game of All-Time*.

Shawn had a lot of media coverage following the season's closing. With him being the number one player in the country and all, analysts and local writers wanted to know where he was thinking about attending college. But even more so, they wanted to know if choosing to go pro, right out of high school, was an option for him. The boy loved the game so much that he rarely ever thought about making a decision so soon. Of course, he was not naïve to the possibilities, but he was enjoying the time he was having with his teammates. In all his years, there was never a point where he did not have fun on the diamond. Even on his toughest days at the yard, the game still captured his imagination and fueled his desire to become better. He did it for the love. But he was now facing the realities of being the center of American attention. It's crazy how noisy everything becomes because of the speculations of outsiders. Many were thinking he was going to go all the way west and play for a top-brand like USC or Arizona State. Some even though he would go play up in Idaho. The reason why was because Cali, Arizona, and Idaho were all states that bred the nation's top offensive talent year-in and year-out. For an Oklahoma kid to make the transition to over there, he had to be the real deal. And, indeed, Shawn was.

Still, Shawn chose to remain undecided. For an almost-seventeen-year-old, he had great awareness and knowledge of how things worked. He knew that 98% of the people around him were only there to benefit from his image and status. He knew that journalists were out for a story and understood how to keep them at arm's length. Ever since he began kid pitch, Marvin would interview him after games with a couple pieces of rolled up paper as the pretend microphone. For example, he would ask him, "So, Shawn, what do you think of your performance this weekend at E-City?" Shawn, usually angry, would say something like, "I hate playing here and never want to come back." But as he got older and matured, whenever he would underperform at E-City, his responses evolved. Shawn would then tell his father, "Well, sir, I just didn't feel comfortable in the box or on defense all weekend. Playing at nighttime here can be a bit of a challenge, and, tonight, I think people recognized how difficult it can be. But this game, itself, is difficult. So, there are really no excuses at the end of the day." By middle school, Shawn was ready to answer questions by the toughest media outlets in the country. Heck, then, he was already more articulate than a lot of pro superstars. That might just be a testament as to how beneficial it was to have a dad (a leader) who was almost Yale's valedictorian. Marvin never ceased to challenge Shawn's brain. He made sure it stayed working at all times, which is something that helped Shawn in baseball as well. You might have heard the phrase, "baseball is a thinking man's game." Well, Shawn inherited the genes of Oklahoma's best academic/business mind in the past 50 years. It just so happened that his other half of chromosomes came from, arguably, the greatest softball player to ever breathe air. Talk about being born to play the game. Shawn was the literal actualization of this.

Schools had let out for summer on Thursday, May 24th, which was a week and a half after the baseball playoffs ended (by the way, the Creek Warriors won the whole thing – 8-5, against the Lawrence Lions). May was always the most thrilling time because it brought the two most anticipated parts of the school year: baseball championships and the last days of school. Well, maybe the former is a little less universal, but the latter is definitely fitting. Summer was bringing freedom for students. They could finally relax their brains, let their hair down, and find time for self-development. By Shawn choosing to remain uncommitted, he escaped a summer full of unneeded stress. He even chose to not play summer ball, giving his body time to heal from an arduous spring campaign. Instead of throwing and hitting balls in the Oklahoma heat all summer, he chose, instead, to get a summer job. Particularly, he wanted to work at one of the local car shops. The moment he saw the Malibu that Marvin and Alicia got for him was the moment he fell in love with cars. As much as he knew his Chevy was special, he knew it was an antique. Vehicles within this realm are not always the easiest to deal with, for many obvious reasons. Technology advancements. Changes in vehicle production. Car body trend changes. Environmental changes. The Internet and Bluetooth. Shawn loved being a part of generation Z, but he wanted to reach back into the days of Millennials, Gen X and Baby Boomers. He did not always like the everyday instant gratification that was made available to him. Marvin had molded his son into an old soul. In other words, Shawn was interested in learning the prototypical functions that directly preceded his time. Working on cars was the perfect way to do this, for he would soon have to practice patience, develop competency (almost from scratch), and deal with brand new challenges head-on.

Just eight days after school released students for summer, Shawn started his new job as an apprentice mechanic. Running Great Motors (RGM) was the name of the shop. Courtland Carter, the younger brother of Marvin's best friend, Quentin, was the owner and head mechanic of the place. It took Shawn about thirteen minutes to get from his house to RGM (in Edmond, right off 15th and Broadway). When Shawn arrived at the shop that morning, leading staff members helped him get situated. Shawn was so excited that even his working clothes gave him a ton of energy. Courtland had an XL pair of black, mechanic-style coveralls prepared for him. On the left side of them, right around the left pectoral area, read his name and abbreviation, *Shawn C.*, in white stitching. He also had some work boots available for him, but Shawn chose to bring his own – his dad was a multi-millionaire, even his work boots were custom and stylish. Anyway, his first job of the day was aiding one of the guys in changing the engine oil of a red 2015 Chrysler 200. Then, Shawn rolled underneath a classic Ford Mustang and watched that same mechanic replace some rusted exhaust pipes with brand-new ones. It was funny to him that he would run into this car on his first day, given that Lisa was a Mustang fanatic. Yet, Shawn's third and final job of the day was helping Courtland bring in and arrange boxed shipments that had arrived earlier that week. His goal for Shawn was to give him a small peek into what goes on every day at RGM. Courtland did not want him to come in thinking that he would immediately be designated to one space. Instead, he urged him to prepare for working in several different areas so that his knowledge could grow thoroughly and organically. His exact words were, "Shawn, I know you're book smart and baseball smart. But you're a baby in the car game. It's time to grow you up, son." And Shawn accepted the challenge. Though, considering that his first day was on a Friday, Courtland made sure his young, new employee did not work a full shift, which allowed Shawn the time to process his experience and come back even more energized.

Later that day, after showering up, Shawn went out to dinner with his parents at a Mexican restaurant just west of downtown. Marvin and Alicia were surprised to see Shawn in such good spirits after losing in the postseason. Of course, everyone loses, but it's different when you are the defending state champs and then lose in the first round. It has a different sting, and Shawn very well felt it. But he managed to get over it very quickly, which helped him focus on his summer goals. His parents were getting ready to go to a resort in Florida for a seven-day getaway trip. It was also a celebration for them. Their first wedding anniversary had passed in the previous December, and they ended up going on a trip to Puerto Rico a week before Christmas. But they also wanted to continue celebrating the anniversary of when they first met, which was in March of 2014. They looked at it as a chance to be intentional about dating one another and eluding the trend of becoming bored and settled. Ironically, they were the *opposite* of bored during that time. March and April were two very busy times for both Alicia and Marvin. They could not find the time to really do what they had initially hoped, which was to take a flight to a destination of their choice (whoever's turn it was to pick). In addition, Shawn was in the middle of baseball season. They were choosing to support him as much as they could, so whenever they were not busy for work, they were at a ballgame rooting for their son. But now, with Shawn not playing summer ball, their schedules could have a lot more flexibility. Thus, they left the next morning around 8, and arrived in Orlando four hours later, at 12:12. As wealthy as they were, they still flew commercial. They both liked flying anyway, so they wanted to have the full experience together as much as possible. Their dynamic was definitely still akin to the time of their honeymoon.

Even so, the Clement household was racking up bread at a more prolific pace than ever. At the beginning of May, Marvin launched his own financial literacy app, which was titled *Marvin's Money Terms*. The goal of the app was to teach teens and young adults how to manage money and wisely use credit. Only, he made sure to use a mixture of urban language and scientific terms that would register in their minds more firmly. This meant that he veered away from the common verbiages of prominent financial teachers. For example, instead of telling kids to *save* money, he told them to develop a *steady threshold* that gradually increases month-by-month. Also, instead saying do not overspend, he told them, "do not *wild out* in quickly going over budget." It was a brilliant electronic tool for youngsters, and it blew up right away, earning Marvin about seven million dollars in the first four weeks. During that same span, Alicia had put out three beautiful pieces that sold for over 30 million dollars collectively. What's crazy is that each of them was a portrait of a girl named Gabriella, who sat and modeled for Alicia in the early parts of January. While studying Gabriella, she had her pose and dress differently for each piece. Each garment was a beautiful dress designed by the country's top fashion designers. The color themes, respectively, were bright green, turquoise, and gold – all of which complemented the model's beautiful brown skin and long black hair.

Alicia's creative talent, and introspective painting style, made each one its own distinct portrait. When looking at them, you knew it was the same girl at the center, but your mood transitioned from piece to piece. For instance, the gold piece presented a mood of prosperity and fulfillment; the turquoise one simulated attitudes of power and prestige; lastly, the green painting simply made you feel a sense of safety. The titles were *G Phase I*, *G Phase II*, and *G Phase III*. But no matter which one you viewed, you felt a wave a freshness gushing through the room, along with an aura of stillness. You also felt a momentary depression that was rooted in the fact that you could not stare at it forever. That you had to leave the exhibit at some point and depart from the frames (unless, of course, you were the buyer). See, that is what makes art so beautiful and worth the money it draws year-in and year-out. Alicia understood this from a very early age and ended up making a lucrative career out of it. But even so, you have to think: a girl must be extremely beautiful for her image to sell *that* good. Sure, Alicia had made 30 million before. But never did she do so in the form of three paintings that sold for 12, 8, and 10 million, all in one showing. Quite honestly, the paintings should have shattered all purchase records from the past two centuries, all the while superseding Leonardo da Vinci's *Mona Lisa* as the greatest portrait work in the history of earth. No doubt about it. And on top of all of that, the pieces did their subject's *actual appearance* zero justice. Even the best books of love poetry, the greatest romance songs and movies, and the smoothest feelings of gratification and excitement, could not describe Gabriella's effortless aesthetic and gleaming glow in real-time. In other words, the only true way to process it was to be in her physical presence for yourself. You would have to feel breath leaving your body, soon becoming aware that Gabriella took it away from you. You would have to feel your inspiration travel to heights that are rarely ever accomplished by the human mind. And, lastly, you would have to understand the true weight of the moment. Because you came across one of earth's hidden gemstones, wrapped up in the flesh of a northern California girl.

Anyhow, when Shawn's parents' flight first took off that morning, he was still sleeping in his bedroom. Once the clock struck nine, though, his alarm went off, and he finally rose and shone. It was nearing the time for him to meet up with Lisa for another morning breakfast date. Shawn had texted her on the preceding Tuesday to see if she was down to go. Lisa, like she had promised him in the baseball season, was giving him a little more space to focus on what he was trying to accomplish. Shawn never asked her to do so, but he knew that it was the best thing for him. Everything was becoming very hectic, and the only way he would have been able to keep the pace with Lisa was to have the ability to create extra time in the day. And Shawn was never one to covet after the quality of omnipresence. He knew how important it was to expend his energy as efficiently as possible, which was, yet, another principle that Marvin taught him. Even so, he knew that he and Lisa would be able to resume dating as soon as they could. In actuality, implementing this boundary of space allowed for them to develop a healthier desire to date one another, avoiding the mistake of getting overzealous. A palpable electricity was present between them, and it was important to cultivate this through healthy practices, instead of turning it into a selfish opportunity to experience bliss through lustful avenues. No one deserves, or wants, for that matter, to be objectified. People and their personalities are neither escapes nor crutches. Rather, people should be genuinely learned and loved – a process that is both arduous and perpetual.

Shawn arrived at Mocha Time close to 10:30, and Lisa got there only about five minutes after him. After greeting, the two of them sat together in a booth near the shop's entrance, right along one of its large windows. It was a bright and lovely morning in June (the 2nd).

Lisa, excited, studied Shawn as if she had never been out with him before. Perhaps, it was because the two of them had not been out together in a good minute. Or, it may have been that Shawn had an added aura about him because of his new job. More than anything, her energy, and overall good feeling about their date, confirmed to her that they had done the right thing in choosing to take a short pause. How great a thing it is when these types of situations resume naturally. When the heart, after a period of necessary delay, receives its exact desire. It was like the two of them could have written an entire book on how to date as a teenager. Goodness, the two of them were blessed. So, they started to catch up with one another.

"Shawn, I'm so happy to see you again. I mean, I saw you around at school after y'all finished up the season, but we all were so hammered down by our final tests. I tried catching you on the last day, but Oliver told me that you had left a little after 5th period. Regardless, I'm glad you reached out to me. I hoped that you would." Lisa said.

"It's good to see you, too. Yeah, I actually did see you on the last day during lunch, but you were mobbing around with your friends. I knew you were locked in about finals and taking your SAT. How was that, by the way?" Shawn replied.

"Everything went good. I still got about three more weeks before I get my results back. But as far as our tests at school, they were fairly challenging, but I did well. *Hey*, what did you think about Mrs. Gates' final?"

"I thought it was hard. She put a lot of stuff on there that wasn't even on the study guide. I hate when teachers do that."

"Right? I'm glad you saw the same thing I saw. But you know how she is, she's always trying to keep us on our toes. I still made an A on it, though." Lisa stated.

"Of course you did. I made a freakin' 87! Luckily, though, it didn't bring my grade to a B. I finished her class with a 91.6, which was my lowest grade this year. But, hey. An A is an A, right?" Said Shawn.

Lisa smiled. "Yeah, you're right, Shawn."

The waiter came up to them to take their orders. Just like last time, Lisa got blueberry muffins and an espresso, while Shawn requested eggs, toast with avocado, and a hot vanilla latte. Inside of the coffee shop, the air conditioning unit was blasting. It probably was around 64 degrees inside. But it had that amazing breakfast smell, blended in with the aroma of whole bean and ground coffee. If you were to step inside, you would feel like everything you wanted for breakfast was already waiting for you. Like you were at your home away from home. *That is*, of course, if you don't mind a chilly indoor climate. Even so, the sun was shining directly into the spot where Shawn and Lisa were sitting. For the first time, Shawn saw the enhancement of Lisa's immaculate brown eyes whenever the sun lit into them. And the ambiance supported Shawn, too, but in a different way. To Lisa, the light exposure gave Shawn's presence a stronger sense of comfort and safety. Thus, they continued to interact with ease. Had a professional photographer been there taking shots of them, any one of the photos would have been worthy of the cover of, like, an award-winning romantic movie. Or, at least it would be one of the most liked and talked about photos on the internet. The energetic ray of light was, most likely, The Lord signaling His pleasure and approval for what they had going. Some people think that the morning time is, perhaps, God's favorite part of the day. Light signifies exposure and knowledge, which are things that are directly associated with Him. To add, people usually have more energy during the morning time, which is due to the universal principle of rest. Regardless of if morning is His favorite or not, it often sets the stage for healthy dating settings. Breakfast at ten is so much safer than dinner at eight. But, of course, it is up to the participants to ensure that proper boundaries are applied and maintained.

Lisa and Shawn stayed in Mocha Time for about 45 minutes. Upon leaving, instead of getting into their cars and going their separate ways, they chose to walk the downtown sidewalks. In all of their prior dates, they either skated together, or sat down and talked. With their schedules being a little more free due to summer break, they could now extend their time spent together (another reward of practicing patience). But everyone knows the sparkling feeling you get when you walk around with someone you're attracted to, especially for the very first time. So, they wanted to check this box off of their dating list.

As they walked through downtown, they took in the up-close scenery of all of Oklahoma City's beautiful business buildings. The city does not have the skyline of major metropolitan places like Chicago or Los Angeles, but it is substantial and gorgeous in its own intimate way. It is very fitting of the personality of the city. Anyhow, Lisa pointed out the newly built park that was just north of where the OKC Journeymen played its ball games. She told Shawn that she wanted to head in its direction. He, wanting to go so that the date could last a little longer, agreed. Walking in, they saw a beautiful LED fountain that was at the very center of the park. Right in front of it was a large stone mosaic that read, "OKC," in beige-colored rocks. They proceeded to walk on it, taking in the view of the fountain and all the park features surrounding them. While doing so, they continued their conversation. At this point, they were evaluating how things were going between them.

"So, I know I was late to our last breakfast date. I hope I've done a good job of keeping my word of communicating more." Lisa said.

"Yeah, you have. In fact, you've done an excellent job. I never meant to come off as an insecure guy who is constantly checking the

location of the girl he's dating. I understand how important space is."
Shawn replied.

"I get you. But, hey, you said you had girls leave you hanging before, so I understand that it may have been triggering. Now, don't get me wrong, I'm happy you still chose to wait on me. But if you don't mind me asking, why didn't you leave that day when I was late?"

Lisa was smart. Despite how great everything had been between them, she still took a moment to check his motives. And Shawn both knew and respected it.

"Well... I guess my actual desire of being there overwrote my instincts. Sometimes, I struggle with projecting the attitudes and actions of people from my past onto the people in my present. I thought that my fifteen-minute rule was for my protection, but it really turned out to be a defense mechanism. Because, deep within it was the expectation that someone would do it to me again." Shawn said.

"Shawn, I understand that completely."

Shawn was taking in information as well. His instincts wanted him to be defensive and assume the worst. In the back of his mind, he suspected that by asking him the question, she was trying to get him to compliment her looks, mind, and style as the reasons why he chose to stay. This is what he had done in his previous dating relationships, and after he did it, the relationship always fell through He felt like his vulnerability had backfired on him. But really, it was protecting him, leading him to the very moment he was in now. God is a Protector.

Lisa continued. "In many ways, our dates are like therapy. It feels like I leave better after every time we spend together. Many guys made me feel extremely anxious after dates, but you make me feel the complete opposite. You help calm me, both by your behaviors and the person you are overall."

This statement struck the most tender chord of Shawn's heart. For, Lisa had just said the very thing that he wanted to say to her but could not find the words to do so (Alicia was still helping him with this sort of thing). But it pointed to something within Lisa's character, reassuring him that he was in safe territory. He then chose to sum it up the best way he could.

"You're a beautiful person. Thanks for understanding me." Shawn said.

Lisa then reached out to grab his hand, and they interlocked fingers for the remainder of their walk in the park. This was another one of those times where a photographer should have been in the distance to capture youthful purity at its finest. After they exited the park, Shawn walked Lisa to her Mustang and wished her safe travels. Once again, they shared an innocent hug.

Shawn then went up to his mom's facility to get some swing work in. It was only about eleven minutes away from Mocha Time. The place was fairly empty for a Saturday, but it was likely due to the summer being so fresh and kids wanting to go swimming – or go do something else with their friends and family. Still, though, there were some other boys and girls inside getting in some practice. All of them were about to start their summer baseball/softball season. They, like Shawn, were just there to do some fine tuning. Still, people's faces always lit up whenever Shawn walked through the front entrance doors of Claire's Corner. Everyone knew Claire's story, especially how magnificent she was on the diamond. To see her own flesh and blood duplicating that success was both inspiring and full circle. It was like one of those things that lead you to believe in happy endings, even when the story has not even reached its midway point. You just know that everything will work out. Shawn was carrying the legacy of his mother with great substance, added with his own touch of style.

Inside of the cage, he worked on getting his swing path restructured. Back in the spring, he had some trouble with his right hip and knee, which were caused by a hard face-first dive he had taken in the first game of the season (he caught the ball). At first, it bothered him mightily, even though he never complained to anyone about it. But soon he realized that he could work his way around it by lessening his repetitions. Though he healed quickly, the soreness would creep back in every once in a while, lingering and causing discomfort. All baseball players know that any discomfort can create a bad habit in a baseball-specific movement. Since it was the season, he had no time to heal properly and give his swing rest. Now that it was summer, though, he could hit only when he felt it was necessary. He went strictly off of the messages his body relayed to his brain. If the body said no, then he would delay hitting. But if it said yes, he would hurry into the closest field or facility that was available.

Shawn ended up taking three rounds of his tee progression. He then brought in his personal soft toss machine and took two rounds of side toss. Lastly, he finished with one short round of front toss. Shawn hit most of the balls very hard, but his swing was not violent whatsoever. A good way to describe his motion is through art terms. Every swing was a skillful stroke onto a canvas, making up an end product that would, hopefully, portray competence and expertise when tested by the rest of the world. And there was no doubt about his excellence. When he took his final swing of the day, it was number 53 – a low number, for Shawn's practice standards. But his minor injuries made him appreciate the principle of *quality over quantity*. His work was quick, purposeful, and, like always, beautiful to behold.

Once Shawn left the facility, he went to grab some late lunch from the mall off Penn and Northwest Expressway. Of course, he was still rolling in his gorgeous Malibu. So far, the car had been driving perfectly, as he had got its oil changed earlier in the week. His next plan for it was to have someone detail the inside for him. Marvin had exhorted him to learn how to do it himself so that he could save money in the long run. Shawn was not necessarily opposed to it, either. His new summer job was during the weekdays, from 9 to 5, which made it harder to even get his car *to* the detail shop. But Shawn was not willing to do that work himself yet, so he figured he would catch time on his next first off day to get it done. Regardless, going to the mall always made him feel like he was recharging. The crazy thing is, he never really bought a lot of things for himself at once. He mainly liked walking around, seeing people get in their retail therapy. Every once in a while, he would go in and buy a $350 bottle of cologne or $800 worth of clothes and hats (he loved hats, specifically low-profiled baseball caps). He was not the biggest shoe guy, though. Most of his sneakers were within the $80-160 range. But he did pick colors that blended in with his clothing aesthetic. It's fair to say that he had a good eye for fashion. That day, though, he bought a new pair of designer frames (they were rimless, with silver accents). Even though Shawn had great vision and needed no prescription at all, he liked the look of sophistication that glasses brought to his appearance. This complex was probably just the inner geek that Marvin had passed down to him. After getting the glasses, he went inside of the food court and purchased some Cajun food: rice, veggies, blackened chicken, and bourbon chicken. He got an iced lemonade for his drink.

As he sat at one of the tables and began eating, he looked and observed the mall's busy Saturday rush. He then thought to himself how grateful he was to have been taught how to wisely use his time and money. He visualized how well off he would be once he left his parents' house. Shortly after, he started thinking about how his summer break would go. It was the first summer, since middle school, where he did not play baseball. He usually played in Seminole and Muskogee, but some OKC metro area schools held tournaments as well. Shawn always played looser in the summer, too. There was something relieving about just going out there to have fun, not worrying about getting to the playoffs or beating out a guy for an outfield spot. Summer ball, for him, was about getting better and meeting fellow ballplayers. Shawn was a true sportsman. But that was then. In the now, his summer of fun was beginning to evolve into something new and unexpected. For one, Lisa was the first substantial dating relationship he had ever had before. Plus, he now had a car, which allowed him to explore the city a whole lot more. In addition, working at RGM was his first actual job. All the money he had made before came from Marvin giving him allowances for doing chores and making good grades – boy, allowances from a multi-millionaire *has* to be the coolest thing ever. Shawn's sense of responsibility was starting to grow at its quickest rate so far in his lifetime. Though taxing at times, it was something he grew excited about more and more as days passed. Baseball is great, he thought, but it is not the only thing that life has to offer. So much more was waiting for him, and he could feel it.

Over east, about 1,300 miles away from Oklahoma, sat Marvin and Alicia in room 541 of a hotel just thirty miles south of the Orlando airport. The name of the place was *Summer Summer Hotel & Resort*, but everyone always called it "the SS," for short. Built in 2003, it was the leading tourist attraction in Florida for the past seven years running. In fact, in 2017 (the year prior), it received a national award for being one of the country's best travel stays, as it consistently received high praises from visitors. Right after getting the award, it received its 5-star hotel status. It had everything there. Its own restaurant. A bowling alley. Swimming pools and water slides. Baseball and soccer fields. A golf course. A music studio. Tennis and basketball courts – which often hosted large pickleball tournaments annually. A top-tier weight room. SS even had its own custom arcade. Of course, it was made as a rival to some of the other premier places in the area (surely, you're familiar with them). But Alicia and Marvin had been wanting to go there for the longest time.

Marvin felt a little anxious being away from Oklahoma, for, he was working almost 24/7. 2018's early economy struggles had forced him to restructure a lot of investment and retirement plans for his clients. The added responsibility of his mobile business app only made things more strenuous. He was somewhat of a workaholic, but he would never admit it to anyone. But Alicia recognized it right from the get-go. Good for him, *she* was a little more accustomed to traveling and, thus, sought to help him relax. While they unpacked their things, she began solacing her husband.

"Honey, everything is going to be fine. This seven-day trip is about *us*. All of that stuff back home will be waiting for us when we get back."

"Yeah, I know. I'm just so used to doing something productive every single day. I hate feeling like I'm missing out on business. Plus, Shawn is home by himself, and –"

"Shawn is almost seventeen years old, Marvin." She told him. "He will take care of the house, and all of his other responsibilities, just fine. Besides, he needs to practice being more by himself anyway."

Marvin then sat down on their bed and kept overthinking. Soon, Alicia hopped up behind him and sat with her legs crossed together. She started massaging his tense upper body – his back and shoulders being the places she applied the firmest pressure. She was always good at relieving his stress because she understood and appreciated how hard he worked. Marvin Clement was a genius in business. However, that genius often led to him being pulled in many directions simultaneously, and, over time, it created a complex of ubiquity in him. Of course, he was built for the challenge and had put in the proper amount of work to be able to sustain his success over the years. Even so, that did not mean that he was immune to the brain and bodily consequences that came with it. He was unaware that he was on the brink of being unable to manage everything at its demanding pace. But God was his Healer, working through his dear wife to fortify him. Hence, it was fitting that she was relieving the pressure from his neck and shoulders. For, he was carrying the world. Still rubbing him, she continued calming him with her words.

"You're the greatest man I know, babe. But even the greatest men deserve a time of relaxation. Be kind to yourself. You just made seven million bucks last month. That's an accomplishment and worthy of celebration. Even more so, you've earned your right to rest." Alicia said to him.

Marvin looked back at her and grinned.

"*You* made 30 million." He said, immediately beginning to laugh. Alicia laughed with him.

"And see, I'm not over here stressing!" She then wrapped her arms around Marvin's torso and put her chin on his left shoulder. "I'm here to enjoy time with my man. That's *all* I'm here to do."

Of course, Alicia succeeded in helping Marvin see that this time away was meant to be worry-free. As a result, he was able to turn all of that built up stress into physical and emotional love towards his wife. Later that night, they spent thirty minutes inside of a bubble-filled bathtub, just holding each other. They talked about the first time they met in New York, mentioning how crazy it was that Alicia had painted an image inspired by Claire Hollins. Marvin joked with her and said that he was actually supposed to be at a Knicks game that night, but he then calmly added that he was glad that he didn't go. It was undeniable how connected their stories were. Yes, the Lord had made Claire for Marvin and, together, they created a beautiful human in Shawn. But He also allowed her to be taken away. Many would deem that cruel of Him. Others may simply think that it was just her time to go. Regardless, He remained faithful to His son Marvin. Alicia was an actualization of all of the time he spent healing in isolation. She was the gift of all of his sacrifices and healthy decision making over the span of twelve years. No, as you are aware, Marvin was not perfect in the process. But the important thing is, he was intentional about getting to the other side of things. And, for things that are worth time and energy, the only way to, is through. So now, instead of trying to replace Claire, he was able to fully love the woman God brought into his life next. Never did he expect to love as hard as he once did with Claire, but it was now happening again for him. God is a Redeemer.

Even so, you would have almost mistaken the two of them as teenagers, as much fun as they had that week. They did everything from swimming and going down intense water slides, to bowling, to playing arcade games, to even playing a game of pickup basketball. Marvin and Alicia did life together like they were the best of friends. The both of them were so thoughtful. Midway through the week, Marvin surprised Alicia by having a custom dress delivered to their hotel room. It was the same one she had tried on during their trip in Puerto Rico. She chose not to buy it then because she did not want to pay so much money (the dress was 11,000 dollars). In typical fashion, Marvin took a mental note and planned on purchasing it shortly after. It was a stunning dress that was created by Puerto Rico's top designer, Antonio Rivera. Its color was a light orange but looked as if it was completely blended with a vanilla cream color. It was less formal than a wedding dress but fitting for an occasion like a themed party or, of course, a date night in Orlando, Florida. It was perfect for Alicia's style. And boy, could she wear that thing. To be candid, Marvin had bought it, not only because Alicia strongly desired to have it, but so that he could just stare at her in it. So that he could take her out and just be in amazement of her grace. It deepened his desire to please her. In the past, whenever he would buy her dresses, he joked to her that he just bought them so that he could take them off of her in the evening time. But *this* dress was so perfect on her that he would not have even dared to bother. Even so, Alicia had a surprise for him as well. Back in January, when she was painting Gabriella's portrait, she ran into Alvin Wake, a prominent financial advisor on the western coast. He also happened to be one of the people Marvin looked up to the most. He had read Alvin's book, *Spend More & Earn More*, which served as the foundation for several of his financial practices. When Alicia met him, she asked if he could record a voice memo for Marvin. He did as requested, but also pulled out one of his books, signed it (to Marvin), and gave it to her. So after thanking him for the dress, and, of course, looking at herself in the mirror with it, she went over and grabbed Marvin's hand. She led him over to the closet and told him to close his eyes. When he did, she pulled out an orange shoe box and gave it to him. Inside of it was the book by his hero. Marvin, seeing it was signed to him, began to get emotional.

"Where did you meet him?" He asked Alicia.

"I ran into him a couple of months back. But wait, there's more." She then pulled out her phone and played the voice memo for him, which said the following:

Hi, there, Marvin. I'm here with your wonderful wife, and she told me how much of a fan you are of mine. Well, sir, I must say that the feeling is mutual. I have been hearing about an Oklahoma man who was ruling the region in terms of investment returns and successful business plans. I had heard your name before, but it was in a short conversation with some guys I know from Texas and Missouri. But just know, I am proud that a fellow black man is creating new thresholds for purchasing power. Hopefully, I can meet you one day in person. Until then, I wish you and your family the very best blessings. See ya soon, Marvin.

After listening to it, Marvin hugged Alicia with a very tight grasp and started to cry. Alvin Wake was his biggest influence in the finance world. The fact that he was complimenting Marvin only confirmed to him that he was making the right moves. Yes, even millionaires tend to question their own successes. It gave him motivation to continue moving forward with his overall plans. But the level of consideration that Alicia had for her man was beyond honorable. She had done many nice things for him before, but, to date, this was the best gift she had given him. And she paid zero dollars for it. Just thoughtfulness, time, and *effort*.

For the rest of their time in Florida, they went out on dates to some of the area's top restaurants. They had everything from Mexican to BBQ to Italian to American-style buffet. In total, they went on ten meal dates. Prior to the getaway, they had only been on seven meal dates since the beginning of the year (all of them being dinners). Now, they planned on creating more time for dating, and their marriage soon became so much more refreshed because of their intentionality. Back when they first got together, the spark between them was exciting. But now, in marriage, the spark was a little different. Not in a negative way, either. Their connection was, instead, evolving into something better. Something more substantial. Each day, they got to know one another in a way they didn't before, and every moment of their vacation was a realization that they, God-willing, had a lifetime of doing so. Is this not one of life's best offerings? To become one with someone who is suitable *and* healthy for you at the same time? To enjoy life alongside your closest earthly companion? To, every day, be motivated to make this special person's dreams come to reality and then actually do it? Yeah, marriage is definitely worth the struggle and wait.

On the outside, everything seemed to be going great. It just so happened that for Lisa and Shawn, as well as for Marvin and Alicia, it was actually true if one was to study them up close. Maybe it was because each person, as an individual, had enough courage and security to do their inner work. So often, it is easy to bypass such a process and rush into relationships that are not vetted properly.

Really, it points to people's issues concerning availability. Or maybe it exposes the plague of poor self-esteem that causes said availability. But these four individuals managed to overcome these obstacles, creating something that should be modeled and studied by those with aspirations of being in healthy dating and marriage situations. They act like a compass, sending directional coordinates to others that are trying to reach the same destination; or at least, get to one that is very near. All things considered, it is not an easy thing to do (like with anything associated with healthy living). There are many roadblocks, speed bumps, and despicable people along the way that tempt you to give up in trying to reach your desired end goal. All parts of your being will be challenged in one way or another. You then learn that the biggest threat to your future is your own self. Self-sabotage is one of the easiest feats out there, and millions of people do this on a regular basis. Life is consequential, and, as a result, some people just have to learn the hard way.

CHAPTER 7:

TIME NEVER LIES

Things were getting heated inside of the Bowen home on the evening of Saturday, June 9th, 2018. Shelby had been trying to get Bobby to take better care of the house because, now that school was out, he was the person who was home majority of the time. She would often get home from the hospital to a dirty living room, kitchen, and guest bathroom. Plus, only to see that Bobby was nowhere to be found. This made her angry because she knew he was usually somewhere with JoJo. She and her son, each on one side of their kitchen island, stared at each other intensely.

"Bobby, I need you to, *for once*, be a responsible individual. I cannot work fifty plus hours every week and still find time to make sure this house is cleaned thoroughly. This is YOUR house, too!"

"Well, you're acting like I don't ever have things to do." Bobby responded. "It's literally the beginning of summer, and I don't feel like being in the house all day. Maybe you should get a maid or something."

This pissed her off, for, he was blatantly dismissing the fact that he was choosing to leave chores undone. She wanted to throw a pot at him, but she started to take deep breaths in order to calm down.

"Son, I get that you want to be out playing baseball or with your friends. Hell, I know that you want to be with JoJo as much as you can this summer. But this house should come first. End of story. If I have to punish you on your time off, I will. This is an order. And if you ever make your little *'maid'* comment again, I promise you, you will be restricted to this house for your whole junior year. I dare you to try me, Bobby." Shelby told her son.

"Whatever."

"That's the last pass I'm gonna give you. You either clean this damn house, or you'll be grounded until I say otherwise. I'm so serious. Get it done."

Bobby then stormed over to the kitchen sink and slammed the dirty dishes into its left side. In doing so, he splashed water and bleach all over his dark blue shirt. But he did not care one bit. He felt like his mom was being completely unfair to him. For all he knew, his friends and teammates were all out kicking it that night. Bobby would have been right along with them if his mom did not force him to stay home and do chores. But being grounded for the whole summer meant that, for one, he could not play summer ball. And two, and more important to him, it meant that he could not be with his girlfriend. So as frustrated as he was, he obeyed Shelby and cleaned up the kitchen, making it look like a brand-new space. Right after, he straightened up the living room and freshened it back up. Lastly, he half-did the bathrooms, as he had expended all of the cleaning energy that was left in him.

Overall, it took Bobby about two hours and twenty minutes to finally finish his chores. Once everything was complete, he walked by his mother's open bedroom door. Peeking in, he saw her passed out in her pajamas, having no cover on. Feeling empathy, he walked up to her and put her comforter over her body. After plugging her cell phone into its charger, he then turned off her bedside lamp. Finally walking out of her room, he started to realize how out of line he had been. Deep down, Bobby knew he was wrong and needed to put forth greater effort. Shelby worked so hard for them. It was about time that he followed suit in all the ways he was able. She needed him to have her back like she had his, but something always kept getting in the way.

Bobby then went back into his room to think about what he was gonna do, since it was already so late. The clock read 9:19, and all of the parties he was hoping to attend were already jumping. He had already seen his friends posting videos on social media, showing how great a time they were having. Given that attending a party was out of the question, guess what his next option was. Yeah, you're right again. JoJo, his bae – (b)efore (a)nyone (e)lse.

When he picked up his phone to contact her, he saw that she had already tried to reach him. He had left his phone in the living room, and it was on vibrate. JoJo both called and texted him around 6:40 that evening, right when Bobby and Shelby's argument began. Even so, her text read the following:

"Hey baby, I'm sorry I didn't call back last night, I was so tired. But anyway, I wanna go watch the horse races tonight at the track. You know, the one across from the movie theater? You wanna meet me there? We can eat at the diner spot if you want? Hit me back soon, love you."

When he read it, he immediately started freaking out. At this point, most of the races were over. Bobby quickly gave her a call, but she did not answer. He called a second time, but still nothing. Both times, she had pressed decline. Bobby was starting to figure that she was probably mad at him for not getting back with her right away, even though it was all on such a short notice (a detail that he never considered). All he knew was that he had missed a fun night with JoJo because of his mom making efforts to teach him valuable lessons. He then called for a third time. In this instance, the phone rung for the maximum number of dials. As it did, Bobby steadily grew hopeful that she finally would pick up for him. Yet, even still, she did not answer. Frustrated, he tossed his phone onto the floor, laid down on the bed, and stared at his bedroom ceiling. Thoughts spun through his brain like a wild tornado. As much as he could, he envisioned the best possible outcome. This, of course, looked like JoJo being understanding and not getting angry with him. However, he could not help but sink in the fear of all the negative scenarios he imagined. It was hard for him because, at times, JoJo was completely undetectable on the emotional radar. Once twenty minutes passed, though, his phone finally vibrated. It was JoJo calling him back. Bobby swiftly hopped off his bed and picked his phone up from the carpet. Then, he answered.

"Hey, JoJo!"

"Hey, babe, what's up?"

"I was seeing if you were at the track still! Baby, I'm sorry, I had to finish cleaning the house tonight. My phone was on silent, and I didn't see you called me!" Bobby said.

"Baby, it's all good. We can go next week or something. You alright? You sound out of breath." JoJo responded to him.

"Yeah, I'm good, baby. I was just panicking a little. I didn't want you to think I was ignoring you or anything. But next week will definitely work. I probably can still see you tomorrow, though."

"Ummm.. I'm going to Tulsa tomorrow with my friends. We're going to a summer festival. How about this: I'll give you a call tomorrow, well before the time we leave. Call you around, say, ten?"

"That works, JoJo."

"Okay, I'm gonna get back to the races, babe. I'm about to make my bets at the booth, right after I see the next horses come through the paddock. Some of my cousins are here, too. We're about to make our way down. Talk to you soon, *Bobby Ray*."

"Bye, honey. Love you." Bobby responded.

"Love you, too." JoJo said.

Bobby felt tremendously better after their phone call. Horse racing was not really his thing, anyway, but it still comforted him that his girlfriend was out doing something she liked. Now, instead of staying up all night worrying about her, he could go to sleep in peace. But like he had feared, JoJo felt some type of way about it all. In her head, Bobby was intentionally ignoring her again. This stemmed from all the other times he had denied spending time with her because of baseball and school schedules. Though she had been getting her way a lot more, this brought the issue right back to the forefront.

The time now read 9:43, and the horses for race number nine were just now exiting the paddock. JoJo ended up betting on the horse wearing number 3, which was named Jacking Fire, to win. She had lied to Bobby over the phone, as she was not there with her cousins. Only, she said that because she knew that it would make him leave her alone. She didn't want him continuing to text her long romantic messages about how much he loved her and wanted to be with her "till the end of time." Her mind and heart were bothered because she felt like Bobby was taking her for granted. After all, it was summer. What the hell else could he be doing on a weekend night, she thought. Even so, she sat on one of the spectators' benches and watched race nine develop. It was marked as the night's most balanced race. Eight more minutes later, all riders were up, and all horses were loaded in. Then, at 9:56, the bell rung loudly. Coming out of the gate, Jacking Fire led the pack, but all of the horses followed closely and stayed tight. Excitement started to build as the horses rumbled near the first turn. Midway, as Jacking Fire tried to pull away from the other competitors, he was being hunted down by the horse wearing number 5, Killer Speed, who had been sprinting on the outside. Seeing him draw closer, Jacking Fire's jockey remained calm. His horse was on a beautiful pace, stretching out each step like a Triple Crown champion. Thus, he refused to beat on him for more acceleration. Around the second turn and into the final stretch, Killer Speed finally caught all the way up to Jacking Fire. And from that point on, they were nose for nose, stride for stride. The other five horses were about six or seven lengths back, as they were all proving to be in need of more conditioning. But no one really paid them much mind. The *real* scene was Killer Speed and Jacking Fire battling out the final parts of the mile. When they neared the finish line, Killer Speed appeared to have it won by a nose.

But for the final strides, Jacking Fire reached out and defeated him by the smallest possible margin: a photo finish. When they checked, Jacking Fire had indeed won it by about four inches. Reacting to the official announcement, JoJo ran across the front of the rails, jumping for joy that her horse had won. But everyone else were on their feet, too, as it was the most exciting race of the weekend. Thus, JoJo came up, flipping her $25 into $300.

In the winner's circle stood the gorgeous bay-colored stallion with his jockey, trainers, and owners. The purse for the race was a solid $47,000, which was a typical day at the yard for head trainer Nelson Brooks (out of Edmond). Crazy enough, this was also the father of Terrell Brooks – the Worth ballplayer that got into it with Shawn at Bella's that one night. Terrell was at the track, too. From the rail, he had watched several of his father's horses run earlier that night. But he had got hungry around the time of race 7, so he went inside of the restaurant and ordered a medium supreme pizza and fries. Interestingly enough, JoJo had known Terrell ever since the age of twelve, as they first met at the 2013 state spelling bee competition. Each of them represented their district. Neither of them won, but they became good friends afterwards, exchanging numbers and social media handles. Terrell always thought JoJo was very attractive. He had even asked her out to the movies one time in 2016, but she never responded to his DM. She did not think the timing was right. Plus, he was all the way in Edmond, while she was all the way in Spencer. It would have been more work than she desired.

Anyhow, after she went and collected her money, she walked back up near the spectator entrance doors. Before she could enter back in, she glanced over into the windows of the restaurant that was connected to the lobby. Through them, she saw Terrell sitting in his booth, lifting a piece of pizza to his mouth. She had not seen him in about a year or so (she saw him, from a distance, at a concert during the previous summer). After spotting him, she briefly looked down at the ground and smiled. Somehow, she knew that she would run into him again one day. How perfect, she thought, was *this* timing. She then hurried in there to say hi. She snuck up on him.

"Yo, Terrell! What's up, man?"

Surprised, with a mouth full of pizza, Terrell's countenance immediately brightened at the sight of her.

"What's up, JoJo?" Terrell said, covering his mouth.

"You mind if I sit?" JoJo asked.

"Not at all, go ahead."

"So what you doing up here at the race track?"

"Actually, JoJo, I'm here supporting my dad. He just won the last race."

"You mean, Jacking Fire is *your* horse?" She said, growing excited.

"He sure is. He was injured for a lot of last year, but Dad finally got him back ready for this summer. It was only his third race of the meet."

"That is so cool. Even cooler, though, I actually picked him to win tonight. I thought he looked pretty good in the paddock, and something told me that he was the one. I guess I have you to thank for making me 300 dollars richer." She said.

Terrell started laughing. "No, that's you just making a great choice. Picking horses is a science. You seem to have it down."

"I guess you're right," she said, laughing with great charm.

Terrell then made eye contact with her and then quickly looked away. His light began to dim slightly, causing his chest to cave in. JoJo noticed it, too, and immediately knew what it was about: Terrell was still salty about being left on read. But she also knew that she ignited his imagination every time she was in his presence. So, she took it upon herself to address the situation.

"Hey, about your message from a while back – "

"No, JoJo, it's all good." He said, cutting her off. "I know you're with someone now. I be seeing y'all online. Y'all seem like a great couple. I ain't tripping."

JoJo saw the despair that was still lingering within him. Now in front of her was a new opportunity for self-fulfillment. In her mind, her boyfriend had made his choice that day. And it wasn't her. Exactly four and a half feet away from her was a young man who had been desperately seeking to be with her since their days of middle school. Like she had done with many others, she could perform her persuasive magic on him, getting him to do exactly what she wanted. Sitting there, she looked down at her jean shorts and white low-top Chuck Taylor's. Thoughts of Bobby arose for a second, but she quickly forced herself to only be concerned about the present moment. Another five seconds passed, and then she looked back up at Terrell.

"Terrell, me and my boyfriend are not on the best terms. In fact, I would not necessarily say we're even a thing right now. So, *again*, I'd like to talk about the message you sent me. I'm sorry that I left you hanging, but I wanna make things right."

Before continuing, she got up and went over to his side of the booth. Sitting close to him, she put her arm around him and gently whispered, "We can go wherever you wanna go and do *whatever* you wanna do."

Terrell was shocked. Had this been Lisa, he would have said yes with zero hesitation. He was still seeking to get Shawn back in whatever way possible. Instead, though, he was presented a chance to help break the heart of a boy he never met or said words to. Sure, he knew *of* Bobby and had seen him play at E-City the year before. But that was the extent of it. Terrell thought very carefully of how he would handle the situation. Did he go through with it and conquer the girl he had been waiting for? Or, did he resist his built-up urges and decline JoJo's out-of-nowhere request? Decisions, decisions. It didn't take the boy long, though.

"Ummm, I guess we can go back to my place in Edmond, if you want. My mom is in New York, and my dad, here, has to get his horses tested and then complete winners' paperwork. He won't be back until around one in the morning, I'm sure. That gives us plenty of time, right?"

She moved in even closer and whispered into his ear. "*Plenty.*" When she said it, the tip of her tongue brushed against the bottom of his ear. Terrell's excitement would have broken the *excitement scale*, if there ever was such a thing.

Minutes later, Terrell led JoJo out of the restaurant and into the parking lot, which was on the far western side of the track. As they approached his car, JoJo's heart melted. Terrell was driving a 1969 Camaro SS convertible. It was golden, with cream racing stripes across its hood and rear. Its rims were a sparkling chrome, about 18 to 20 inches wide. The license plate read, WORTH43, as he was number 43 for Worth's baseball team. It was as picturesque of a car that you can get. Or, maybe instead, it was the perfect representation of the lust that was present between them. Regardless, they were soon riding in its front seats.

Soon, Terrell was zooming northward on I-35 with his car's top down. The wind was rushing against JoJo's face and curly hair, giving a perfect cool balance to the 82-degree night it that was. As he drove, she felt as if she had just been freed from a jail cell. Meaning, her commitment and loyalty to Bobby had become tedious and uneventful for her. Terrell was the change that she was so desperately seeking. Fresh spontaneity, which rekindled her romantic core. Thus, she had no question of what was going to happen when they got to his house. But just the journey getting there gave her an unprecedented thrill. JoJo, herself, did not yet have a vehicle. Neither did Bobby, which was something she oddly held against him, even though he was still fifteen and unable to drive legally. Terrell was seventeen and approaching his senior year. Despite having blown his cover to her over direct messaging, he had a mysterious edge to his personality. Even though Bobby was ideal for JoJo, she did not always like dealing with the realities of their relationship. In Terrell, she willingly folded into their situation's unpredictability. That she could, if she wanted, keep this thing going on occasion and utilize it during times where Bobby's behavior was unyielding. JoJo always managed to have her way. Truly, her feminine flair was very difficult to fight against. But Terrell was not clueless, even though his actions said otherwise. At the end of the day, he knew what it was. Doing this was just a check off his box, anyway. He did not want to go the whole summer without catching a body of his own. Yeah, pretty shallow, but he, *too*, was not used to going without. It was a love affair of the mightily spoiled.

At this point, the time was 10:41, and they finally had reached Terrell's house. After pulling in and then placing the car in park, he turned off the ignition and went to open the passenger door for her. JoJo thanked him and grabbed his hand as they went towards the front entrance of the home. But before her feet could reach the porch, she had a brief thought of resistance. As it looked, she was moments away from doing the lowest, most dirty deed she had ever done. There was still time left to change her mind. She could tell him no and just ask for him to take her home. Or maybe, she thought, they could just spend the rest of the night looking into the stars from Terrell's masterpiece of a vehicle, talking about how their lives had gone since the last time they connected. Hypothetically, there were several alternatives. Yet, she could not deny her current reality any longer. The palpation of Terrell's hand, and the wonder of the depth of his intimacy, reigned supreme in JoJo's mind. There was no going back now. It was time to test all of what her new lover could accomplish. So, he then took her upstairs into his loft-style bedroom. It was clean and fresh, almost like he had already known he would have a girl over. Or, maybe he was just a guy who kept his space organized. Regardless, in there, the two of them undressed each other and passionately became one.

After, JoJo and Terrell laid next to each other in amazement of their shared experience. All of Terrell's physical features satisfied JoJo. She thought him, by miles and miles, better than Bobby. At this point, her boyfriend was merely a thought of once was. JoJo's mind and heart were now in the hands of a new person. Terrell ravished in the experience, too. Before her, he had been with four girls. On three of the times, he went to the girl's house while her parents were gone. On the fourth instance, though, he had a girl inside of a hotel room in Missouri (he was playing in a summer tournament there). But JoJo had been the first in his very own abode, which was something he saw as a milestone, especially since it was the person he had been waiting on for quite some time. Anyhow, both of them were sweating and out of breath. To gather more strength and energy, Terrell rolled over and sipped on the bottle of water that was on his nightstand. After doing so, he rested back on his pillow and resumed catching wind. When JoJo was finally able to recover, she climbed back on top of him. She did not restart the process, though. Instead, she sparked a conversation with him. Any part of his mind that was not yet accessed, she was gunning for it. She was also trying to make the moment as memorable and euphoric as possible. And as you may assume, he was more than happy to entertain her.

"Okay, Terrell," she said, "I don't know where you've been for the past couple of years, but all I know is, I'm glad I finally caught up with you."

"Oh, really? My messages show otherwise." He said, jokingly.

"Yeah, I know I never responded. But that never meant that I was not interested in you. Many guys message me online, and I don't always feel like paying it any attention. You just caught me on one of those days."

With every word, she was redeeming all of the bitterness that had built up in Terrell since the day he sent her the message. For her, it was like slicing a piece of cake: little resistance.

"I got you. No worries here, especially after tonight." Terrell replied.

"What do you mean after? Tonight doesn't have to be *over*." JoJo said to him.

Still resting on top of him, she gave Terrell a kiss on his collarbone and then on his lips. She slightly pulled away and then looked at him with great intensity. And Terrell, finally ready, yielded to her again.

In the end, Terrell took JoJo home around 1:15 in the morning. She had a key hidden underneath the doormat near her front door, which was usually used whenever she came home late from Bobby's house. This time felt different than all of those times for obvious reasons. Terrell gave her exactly what she wanted. She felt safe and secure with him. Even though she knew she was out of line, she had fun. Guess it's true what they say: at the end of the day, people will always do what they really want to do.

After getting freshened up inside of her home, JoJo hopped right into her bed and fell asleep. She had no remorse whatsoever. About thirty minutes after dozing off, her phone lit up her very dark room, as it was on the charger and atop her bedside dresser. The notification was a text from a person you would never guess. Okay, fine, you're an expert at this now. It was Bobby. He, too, had been sleeping like a baby, but had just got up to go use the restroom. When he did, he figured he'd send his girlfriend a sweet message that she could see right then or wake up to the next morning. Bobby never failed in being a thoughtful boyfriend. The text message read as the following:

JoJo, I just hope you know that our relationship has been the greatest time of my life. I never thought that I could enjoy someone's presence so much. You help me to be a better person. I know you have had to be patient with me in a lot of ways, and I thank you for sticking by my side. But, babe, I want you to know that I love you more than anything else in the world. I hope we can continue growing together this whole summer. You got me, and I got you. Love u babe.

The next morning, JoJo woke up and read it. She didn't respond. Instead, she chose to send Terrell a good morning text. *Here* is what she said to him:

Good morning, Terrell. You were such a phenomenal person last night. I enjoyed every second of our time together, and I hope that we can continue hooking up. It's VERY fun. Hope to talk to you soon, maybe later on this week or so. But if not, just hit me up when you can. Kisses.

After sending this to him, she reopened her message thread with Bobby and read through it again. Soon, she started to think of a creative way to break things off with him. Maybe she could go about it in the classic, "we need to talk" text. Maybe she could go over to his house and break it to him in person. Or, she could just wait to tell him. As great as the previous night was with Terrell, she thought, there was no guarantee that he wouldn't ghost her. With this, she would have to cross all t's and dot all i's. Whichever way, though, she knew that she had the upper hand. She knew that Bobby was the one who was doing the chasing. "He'll be alright and find someone else. I'm tired of waiting for him to prioritize me, anyway," she whispered to herself. As a result of her thoughts, she went ahead and called him. Bobby was still asleep, but the buzzing from her call startled and woke him. Realizing it was her, he calmed down and answered.

"Hey, JoJo, good morning," he said, in his half-sleep voice.

"Morning, Bobby. What are you up to?"

"Well, you actually were my morning alarm. I needed to get up anyway, it's almost eleven o'clock. But I'm gonna be chilling for the day. My mom is getting ready to leave for work in about forty-five minutes. You getting ready to go to Tulsa?" He asked her.

"No, we cancelled the trip." In truth, there was really no trip to begin with. Bobby failed to detect the lie, though.

"Oh, okay! So does that mean you can come over? I can get the popcorn ready!"

"Actually, that's the thing. I don't know if I can keep doing this." JoJo responded.

"Doing what?" Bobby said, slightly perplexed. "You want me to come to your place instead?"

JoJo paused, as she realized that she was blind-siding him pretty hard. She knew it would take a little more effort and focus. She responded.

"No, Bobby, that's not what I mean."

They had a silent ten seconds or so.

"Okay... so what *do* you mean exactly?" He said, growing more concerned. "Is everything okay, babe?"

JoJo then locked in on telling him the truth. She did not want to dance around it for any longer than she had to. One thing about her, she understood that her energy could not be in two places at the same time. Though Bobby was drowning in irrationality, it wouldn't have taken him long to detect the changes in her that were rooted in her unfaithfulness. He was not the brightest fish in the pond, but he was no fool.

"Bobby Ray, I have to tell you something." JoJo said.

"I'm listening."

"I had sex with someone else last night." She admitted.

Bobby started laughing. "Okay, JoJo, that's real funny. So are you gonna come over or what? We can binge on that new show you been wanting to watch. Cycles, isn't it called? After that, we can... *you know*."

JoJo kept her game face on, though she was slightly intrigued by the idea that Bobby was presenting her with. Fornication was one of her favorite things in the entire world. Only, she no longer required for her counterpart to be her dear Bobby Ray. She stuck to her guns.

"Bobby, I'm not lying to you. I'm being for real. I slept with another person. He goes to Worth, but I've known him for a few years. I bumped into him at the track last night. I'm actually telling you this because I think it's gonna continue happening. Me and you are done, Bobby."

To prevent the foreseeable argument that was just seconds away from happening, she hung up in his face. Yeah, before the poor guy could even respond to her or make any of his feelings known. Talk about starting your day off on a bad note.

Bobby genuinely thought that she was just messing with him. But when he heard her say it for the second time, with added details, he knew that it was true. Even though she had just pressed end, he still had the phone up to his ear as if she was still on the other line. Trauma was beginning to take its first sucker punches: one to the head, and three to the body. How unfair. Defenseless and completely unaware of the volatility that had been resting in JoJo's bosom for *however* long. Bobby figured that she would have just told him that she was unhappy with their relationship. After all, she never backed down when it came to voicing her disappointments. Their communication was always solid, which was why this was so puzzling for him. But he was dealing with an individual that was never in it for him to begin with. Instead, JoJo liked the *idea* of Bobby. Someone who would never cease to be head over heels for her, no matter what she did. A person who was a top athlete, which brought desirable social status (which brought attention). She partnered that with her own shallow tendencies and reputation as one of the prettiest girls in the area. The result was a relationship that she could dictate at all points. For, she knew that Bobby was going to hold on tight to her because of his strong desire for companionship. But in actuality, Bobby's emptiness is what led him to be with her in the first place. Once they became an item, JoJo filled him up for as long as she was willing, and it made it him happy. He made her happy, too, as long as he remained malleable. In Bobby's eyes, though, easily bending to her will was what being a considerate boyfriend looked like. A person who was open-minded and fair. Someone who made provisions for his girl, whenever and wherever. But even though he gave it his best shot, she still abandoned him. And as a consequence, Bobby was made empty again.

It angered Bobby that she had the nerve to be smug in her confession. The fact that she, somehow, made him seem like the guilty person. By the way she persuaded him so easily, she could have told him that the sky was purple, and he would have looked outside to see for himself. It was natural for him to be so moved by a young lady, but JoJo took it to a whole new level. She managed to dig further into the depths of his mind and soul. It's crazy, though. Half of him was wishing that he would have never met her at that Halloween party. That he would have chosen to go into a different room and conversate with a different girl, or any other person, for that matter. Yet, the other half of him wanted to absolve her for her transgressions, leading to a comforting reunion between them. This was the reality of where he was. He was, very much so, an idealist. He imagined an entire future with JoJo, and yet, she couldn't even imagine another 24 more hours with him. How can two people, with such different motives, find themselves stuck in a mess as great as this one? What were the things that really drew them together? Of course, there was physical attraction, but what was really lying underneath it? These are the things that Bobby never really thought about, and his heartbroken state was the evidence. One thing he did know, though, was that rage was building up in him. And very fast. He wanted to, somehow, activate the powers of a great superhero and destroy everything within a ten-mile radius. He especially wanted to vandalize the Gonzalez residence. If only, he thought, he had a car to run directly into the front room of their space. If only he could take a sack of stones and obliterate every one of the house's windows. Or maybe he could just take a tank of gasoline, along with some matches, and burn down the entire damn thing. These were real thoughts. Deep connections, gone wrong, can easily make people go crazy.

But to his credit, Bobby was able to fight off these irate urges. *Something* in him told him to put his mind on something, *anything*, other than her. Thus, he slowly got up off of his bed and walked over to his window to look outside. Opening the blinds, he took in the view of the morning scenery. He saw all of morning birds gathering along the power lines. One particular bird caught his eye. A cardinal, with one of the most beautiful shades of bright red, was flying back and forth between the mulberry tree and the fresh green grass. As if it could feel Bobby's gaze, the bird then flew onto the layered brick that was protruding from Bobby's window. It stayed there for about thirty seconds. During such time, Bobby felt a peace that surpassed all understanding. Like it had been a Spirit dove in disguise, coming to reassure him that he was going to be okay. But when it departed, Bobby's thoughts and feelings started to settle back in. With each second passing, he became more aware of how wrong JoJo had done him. Eventually, he could not help but begin crying. His heart started throbbing, like someone was striking at it, nonstop, with a great spear. A relentless wave emotions cycled through his body. Confusion. Passion. Hate. Anger. Love, love, and love. Bitterness. Malice. Resentment. But one particular emotion overtook him the most: *pain*.

Moments later, Shelby walked into his room to tell him that breakfast was ready. When she did, he continued looking through his window, frozen. She noticed this and approached him. Getting closer, she saw that he was crying. Immediately, she grabbed him and hugged him, as he continued to sob uncontrollably. It was no secret to Shelby as to what this was all about. She knew her son more than he knew himself. Thus, she made the simple decision to let her presence be all that he needed. She hated seeing him hurt. His current state reminded her, so vividly, of a hard break-up she experienced in high school. She, too, was looking through a window, crying her eyes out. Like her son, she often wore her emotions on her sleeve, and it would backfire in unexpected ways. But even so, as she was holding him, she felt a great sense of relief come over her. For weeks, she had sensed that Bobby was growing more distant and bothered. She had already tried talking to him, but none of what she said was truly registering. So now she chose to talk to someone else: God. She started praying for him a lot more than she usually did. Praying that God would keep him safe wherever he went, and that He would remove the people who were not seeking out his best interest. Praying that her son would live to experience wholeness, evading a life full of misery and disappointment. She prayed that he would, one day, be better than she was. And now, here it was. Her prayers, answered.

Bobby finally sat back down on his bed, and Shelby remained there with him.

"Son, you can tell me everything when you're ready. But what I want to know is, are you done?"

"What do you mean?" He answered her, still drying his tears.

"Bobby, are you going to leave this girl alone? Can you not see how much she was taking from you? Your time, your energy, your space. Son, you are about to be sixteen. Now is not the time to allow another person to determine how you live. You are way too young." She added.

"Yeah. I guess I don't really have a choice, though. She just up and left me for another dude, anyway." Bobby said.

"Well, I'm sorry to hear that. But I have to tell you this. It's still your responsibility to move on. This means that you can't call her. You can't go over to her place, just out of the blue. You can't even ask her how her day was today, tomorrow, or any other day, for that matter. All because you miss her. Son, simply missing someone is never enough to alter reality. Everything is changed now. *Oh*, and you're going to have to get rid of all of these pictures you got in here."

Bobby looked around his room. On his walls were several printed-out photos of him and JoJo. Out on dates. At school dances. At the Oklahoma state capitol. Selfies from the ballpark right after some of his games. Mirror photos. He even had naked photos of her inside of his dresser, but he didn't dare letting his mother know about them.

"Gotchu, Ma. I'm throwing them out today."

"Good, son. And remember this: there are so many other girls out there. So many that are, honestly, heads and shoulders above Joleen. You just have to become a better person so that one day, you'll be ready for her to enter into your life. But before anything, you have to heal."

Bobby looked at her and nodded in agreement.

"You're right. Thank you, Ma. Love you."

"Love you, son." She said, hugging him tightly. "I'll have your plate in the oven for you so it can stay warm. I'll let you do what you need to do first."

After Shelby left his room, Bobby hurried up and ripped down all of the photos. And yes, he even took the naked ones out of his drawer. He then went and got a plastic bag to put all of them in. As he fumbled through the pictures, each one struck him with a sting of grief. Trashing months and months' worth of memories is never easy, especially when they attach to the areas of the heart and brain in a way that most memories do not. Bobby was never one to think about the potency of his decisions, so he was unaware that he was the type of person who carried experiences past their initial occurrences. For example, he could smell her scent flowing throughout his room, even though she hadn't been there in over a week or so. She had a pink oversized sweater resting on one of his chairs, and it was drowned in her fragrance. Before she called him, he thought nothing about it. He was used to it blending in with the natural smell of his room. But now, after the fact, his senses went into selective mode, detecting JoJo in whatever way possible. Each time he licked his lips, he could taste her smooth and soft skin. The hairs on his body would stand up whenever he would close his eyes and imagine a night with her, simultaneously making his muscles tense up like he was seconds away from a war-like experience. His anger, sexual frustration, and ever-changing visualizations made his testosterone reach peak thresholds. And with each thought of her, he felt as though she would magically reappear. Maybe she would come back and turn his nightmare back into the blissful dream that it had been for so long. What a misery. For him to be experiencing everything that she made him feel, as if she was right there in his midst. Only to be countered by the realization that she was gone, and, most likely, gone *for good*.

The enclosed space in his house was beginning to drive him nuts. Quite frankly, he couldn't even be in his *own* room long because every time he would look at his bed, he imagined JoJo sitting or lying down on it. All of the times they were intimate was an obvious trigger. But it was the non-sexual occurrences that got him the most. JoJo lying down on his bed, going through all of his childhood photos. Her going through his baseball gear and trying on his old jerseys. Him holding her up close as they binge watched their favorite shows. The times they were playfully wrestling with each other. And JoJo sitting on his lap with her arms wrapped around his neck, asking him what his hopes and dreams were. It was too much for him to think about all at once because even though JoJo was gone, he still had to abide in the spaces she had infiltrated. Most likely, he was going to have to get some new bedroom pillows and blankets that would create new pathways in his mind. Hell, he probably should have thought about even painting his room a different color. But right in this moment, all he could do was try to stop torturing himself. So, he went into the kitchen and met Shelby for their morning breakfast.

At the table, Shelby poured more wisdom into her son. Ultimately, she knew that nothing she said was going to magically make him whole. But she wanted to help as much as she could. As passionate as her son was, she was surprised that he was fairly calm. Shelby was not giving her parenting skills enough credit, though. Had she not been present to comfort him, he would have likely done something very idiotic. Bobby could have ended up in someone's jail or worse. Rage, at the core of one's soul, can stir up something ugly and unforeseen. It can ruin, even, the greatest of people. All it takes is one decision, which can happen in seconds. In a way, it was a blessing in disguise that Bobby was hungry and still a bit sleepy from a full night of rest. It gave him something to do. Something to complete, even though it was just breakfast. But it was *something*.

After eating, he walked his mom out to her car. She was still concerned about him and thought about maybe taking the day off. She decided to ask him.

"Son, I can stay home today. I don't want you to be here alone thinking about *that girl* all day. I can call in." Shelby told him.

"No, it's okay. I'll be fine, I promise. I appreciate you having my back, though, Ma. I'll clean up the kitchen and watch Fountain or something. I'm pissed, but I'm not going to do anything to ruin my future. She obviously ain't worth it." Bobby responded.

"Okay. I'm proud of you for handling this like you are. Call me if you need to talk some more, okay?"

"Okay."

"Love you, Bobby."

"Love you, too, Ma."

And so, Bobby ended up doing the dishes. He turned on some music on the TV to help him focus more. For someone hours removed from having his heart broken, he was taking the blows like a true champion. It probably was because of the way that JoJo chose to go about it. For her to just choose to be with Terrell at the drop of a dime. It would have been different if Bobby was caught doing dirt on her, or something, and had it coming back to bite him. Like, if one of JoJo's friends had sent her screenshots of Bobby sending DM's of God knows what. Well, maybe you know, too. However, none of this was the case. Bobby was victimized all because he made the mistake of being unavailable. It spoke volumes about JoJo more than it did about Bobby, which is why he didn't put up much of a fight. He never called her back. Neither did he send her a text or voice message. He just continued to do what he was already doing the day before: taking care of his responsibilities.

Once he finished cleaning, he went and hopped into the shower. It must have been the longest shower that he ever took. It warmed his body, which had previously been cooling as a result of his heart growing colder. The guy stayed in there for about 22 minutes, and it was extremely therapeutic for him. When he finally got out and dried off, he went into the living room and turned on a show he had never watched before. The name of it was Shelly, and it was about a woman who was a private investigator in Tulsa, OK. Everyone had been talking about it, as it was one of the first shows to blow up with an Oklahoma setting. Bobby had desired to watch it with JoJo, but she wanted to watch Cycles instead. So, in spite of her, he watched Shelly for three hours.

After the conclusion of the sixth episode, the clock read 4:22 in the afternoon. Shelby still had six more hours at work, but she had checked in on Bobby periodically, texting him messages along the lines of, "how are you," and, "what are you doing?" He made sure to tell her that he was fine. But now that it had been a good while, and he no longer wanted to watch television, his mind began to develop anxiety. How in the world else could he spend the rest of his evening, after spending most of the past 200+ days in connection with another human? Well, one thing he knew for sure, he needed to get some fresh air. Thus, he went and put on a light grey tank top that read HAPPS across the chest. Paired with it were shorts that were just a shade darker. For his feet, he put on some white ankle socks and lime green running shoes. Running was his initial plan. At this point, his body was chemically conditioned like that of a first-time Olympian. Soon, though, he realized that distance running would do nothing but drain him for the next couple of days. His first summer league game was Tuesday, and he wanted to be fresh. Therefore, running was out of the question. Still thinking, he grabbed his house key, locked everything up, and left. He walked to the bus stop that was just about a third of a mile west of his neighborhood. The 4:45 bus was headed for downtown, and it pulled up to the stop just as scheduled. Bobby then hopped on and sat on the first row of seating.

The summer sun was still shining magnificently. It was about 85 degrees out, which was, surprisingly, the high for the day. Bobby didn't mind it. Had he had to deal with excruciating heat, too, it would have made him feel even more miserable. Summer temperatures in Oklahoma are usually unforgiving. Yet, on this day, the sun showed mercy. Anyway, the bus made its way southwest. As it rode, Bobby, sitting on the window seat, took in all of the sights of the city. Behind him were only about three other people, and they were all catching rides for their evening shifts. It took the bus about thirty minutes to reach destination, as it only made two additional stops. When Bobby stepped off, he was about a third of a mile east of the stadium where the OKC Journeymen played. That evening, they were hosting the last of their 10-game home stretch. Opposite of them were the Sacramento Steelers. First pitch was at 6:00. Perfect timing, as it was just now 5:27. Bobby then made his way towards the stadium.

When he got to the ticket booth, he purchased a ticket for the lawn seating area (just beyond the outfield fence). And for the next three hours, Bobby laid across some of the softest grass you could ever imagine. It may have even been softer than the Journeymen's infield. In addition, the stadium had great energy from start to finish. There were about 18,000 people spectating from the bleachers. Bobby watched the game periodically, checking to see what happened in crucial moments. He also made sure to react to all fly balls, ensuring that none of them were out for his head. But for most of the time, he laid down and relaxed. He closed his eyes and took in the game through his ears. The crowd and its various reactions. The crack of the bat. Walk-up songs and the music that was played between innings. The sound of the pitchers warming up in the bullpen. The faint sound of the umpires calling men safe or out. Also, the silence between every play. It was similar to a symphony orchestra. At some points, forte. At others, piano. But, overall, a perpetual flow of different parts that came together to create a wholesome piece. And so, on the day of being dumped, Bobby managed to drown out all the noise and experience peace. For a brief moment, he had transcended reality. And God, through baseball – and a wise mother – provided a great escape for him.

CHAPTER 8: GRACE & CONSEQUENCE

As great as Bobby dealt with the breakup on the first day, the next 48 hours were filled with extreme withdrawals. His body would often shake while he was in bed, and wherever he walked, he felt numb to all of his normal sensations. When it was time to eat, he barely ate ¼ of what was prepared. And as a result of it all, he only slept for two hours Monday night. Shelby ended up taking off work Tuesday just so that she could be in the house to monitor him. The most important thing to her was making sure that he finally got some sleep. In the process, she was also gauging where he was, hoping for improvements as the day progressed. Bobby was not as talkative as he was Sunday, either. All he did was scroll through his phone. Whenever he went away from it, he made sure to turn up his ringer so that he would be quickly notified if JoJo tried to reach out to him. Unavailability, he thought, would never again be a determining factor in his relationships. Even though he was blameless in the situation, he could not help but put on the coat of guilt. His mind was playing tricks on him. *Yearning* might not be the best word to describe the state that he was in. The boy was, flat out, thirsty. It was like he was a wealthy man in an African village who suddenly had everything stolen from him; and now, he was all alone in the middle of a desert. Oh, and at peak temperatures. In terms of what was in his heart, he held all of the sentiments of a man that was preparing to take his girlfriend out on a romantic date that would ultimately end in a proposal. But he had experienced her already, just as a man experiences his *wife*: in fullness. So, in real-time, there was nothing left to explore about JoJo. Even so, her abrupt departure from his life made him reminiscent of what once was, and imaginative about what could still be if she was still present.

Anyhow, because he became heavily sleep deprived, he missed out on his first summer league game on Tuesday. First pitch was scheduled for 3:15 at E-City, and while all the other guys were loosening up their arms and legs, Bobby was underneath his bedroom comforter, with his mother right next to him. Shelby had urged him to get out of his room for a change, but he was insistent on staying in. So, she brought all of his meals to him at his bedside dresser. He had a little bit more of an appetite now, as a result of barely eating the day before. The guy was having to eat spicy noodles and drink strong tea in order to clear respiratory pathways from all of the sobbing he had done. Eating made him feel slightly better but not enough to make him sleep. So, he just scrolled through news posts and looked at social media reels. Even though his eyes were locked in on the screen, none of the content really registered. Instead, his mind played out scenes of various experiences he had with his former girlfriend. And to have spent so much time with her, you have to know that his imagination was very vast.

Bobby eventually fell asleep around 9:40 later that night. Shelby had just made him a sandwich and chips, and this time, the food finally settled in. One key factor in it all, though, was that she also took time to fervently pray over him. It was the strongest prayer Bobby had ever heard before, and it softened his heart and comforted his spirit. He ended up sleeping the entire night (a solid 10 hours). When Wednesday morning came, he woke up refreshed and energized. His mother immediately seized the opportunity to capitalize on this. She drove him up to Mocha Time so that she could get him out of the house. Ironically, Mocha Time was not the usual date destination for Bobby and JoJo – JoJo hated coffee. Thus, he really didn't have any memories to reach into, as far as setting was concerned. Shelby always managed to effectively implement creativity in her parenting approaches. Like Bobby, she had idealist attributes. At a critical time like this, however, her practices were put to the toughest test. Somehow, she had to figure out a way to help her kid see the light at the end of the tunnel. And for Bobby, this tunnel seemed to stretch for thousands of miles. But he had a mother that was going to keep him accountable. Regardless of how much work was going to be required of Bobby, she was determined to guide him to a position where he could steadily gain ground.

The two of them sat across each other, in a booth right in the center of the place. While they were waiting for the waiter, Shelby tried getting her son to express what he was now feeling. She asked him how he felt about missing his first summer league game and how he was going to explain everything to the team's coach. He told her that he felt like baseball didn't matter the day before. "All that mattered yesterday was that I made it to today. I'll tell coach I had a family emergency," he told his mom. She nodded in agreement. He had definitely been inches away from a mental breakdown. Still, though, she pointed out the cold hard facts, telling him that baseball *should* matter to him more. That it was a part of his health. Baseball gave Bobby a feeling of bliss that no other girl ever gave him – not even Veronica Redding, back on the night when she gave him his first experience of the complete female anatomy. It was because his passion for baseball was genuine. Versus, his lustful passion for girls was rooted in insecurity. Baseball was constructive, while his thirst for girls was *destructive*. The great game often highlighted the fact that life is full of both grace and consequence. Shelby explained this to him more thoroughly.

"Son, whenever I see you out there on that field, you look like you are living your dream. You have a joy that is indescribable, and other people feed off your energy. So many opportunities are ahead of you in this game. But like I told you a couple months back, you have to attain a focus that is immovable. JoJo was only getting in your way. She was a distraction. Why do you think you played so bad and were benched for playoffs?"

"Yeah, I know." Bobby said.

"You can't be distracted in baseball, you *know* that. All it takes is one minor thing to throw your game completely off. The way you played this past year, you should be somewhere showcasing your talent in front of college and pro scouts. But you're not. You're here grieving over someone who was never good for you. She couldn't fit into your life. No, not in a way that allowed you to thrive. Open your eyes, Bobby. Don't sabotage your future over a girl. You have to stay locked in, or you're going to derail yourself."

Bobby listened to everything that she was saying. As much as he wanted to absorb it all, he couldn't. He was too broken. Even so, he showed his mother respect by at least making it seem like he was hearing her fully. She continued her lecture.

"Let me ask you something. Right now, are you on track or are you derailed? Be honest with me." Shelby asked.

"Derailed, I guess." Bobby replied.

"Yeah, *ya are*. But one good thing about it is: you can get back on track. You still have the rest of summer to lock in and reorder your priorities. No longer is JoJo your responsibility or priority. I need you to say it."

"Say what?"

"Literally say, 'JoJo is no longer my responsibility or my priority.'"

Bobby inhaled deeply. Everything in him warred against saying such a thing. He knew that the statement had power to positively disrupt his current chemistry, but insecurity was holding him hostage. Yet, *obeying* his mother had always paid off in some form or fashion, so he just went along with it. He exhaled.

"JoJo is no longer my responsibility or my priority," he repeated back to his mom.

"Say, 'I am worthy of having good things in my life.'" She demanded.

"I am worthy of having good things in my life."

"Say, 'the only person that can stop me, is me.'"

"The only person that can stop me, is me."

"Now, lastly, say this: God loves me, and no weapon formed against me shall prosper." Shelby said.

Bobby paused for another moment of deep thought, looking down at his folded hands. He had greater pushback with this one, as Satan was trying his hardest to muzzle him through disbelief. The boy's recent experiences had given him great leverage to do so. Luckily, though, Shelby already knew what the devil was up to, which was the whole point of having him repeat life-filled statements out loud. Finally, he looked back up at his mom.

"*God loves me, and no weapon formed against me shall prosper.*" Bobby said.

"Good. Now, let's finally put in our orders. What ya thinkin'?"

Soon after she said this, their waiter came up to greet them. Shelby put in an order for some pecan pancakes and sausage. Bobby, on the other hand, requested a stack of original pancakes with scrambled eggs on the side – Mocha Time was known for having the best pancakes in all of downtown (for many customers, the coffee was secondary). Quality service was a big draw as well. It only took about seven minutes for them to prepare their food and bring it out to them. Bobby ate his breakfast like he had never seen pancakes before. He was starving, as his body rhythms were still lagging behind. But his mom was happy to see him so animated. In a subtle way, it gave her hope for his immediate future as a young man. Many kids in his situation would have refused to even leave the house. Bobby was really doing the best he could. Looking at the big picture, his mom could sense that her son had pure intentions. She knew that those same intentions had been used and abused by the girls he chose to mess with. Thus, her mission was to guide him into becoming a person who could regularly detect toxic attributes from people (girls, especially). Regardless of how fast his pace would end up being, she was committed to being his lifeline.

It was only about 10:15 when they walked out of Mocha Time, so Shelby still had a little time to spare before having to drop Bobby back off so that she could go to work. Shelby noticed Bobby's eyes momentarily spark when he saw the Journeymen's ballpark in the distance. Perhaps, he was recalling being at the game just 60 hours earlier, as it brought a peaceful ending to a rather traumatic day. So, Shelby insisted that they take a mini-trip over there. Around the stadium were statues of Oklahoma men who had made it to the big leagues. They walked up to each of them and read their inscriptions. Then, she saw another opportunity to encourage him.

"You know, son, they could build a statue of *you* one day." Shelby said.

"Think so?" Bobby asked.

"Yeah, *if* you work hard and stay determined. Look at all of these players."

He looked up at them with great admiration. Shelby continued.

"They all made it from our state. You don't think that they had to rise up in times of adversity? Oklahoma isn't even known for baseball. Plus, they, undoubtedly, had their own personal struggles coming up as young kids. Their lives were not picture perfect, either, ya know. But their ending turned out beautiful because they stayed the path. Learn from them, son."

Bobby nodded in agreement. He could not deny how inspired he felt when she uttered those words. Really, it was just an overflow of all of the positivity she had already poured into him. Man, having a person who genuinely cares for you has to be one of life's greatest blessings. She wanted nothing from her son, aside from his love and respect. He could have been the biggest nerd walking through the hallways of Happs. Or he could have been a piano player. A painter. A doctor in the making. Anything. She would have found a way to inspire him through whatever he was passionate about. Because *real love* makes people find a way.

So, after walking around downtown, she took Bobby back to Spencer just past eleven o'clock. It was 11:27 when they got back to their home. She let him out of the car, urging him to keep his head up for the rest of the day. "Everything is going to be alright," she told him. After seeing him reply and acknowledge her, she then spun out of the driveway and left for work. When she made it to the hospital, at 11:48, she received a jolt of creativity that was unlike anything she had felt in a while. Her muse was actually her son's heartbreak. Right along with it was her love for the Lord aligning with her natural nurturing abilities. The day's date was June 13th. Bobby's sixteenth birthday was only eighteen days away, on July 1st. For quite some time, Shelby had been stacking up money to buy Bobby a car. She initially wanted him to have it by fifteen so that he could practice driving with a learner's permit, but Bobby had been so busy with baseball and school that he had little time. Partnered with the fact that Shelby worked so much, it just wasn't an ideal thing to do. Now was the perfect time, though. With him having a car, she figured, he could get out of the house whenever he wanted to. He could drive instead of having to take the bus all of the time, which would make her feel so much more comfortable being away from him.

Ever since he was a young kid, Bobby wanted a sports car. He dreamt of having a matte red Nissan Skyline GTR, with chrome rims. It was interesting how he came up with the concept. Back when he was eleven years old, he entered into his pre-teen video game phase. Oh, and he fell into it hard, too. Shooting games. Fighting games. Building games, like Minecraft. Sports games, *of course*. But only one genre truly had his heart: racing. His favorite game of all-time was Stylin' Drivin' 2009, which was a racing game that allowed users to build their own cars to race through the streets of Kansas City, Dallas, and New Orleans. This is where Bobby was first introduced to the Skyline model. The car captured Bobby's eyes and heart, and it was the ride he used to attack the game's campaign with. Once he completed all missions, it transformed into his pride and joy. The way he talked about it to his friends at school, you would have thought the dude already had the car underneath his carport at home.

Even though she would have loved to have purchased his dream car, Shelby had only $25,000 work with. A Skyline would have put her into debt for a good minute. So instead, she began researching other popular Nissan models, and many of the current ones were still north of the money threshold. To work around this, she decided to backtrack in terms of years. Looking on a site called Lee's Keys, she saw that a midnight green 1993 Nissan 240SX was listed for $22,000. Its seller was in Tulsa, OK, a city only a couple hours northeast of OKC. This fit Bobby perfectly. Sporty and stylish, just like the Skyline, except scaled down a bit. Another thing that gave the car value was that it only had 97,000 miles, which was amazing for a vehicle over twenty years old. In its history, all it had was a couple of issues with the transmission and alternator. Nothing major, though, as the car was well-kept by each of the previous owners. Besides, Lee's Keys did a thorough job of ensuring that sellers only listed cars that were in good-to-great condition. In consequence, the car's details intrigued Shelby. She soon took down the provided number and called it. The person who answered was a man named Wilson Montez.

"Hello?"

"Hi, I'd like to speak with Mr. *Wilson Montez*." Shelby said.

"This is him. May I ask who's calling?" Wilson replied.

"My name is Shelby Bowen. I saw your online listing for the '93 Nissan 240. I was just calling to get more information on the vehicle."

"Oh, yes, ma'am. I am so happy you called about this car. I used to get calls about this ride on a daily basis, about three years ago. But no one ever wanted to pay the money. It rides good, though. No engine or interior damage. No accident history. She's still a beauty. How is the price for you?"

"I can do the price. It's actually for my son, who is about to turn sixteen in a couple of weeks. He hasn't seen it, but I know he'll love it. He already loves Nissans, so I figured I'd get him a vintage one. It's definitely a good starter vehicle, I think. Can I get some of the car reports emailed to me?"

"Absolutely. I can schedule a test drive for you as well if you'd like."

"That would be perfect. How does Friday morning sound? Around 9:30?" Shelby asked.

"That works for me, Miss Bowen. And I'll get those reports over to you as soon as possible. I'll send a link of my address as well. Looking for to it!"

"Thank you, Wilson."

For the next two days, Shelby did her best to keep her poker face on. In truth, it actually helped that Bobby was going through all his chaos. He wasn't even thinking about his birthday coming up. The last time he *did* think about it was two weeks earlier. He was on the phone with JoJo (of course), and the two of them were trying to figure out what they were going to do at the end of his birthday night. Bobby had told her that she should just come over and have dinner with him and Shelby. JoJo, on the other hand, argued that she wanted to take him to a downtown restaurant. "You shouldn't be cooped up in the house on your *birthday*," she had told him. It sounded like she was being sincere with him, but she really just wanted to go for the attention. For the photos that would be posted on her story that night and all the comments that would follow. It was how she did things. Bobby just never figured it out in time.

Anyway, though, Shelby was able to stay under the radar with her surprise. When Friday morning finally came, she told Bobby that she had to go to an early morning meeting at the hospital. He thought nothing more about it, simply giving her the "Okay, Ma." After making and eating breakfast with him, she left the house at about 7:45. Getting on the highway, she took the turnpike so that it would knock off about forty-five minutes, making her trip last only an hour and forty. She arrived at Wilson's spot at 9:25 – just five minutes short of scheduled time. Of course, Wilson never worried if she would be a little late. In truth, he would have waited a whole extra hour for her if he had to. Like he said, no one was really calling about the car for a long time. Thus, he was more than ready to get it off of his hands. When she pulled in and hopped out her ride, he happily greeted her.

Wilson took her right inside his garage. He had a couple of shop lights right in its center, and he turned them on. When he did, the lighting exposed a medium-sized vehicle with a brown tarp covering its entire length. He then looked at Shelby and stated, "Moment of truth, Miss Bowen." She grinned with excitement and watched him. Pulling off the tarp, he revealed the jaw-dropping Nissan 240. It was more beautiful than the online photos gave it credit. The car's paint job looked pristine, as if someone had just put the final finishes on it. On the wheels, the rims shined an outstanding chrome, so much so that you could take a mirror selfie through them if you just so felt the urge. And the tires were in very good shape as well, having polished rubber and full tread. All of the windows, lights, and mirrors dazzled with cleanliness. It was very impressive.

"This is a pretty amazing car. Can I take a peek inside?" Shelby asked Wilson.

"You sure can, ma'am."

Shelby then took in the sights and smells of the interior. It wasn't what she was expecting, regarding color. She was thinking that it would be a full black or dark grey inside. That's, at least, what the pictures showed online. Instead, everything was neon green, with black accents. Wilson had customized the interior a couple of months back. Afterwards, he forgot to update the car's online gallery, which was partly because he was beginning to contemplate on keeping it for himself. For, the work he did took the car from just pretty, to magazine-feature worthy. But he was determined to get a nice return on his investment, and, for that, Shelby was grateful. She knew the car was the one. All that was left to do was make sure it ran good. Once she finished inspecting everything, she requested to take it for a spin. Wilson tossed her the key and told her to enjoy (he had no doubts about the test drive). When she got in and turned the key, the engine started easily and had a calm, quiet sound when idling. Soon, she traveled down to a convenient store that was two miles east of Wilson's location. It rode smoothly. The brakes had good grip. The AC was blowing cold air, which was very important, given that it was mid-June. All the electronics seemed to be in full tact. The mirrors were well positioned to give drivers multiple points of view while driving. Seats, soft and comfortable. Shelby could not detect anything displeasing, which acted as confirmation for her.

On the way back to Wilson's, the car drove even smoother. For a quick second, she thought about purchasing it for her own self and just handing down her current car to her son (she had an all-white Sonata, 2015). But she knew how happy it would make him if she was to gift him with such a cool vehicle. It fit Bobby like a glove. Even so, when she returned, she made Wilson an official offer of the full $22,000. Wilson gladly accepted. They then went to fill out all of the paperwork, and, upon completion, Shelby made the payment. When it processed, Wilson gave her his word that he would have the car delivered to OKC in the next three business days. Shelby gave him her approval and shook hands with him.

"Pleasure doin' business, Mr. Montez." Shleby said.

"Pleasure's all mine, ma'am. You have a wonderful day and a safe trip back home." Wilson replied.

So just like that, the man was $22,000 richer, minus the fee from Lee's Keys. What's crazy is, the car that Shelby bought from him was the very first listing he ever posted on the site, as he put it on the market all the way back in 2006. Talk about *persistence*. This was twelve years later. Plus, he never changed his price. He knew the car's value and stuck with it. And in the end, the car sold itself.

Mr. Montez came through on his word regarding the delivery of the car. On the following Wednesday, he arrived to OKC with it. He had one of his men drive the Nissan while he followed him in an all-white Range. You wouldn't believe it, but Wilson's most recent ex-girlfriend happened to stay just outside of Spencer. Hence, he pulled up in his Range just to flex on her. Even so, he arrived pretty early, as it was only 8:45 when they reached the Bowen home. Bobby was still sleeping, but Shelby was wide-eyed awake. As she met Wilson in the driveway, he gave her the final documents and the car keys. "It's all yours, ma'am," he told her. She thanked him for the final time. It was divine timing for her to have come across such a diamond in the rough. This particular car could not be found in any of the surrounding states. All other listings of the vehicle featured sellers that were in the Midwest, west coast, and northeast regions. But even still, none of the ones in those locations had less than 140,000 miles. Plus, several of them had damages to the exterior. It would have been more of a project than a gift for someone's sweet sixteen. Shelby was used to this kind of thing happening to her and always saw it as God's favor and provision. Somehow, He always made a way for her. He always showed up. God is a Provider.

Now that the car had been delivered, Shelby now had to decide what she was going to do with it. There was still another week and a half before her son's birthday. Simply giving it to him early was an option. She did not traditionally give Bobby presents early, but given the circumstances of his current season, it could have been a good spark for him. Yet, she decided to keep it reserved for his big day. She did not want to make his issues with instant gratification any worse than they already were. Wow. Even in her gifts, she taught lessons. She ended up taking the car to the house of one of her coworkers. Her name was Naomi, and she also happened to live in Spencer, probably about seven minutes south of Shelby's place. And so, Bobby's classic Nissan rested in Naomi's garage for the following ten days.

On Sunday, July 1st, Shelby awakened Bobby with the singing of the world-famous melody of "happy birthday to you." He had just got done dreaming about JoJo, and, at first, that is who he thought was waking him up. But when he realized it was mom, his entire body relaxed in safety. Shelby's voice was extremely pleasant and hearing her sing made Bobby feel like the most special person in the world. After concluding the song, she hugged him tightly.

"16! What? I really got a *sixteen-year-old*! How you feel, Bobby?"

"I feel good, Ma. I'm glad to be here." He said it as if his life had been on the brink. Though he was just going through natural pubescent things, his mother did not invalidate him.

"Well, I'm even more happy you're here! Hey, I got breakfast already made. Freshen up so that we can eat."

"Okay."

Shelby had prepared some biscuits, scrambled eggs, bacon, and oatmeal (with peaches). When Bobby met her in the kitchen, they gave God thanks and then enjoyed their meal. Both of them complemented their tastes with a glass of orange juice. After Bobby got done eating, he went over to the sink to wash all of the dishes. Shelby almost stopped him, but she, instead, let him take care of it. She was allowing the surprise to flow naturally. Excited, she went inside of living room, sat on the couch, and turned on the TV. The time had come.

"Don't forget to take out the trash! I know it's your birthday, but you still have responsibilities." Shelby told him.

"Got you, Ma."

After finishing the dishes, Bobby went around the kitchen and wiped everything down. He then swept the floor and threw away any other trash that was left out. Seeing that all of the core work was done, he went over to their trash bin and took out the lavender-scented bag. After tying it up, he immediately replaced it. Finally, he took the trash outside. Hearing the front door open, Shelby hurried out behind him. Bobby had his head down the entire way, so he did not even look under the carport. For all he knew, the only thing there was a white Hyundai, which he saw every single day. Plus, from the vantage point of the trash barrel, his mom's car hid anything else that was on the other side. Discarding the trash bag, he looked up to see his mom standing in the grass of their front yard.

"Hey, mom." Bobby said.

She stood there and said nothing back. All she did was smile at him.

"What are you up to now?" Bobby continued, growing more curious.

"Gosh, son. If it had been a snake, it would've bit you."

"What are you talking about?" Bobby asked.

She walked him over to the carport. When Bobby laid eyes on the car, he froze. So much so that he stood there with his mouth wide open, for like ten seconds or so. He obviously was not expecting it.

"Take it in, son. Right in front of you sits a 1993 –"

"Nissan 240SX!" He interrupted her. "155 horsepower, 4-cylinder engine, and 4-speed automatic transmission. I know exactly what that is!"

"Oh, do you?" Shelby asked.

"Yeah, I wrote a paper on it last year in English class. My teacher knew about my love for the Skyline, because I talked about it a lot during class discussions and brainstorming. So, she challenged me to do research about something else. Me being me, I just chose a *different* Nissan model." Bobby stated, in amazement.

"That is so cool, son. Well, it looks like you manifested that into your life. I bought this car just for you." She handed him the keys, which had a neon blue carabiner. Clipped to it was a baseball bat keychain and a tag that had Bobby's name on it. "Happy birthday, my son."

"Thank you so much, Ma!" He hugged her.

Bobby then hopped inside of his new car and relaxed in the driver's seat. It was still morning out, and the temperature was only about 73 degrees. Shelby knew how much he loved cool rides but had no idea that the car she bought him was one that he wanted just as much as the Skyline. Well, at least, *almost* as much. She was proud of herself for doing such a deed, but even more so grateful to God for directing every step in the process. He is a great Orchestrator. You have to think, what were the odds of Shelby buying her son a car that he had written a *paper* on just ten months before. Almost impossible, right? Well, almost doesn't count. Even so, had she not had a gracious and understanding heart, she would have not purchased him anything for his birthday. Bobby, as you know, was being extremely disrespectful for a good while. Yet, she knew that much of it was because he was under the influence of other people. She had faith that the things she instilled in him would remain his anchor, and it was evident in all of the times he took refuge in her, even after him messing up mightily. That's a picture of grace. And by doing what she did, she gave Bobby a new opportunity to establish who he was as an *individual*. She gave him something that he could call his own. Apart from baseball. Apart from school. Apart from any of his relationships, including the one with his mom. Apart from, even, their own estate. The car was Bobby's and no one else's, which was Shelby's creative way of establishing new mindsets in both her and her son. For her, it gave her an opportunity to be confident that she was raising him into a man of responsibility. And for Bobby, it was a way for him to strong-arm his identity back after all the times that others tried to define him. Now, he could release from the world he once knew and explore things more extensively, all while figuring out what he really desired out of life.

About an hour later, Shelby took Bobby up to the DMV so that he could get his driver's license. He passed his test with ease. When he took the photo, he could not help but smile very big. It was the happiest he had been in a very long time. His birthday was already light years away from what he was expecting it to be. At first, he thought there would be a lot of grief about JoJo not being with him. But instead, it turned out to be what it was supposed to be all along: a day about *him*.

It was also the birthday of another local baseball star. Yes, you guessed it *again*. None other than Shawn Uriah Clement. On this day, he turned seventeen. Marvin and Alicia had just got back from their trip in Florida, but while they were still down there, they found two great gifts for their son. Seven minutes west of their hotel was a local sporting goods store, and they went to it on the day before flying back home. It turned out that the store was having a special on all baseball equipment, 45% off. This was clutch timing for Shawn's parents. And yeah, even though they were millionaires, they still sought deals whenever they could. While looking through the merchandise, Marvin found two items that matched Shawn's exact playing specifications: a 34/32 wood bat and a 12 ¾ inch outfield glove. But there was more to it than just perfect dimensions and a good discount. Both of the items happened to be royal blue. As you remember, blue was Shawn's favorite color and first word as a baby. His mother, Claire, had bought him two blue t-ball gloves on the day she passed away. Thus, as soon as Marvin laid eyes on the items, he immediately knew that they were meant for his son. Where else, he thought, was he going to find matching blue items that were also formed to Shawn's playing preferences. You have to understand that 34/32 bats are not just readily available at most sporting goods stores. And blue gloves are often made for smaller kids who have just entered machine or coach pitch. Any blue leather in adult sizes would usually have to be ordered online. Even so, Alicia loved the items, too, as she was quite fond of the color. She had the literal eye of a world-class painter and would have told her husband if the color was too vibrant or too faded. So, she reassured him that it was a great buy. And for the united cost of $211. Ladies and gentlemen, that is what you would call *a great deal*. On top of that, they got both items personalized. On the inside of the glove read, in white, *Claire Hollins* (top) *Clear High School* (middle) *Class of 2001* (bottom); and on the outside, and also in white, was *Shawn Clement* (top) *Love High School* (middle) *Class of 2019* (bottom). Carved out on sweet spot of the bat was *Specified for* (top*) Shawn Clement* (bottom). How beautiful of a gesture.

When they gifted Shawn with his new equipment that morning, he broke down and cried. No day went by where he did not miss Claire. Soon, though, he was overcome with immense joy and gratitude. In thanks, he hugged both of them. When they took birthday photos of him, he held his new bat and glove, while wearing his mom's letterman jacket. Oh, of course you know that the background was fire, too, as behind him sat his two-toned (sky blue and light green) '65 Malibu. Like Bobby, Shawn was very happy with his birthday gifts. He smiled big, leaning against his car with a cool pose. The pictures came out great, and Shawn posted them on his social media account. The caption for them simply read, "Blue seventeen." Anyhow, after the photos and online posts, they all went back inside to have family breakfast together. Marvin made a wholesome meal: pancakes, scrambled eggs, bacon *and* sausage, and a fruit selection (grapes, bananas, watermelon, and honey crisp apples). Of course, Shawn made sure to have some toast and avocado with his scrambled eggs. But his father had always been the cook in the house, even going all the way back to when Claire was alive. He took pride in feeding his family and then going out in the world so that he could provide all other needs of the household. It was his mission to be a devoted husband and father. That is what fueled him every day.

Anyhow, Shawn soon received a call from Lisa. She, too, wanted to wish him a happy birthday. It was Sunday, so everyone was off work, even her (she worked at a graphic design place, called GrangerTech). The timing of her call was great, as the Clement family had just wrapped up breakfast, and Shawn was almost done cleaning everything up in the kitchen. It was still only 9:45 that morning. When Shawn's phone buzzed, and he saw that it was Lisa, his heart leapt in excitement. He quickly dried off his hands so that he could pick up.

"Hello?" Shawn said.

"Well happy birthday, *my* Shawn! Good morning!" Lisa greeted him.

"Thank you, Lisa. And your Shawn, huh? I like how it sounds when you say that. Can you say it one more time?"

"*My Shawn.*" Lisa said softly, holding her syllable out at the end so that he would know that she meant it. Once she said it again, she started blushing, having a smile as wide as the Atlantic is from the Pacific.

"Okay, you're hot," he said, as the both of them started laughing. "How are you today, though?"

"Well, *sir*, I am doing quite well, especially since I get to hear you so happy on your day. I actually left your gift in your mailbox. You wanna go get it while we're on the phone?"

"Sure, just one second."

He hustled up to his room to put on his shoes. Then, still holding the phone to his ear, he headed outside for the mailbox. When he got there and opened it, though, nothing was inside. It confused him.

"*Umm*, Lisa, are you sure you put it in the right one?"

"Of course, I'm sure. I've been to your house before, ya know." Lisa said.

"Okay, well there's nothing in here. Let me go back inside to see if my parents took it out already. They usually get the mail, anyways."

"Shawn, you don't have to do that."

"What are you talking about?" He said, pausing in the middle of his driveway. Seconds later, he heard the sound of a vehicle approaching. He then turned around and, wouldn't ya know, saw a black Mustang pulling near the curb, right in front of the mailbox. It was Lisa. Seeing her, Shawn started laughing. Inside her car, Lisa was laughing right along with him. She had won style points for the day, knowing that she was doing something unprecedented for him. Soon, Shawn walked over to meet her right as she was opening her car door and stepping out.

"Oh, you think you're slick! What are you doing here?" Shawn said, right before hugging her.

"Well. I wanted to do something memorable for you. You value sentimental things, so I figured showing up for you would be just as good as any gift."

"You were right. It's really good to see you." He leaned in and hugged her again, doing his best not to make a move for a kiss.

"But, Shawn, I still got you a present. I hope you like it."

She popped open her trunk, and a large black gift bag was revealed. She took it out and gave it to him. "Happy birthday, my Shawn," she said again.

Shawn did his very best to keep from embracing her once more, as she was driving his energy through the roof. When he opened the bag, he pulled out a bright orange XL football jersey. On the front of it, across the chest, said LOVER; and on the back, CLEMENT, with the number 18 enlarged underneath it. The collar and sleeves were accented with white. It was yet another custom gift. Along with the jersey was a pair of black shorts that had LOVER on them to match. LOVER was a local brand that was one of the region's leaders in fashion gear. It was thoughtful and poetic of her to buy such gifts for him. Think about it for a moment: both of them were going to *Love* High School. Plus, day by day, he was becoming more of her *lover*. Lisa was a hopeful romantic, and it was showing. Even so, the last thing left in the bag was a card, inside of a pale-yellow envelope. He opened it up and read.

Happy Birthday to the coolest guy around. (FRONT)

For all of the times left for us to share, I just want you to know that I will always care. There'll be many more fun and cool things to do, but before anything, I just want to wish the Happiest of Birthdays to you. (signed) *Lisa.* (INSIDE OF THE CARD)

Shawn, once again, got emotional. Also once again, he hugged Lisa with a very tight grasp. He had not expected for her to add to his life like she was. Just as well, she had no clue that she would end up doing so herself. Their relationship was still new and, very much so, developing. It was obvious that they were beginning to have deeper feelings for one another. Maybe a good way to describe it is that they were, somehow, carefully stewarding lightning inside of a glass bottle. They were having a classic summer romance, except, void of the traditional trend of hooking up all the time – and yes, meaning sexually. To this point, the two of them had never been alone in a secluded room and were not planning on doing so anytime soon. Neither of them wanted to sabotage what they had going. But the more they practiced good boundaries, the easier it got to maintain and, even, fortify them. What a pleasure to behold. Two people with overflowing amounts of purity, both focused and determined on doing great things for themselves – both now and in the future. Crossing paths and enhancing each other's vision, all while still being young teenaged kids. Again, *like* lightning in a bottle.

Before Lisa left, she went in and said hello to Shawn's parents. Shawn had introduced her to them about two weeks prior, right when they got back from Florida (they all went to a restaurant in Edmond). After mingling for about fifteen minutes, she headed out so that Shawn could continue the rest of his day. Holding Lisa's hand, he walked her out to her car, just as he did after all of their dates. Again, where was the freaking camera man in the distance? This was, in actuality, young love. It got no better than them.

Anyway, after his girlfriend left, Shawn prepared to take a trip to Shawnee. He was going there to visit his mother. Marvin usually took Shawn about five times each year, but this was the first time he drove his own self. As he rode in his Malibu, he wore a white muscle shirt that had one of Claire's high school softball pictures on it. Down below, he had on black shorts with the Love Bulldogs' logo on the left side. For sneakers, he wore grey running shoes (with white ankle socks). It was starting to heat up outside, reaching 86 degrees as the time progressed towards noon. It was 11:35 when Shawn reached Shawnee's city limits, and the cemetery was just four more minutes away. When he pulled in close to where his mother was resting, he started to get nervous. He always made it a real goal to talk to her as if she could really hear him. It was part of their bond. Claire took Shawn everywhere when he was a baby. Now that she was gone, it never ceased to bring him pain. She was his partner in crime (figurative).

Getting out of the car, he grabbed a bouquet of yellow and red roses that he had sitting on the passenger seat. He remembered his dad telling him that those were her favorite flowers (Marvin would also bring them to her grave). After closing his door, he put on a pair of shades, as the sun was beaming right in the direction of Claire's tomb. When he got up close to the stone, he kneeled down at about a foot in front of it and placed the flowers down underneath him. With his fingers, he then felt through the texture of all the engraved lettering, which said, *CLAIRE ANNE CLEMENT-HOLLINS* (top), *APRIL 11th, 1983 – DECEMBER 11th, 2004* (middle), *A beautiful wife and devoted mother. One of the greatest softball players of all-time. A humble soul.* (bottom). Shawn felt a wave of deep grief. He longed for his mother to still be present. To see how much she would have evolved in her business. The thought of potentially having a brother or sister. To feel her support in all that he did and see her proud face whenever he would accomplish great things, like being named the nation's number one player, for example. He cried for about a minute, eventually taking off his shades in the process. But when his crying ceased, he put them back on and finally began the conversation.

"Seventeen, Momma. Your boy made it another year. I even started a new job, working as a mechanic in Edmond. You wouldn't believe who I'm working for, too." He paused for a couple of seconds, simulating her response. Then, he resumed. "You remember dad's friend, Quentin? Yeah, well, his little brother, Courtland, is the head mechanic of a shop called RGM – Running Great Motors. I don't know if y'all ever met, but Daddy told me that you always loved when Quentin and Lewis were around. They're still doing good, too, in case you were wondering. But, Momma, check this out. I even got a girlfriend now! Her name is Lisa Webb. No, she ain't an athlete like you, but she keeps a good shape. And man, she is extremely smart and got the looks to match. I think she got a shot at sticking around. Dad and Alicia both like her. I think you'd like her, too, and maybe even get to meet her someday."

He took another pause, this time, for about a full minute. In doing so, he did his best to remember her voice and laugh. Thankfully, Marvin often recorded home videos when he was still a toddler, which captured glimpses of Claire's vibrant personality. Growing up, Shawn would play them on their television for hours and hours on repeat. He did it so much that Marvin, still grieving hard during those times, would have to leave the room or even go outside. It hurt him too much to hear her voice. But back to the moment at hand. Shawn continued to process Claire's voice in his head, thinking of what she might have said back to him. Then, he finally began a conclusion.

"Daddy and Alicia got me a blue glove and bat for my birthday. But I want you to know that I still have the gloves you got for me fourteen years ago. I promise to never lose 'em as long as I live." In tears, Shawn looked around the graveyard as if he was tracking down someone's location. He did his best to refrain from getting angry at the person that shot her. Still, the man had not been found by law authorities. But Shawn wasn't going to let anger ruin the moment and, as well, the rest of his special day. So, he continued. "Momma, I miss you so much. Dad misses you, too. Yeah, I know he married someone else. But he knew that you would understand him. In fact, he even told me that he felt like you were approving Alicia. Something about how she had painted a picture of you for one of her exhibits. At that same exhibit is where they actually met. Up in *New York*, I do believe. Even after everything, though, you will never be replaced. Thank you for having such an amazing heart. I promise to continue your legacy. Love you, Mom."

Shawn then touched his two fingers on his lips and then touched his mom's stone. Visiting her, though difficult, made him feel even better than when his day first started. He drove back to OKC in the greatest of moods. You'd figure, after visiting a lost loved one, it would have dampened him down in a way. Instead, it was the complete opposite. Claire might as well have been right alongside her son the entire trip home, checking out the interior of his new ride. Having a conversation with him about all of the things he used to do as a baby. All of the times he woke her up in the middle of the night, crying. His first, second, and third birthday parties. Maybe even some stories about when she and Marvin were dating, just as some practical advice for him and Lisa. Some insight on how to adjust his swing with different pitches and take better routes on fly balls. Anything whatsoever. They were forever connected.

So, Sunday was a great day for both of the birthday boys. Two days later, on Tuesday, Bobby had another summer league game scheduled at E-City. First pitch was set for noon. He had still yet to appear in any games, as he was continuing to focus on recovery from JoJo. But his birthday experience had given him fresh momentum, plenty enough to push him over that first obstacle he had been confronted with. He ended up having a great day at the yard: 3-for-3 with two stolen bases. The only part of his game that didn't shine was his defense with runners on base. The last time he had caught a game was at Clear, right before getting benched for the postseason. That was nearly two months prior. Therefore, he was very rusty. Bobby was not worried about it, though. He was so much of a natural that it would only take a couple of games for him to get right back to gunning runners out at second and third, as well as succeeding in back picks. The boy had a cannon of a right arm. He was going to be perfectly fine.

As much as he was excited about playing so well, getting another day and chance to drive around in his new car was what really fueled Bobby's energy. Yet, the realities of having a vehicle wasted no time in hawking him down. Immediately after pulling out of the parking lot of the ballpark, Bobby ran over a nail. Had the Nissan's system still been aged, he would have never known about the nail, unless he had kicked the tire or visually realized that its pressure was down. But Wilson had upgraded the panels on the 240's dash. One of the things he added was a light that told the driver whenever tire pressure was lowering. Hence, Bobby knew right away what had happened. He now dreaded the fact that, if the nail was in the wall of the tire, he would have to spend a chunk of his allowance and birthday money on buying a brand-new tire. He pulled over into one of the local convenience stores to search for an auto repair shop. The first one that popped up was RGM. He clicked on it to get the directions and then headed that way.

When Bobby made it to RGM, the time read 3:02. He walked into the lobby and saw several men talking at the desk. Among them: Shawn. He was being reprimanded by Courtland and the other lead mechanics for failing to mark down the particulars of the previous week's shipment. While getting the ear-full, Shawn glanced over and noticed Bobby standing there. This made him even more embarrassed for messing up, as few people even knew that he was working in auto repair for the summer. Even so, he apologized to his superiors and vowed to not make the mistake again. Soon after, Bobby walked up to the counter for help. Courtland greeted him.

"What's up, hoss, how can we help?" Courtland asked him.

"How ya doin', brother, I just need to get my tire looked at. I just ran over a nail about fifteen minutes ago, pulling out of E-City."

"Which car are you?"

"The green Nissan 240."

"Got you. It'll be about a twenty-minute wait." Courtland then looked over at Shawn. "*Shawn*, could you please practice your documenting skills and get this guy a repair form? Make sure to mark the date and time, please."

"Yes, sir." Shawn said to him.

As Shawn walked away from the small group, Bobby finally noticed him, as his initial vantage point had not allowed him to. Though still embarrassed, Shawn was happy to see Bobby again. He retrieved the repair form and gave it to him. They greeted one another.

"What's up, Bobby? How you been, bro?" Shawn asked him.

"Hey, bro. I been cool. Would be a little better had I not run over this stupid nail." Bobby responded.

"Word? When you do that?"

"Just now." Bobby said.

"Dang, that sucks. I didn't even know you had a car."

"Yeah, I just got it two days ago for my birthday."

Shawn looked at him in amazement. "No kidding? *My* birthday was two days ago, too. I'm 7-1-01, how bout you?"

"7-1-02. Ya got me by one year." Bobby said, smiling.

"That's still super crazy, bro. Ay, we need to get together some time. I ain't playing league ball this summer, but I'll definitely be down to get some more work in with you. Or even just kick it, if you down with it."

"That sounds good to me, man. I still got your number." Bobby said.

"Bet, bro. Well, hey, once you fill out everything on the form, just holler at me. I'm gonna be over here with boss man." Shawn said, as he walked back over to Courtland.

"Will do. Thanks, Shawn." Bobby replied.

Lucky for Bobby, the nail was not in the tire's wall. Instead, it was right in the center. Shawn and his fellow worker promptly took out the nail and patched the whole that it created. The whole thing only cost Bobby fifteen bucks, which was extremely better than the $175 it would have costed him for a new tire. As he left, he thanked Shawn again, telling him that he would, for sure, be hitting him up soon. And so it was, the two greatest ballplayers in the state of Oklahoma were getting ready to become good friends. It turns out, *some* detours are really just destiny in disguise.

CHAPTER 9:

GOOD COMPANY

Exactly a week later, on Tuesday, July 10th, Bobby played again in his summer league. This time though, he traveled south all the way to Moore. It was a doubleheader that had been scheduled for 2 o'clock and then five. In the first game, Bobby continued his great play, going a dazzling 4-for-4 with 5 RBI. One particular hit, though, stood out above the other three. It was his second at-bat of the day. The pitcher, a righty that stood about 6'3", looked in and got the signal from his catcher, who then gave him the sign for slider. Usually, breaking pitches like this, in a right-on-right situation, proved detrimental to the batter up at the plate. If the pitcher had solid offspeed stuff, the hitter was in for a tough day. But Bobby was not your average player. In truth, he actually liked sliders more than any other pitch. So, when the guy threw him the 80-miles-per-hour offering, Bobby crushed it in the air to the opposite field. The baseball ended up striking the rounded top of the right field foul pole. The *very* top! This means that he had run out of margin for error. Any higher, the umpire would have most likely called it foul. To the right, everyone would have known it to be out of play as well. And to the left or below, well, it still would have been impressive, but everyone had already witnessed someone do that before. Bobby, once again, did something that no one had ever seen. After gazing at such a remarkable occurrence, everyone's eyes immediately looked at Bobby rounding the bases. The sun glistened through his white jersey and baseball pants, giving him an appearance that was as close to surreal as you can get. With each stride, he was admired by all who paid the price of admission. When Bobby touched home, he pointed up to the sky to give thanks to his Creator. Then, he quickly went inside the dugout to put on his catcher's gear. For him, what he did was casual. Sure, he was pumped about hitting a bomb, and he understood the rarity of how he accomplished it. But he had already moved on to what was in front of him and his team. Everyone else in the park could not do such a thing, however. Going forward, with each play, people carefully watched Bobby to see what amazing thing he would do next. For, they knew that inside of him was something great and once-in-a-lifetime.

In the second game of the header, Bobby focused more on defense. Before the first inning, he notified each of his pitchers that he wanted to work on back picks to both first and second base. They agreed to switch up their looks for him so that, with whatever number of looks they gave, Bobby would know the play was on. Of course, the pitchers made sure to relay the information to the infielders as well, or else, Bobby would have been throwing the ball straight into the outfield due to no one covering the bags. Nonetheless, everyone understood what was going on. By the end of the game, Bobby had thrown out *three* runners on back picks – one at each base. The ones at first and second were intentional. The pitcher had given his looks, and Bobby proceeded to throw darts to first and second after the pitches were thrown. Yet, the play at third was different. No play was on. Instead, the baserunner was simply being overzealous. He was the quickest guy on their team and was used to always getting huge secondary leads from third (in anticipation of a passed ball). In this instance though, while shuffling to achieve his large lead, he slipped and fell as the pitch was being delivered. Bobby noticed him right away out of the corner of his eye. The runner tried to quickly get up and go back to third, but he was, as they call it, dead meat. Bobby had already received the pitch, hopped up from his squat, and thrown a rocket to the third baseman's chest. Three successful back picks. Yeah, it was summer ball, where players usually played a lot less cautious, but it was still an impressive statistic. Oh, and at the plate that game, he went 4-for-4 again – 3 doubles and a single. The guy did whatever he wanted, whenever he wanted. Witnessing his greatness was like watching a world-class thoroughbred win a mile-and-a-half race. Though you already knew it had the best odds to win, watching it happen was a sight for sore eyes. Certain athletes are just different, and Bobby had that "it" factor.

After the games, he headed right back to Spencer. The sun was finally starting to set, which meant that he could soon flip on his headlights. If you are familiar with cars from the 1990s, you know that many of them had headlights that blended into hood like they were hidden. When they were needed, though, they opened up in a way that made the car look like it had eyes. This was one of the things Bobby loved most about it. Not too many people still drove around in cars like his. It was vintage. Even so, before getting back home, he stopped at a local fast-food spot to grab him some dinner. He had leftovers from his mother's cooking at home but was spent from playing ball all day. He did not want to break out everything and then have to clean it all up. So, as an alternative, he got himself a bacon burger and fries, with an iced tea to drink. It cost him just eight bucks, and he got it to-go.

The time read 8:12 when Bobby finally walked through the doors of his home. After entering, he placed his food in the microwave and then went to take a quick shower. Right when he got in, he suddenly started having more withdrawals of JoJo. Anger, frustration, scorn, and passion all swelled up in him, forcing both his heart rate and blood pressure to gradually rise. Still, he did his best to get washed up. As the water steadily beat his brown skin, he succumbed to vivid memories of showering and bathing with her. Maybe it had something to do with the water, as he even thought about the first time they went swimming together, which was only about a week before she broke his heart. That day, she had on a purple-colored bathing suit that emphasized her comely figure. On her ankle was a bracelet Bobby bought for her, and it was just tight enough to stay on while she swam through the waters. Her stunning eyes and perfect smile stood out more that day, due to her hair being tied in a ponytail. And, God, her skin. Every time Bobby touched it, he felt the safety of its softness, right along with the electricity of its warmth. He vividly remembered her embrace while they were at a pool depth of about 5 feet. The scene, a waterpark full of people, as if everyone had the day marked down on their calendars. Clear water, clear skies, and clear intentions. Bobby was holding JoJo up on his back, with her legs wrapped around his torso. Her arms wrapped around his neck like she planned on never letting go of him. And every so often, her lips kissed his cheek, making him feel like he was exempt from the rules of gravity. You couldn't have convinced Bobby that the moment would not last a lifetime. It was very hard for him not to think about doing life with JoJo. Hell, if any random guy was to walk past her at the store or something, she would remain in his mind for quite a while. Soon, he'd probably tell his friends something like, "Ay, yo, I just seen one of the baddest chicks on the planet," and it wouldn't have been hyperbole. JoJo was *that* gorgeous. Ergo, Bobby had the unfortunate task of getting over someone with an elite caliber of beauty, all while still growing up in the United States of America. What an uphill battle! He had been handling everything well for a solid nine days, but this was his most challenging moment yet. For, the withdrawal caught him in his most vulnerable state and at a time completely unexpected. Still washing himself, he turned off the hot water and just let the cold rush over his body. It was out of the blue. To his surprise, though, it helped. He now focused on the intensity of his body rapidly cooling down, instead of the power of intimacy with his former girlfriend. A last-minute escape, as he tricked the body in order to relieve the mind. As you see, though, even after getting his first car, playing great on the ballfield, and enjoying new life patterns, Bobby still had a *long* way to go before reaching wholeness.

After his unique showering experience, Bobby hurried back into the kitchen to eat his meal. His food had slightly cooled down, so, he warmed it back up in the microwave. Then, he pulled up a tray and took a seat on his living room couch. As he began digging into his burger and fries, he turned on the home makeover channel. On it was a show where people renovated old houses and flipped them for a profit. Bobby never really watched anything other than sports, but he was always fascinated by the processes of houses being built. Whenever he would ride past different building projects, especially in Spencer, he would always wonder about how all the different pieces came together. Roofing. Siding. The foundation. Sod-laying. Fencing. All of it sparked the creative space in his mind and, over time, became a hidden passion of his. He never dared to tell anyone about it, though, fearing that people would think he was lame. No one would even care about his eye for residential architecture, he once thought. Everyone had associated him with baseball and popularity, so that was what conditioned his brain. Notwithstanding, it was evident that changes were beginning to happen within him.

When Bobby went to sleep that night, he had a rather interesting dream. He dreamt about renovating his own home in Dallas, Texas. He had one of the most phenomenal properties you could ever think of. His house was two stories, built out of natural earth elements, with steel buildings as its add-ons. Oh, and the front yard was outstanding: plush green grass, a great garden, and rope lighting that accented all edges. The back had a swimming pool, party area, and dance floor. And in his garage, of course, was a red Skyline, but he had his real-life ride in there, too. As cool as all of this sounds, one specific part of the land shined brightest: the baseball field. With it were metal bleachers, dugouts, field lights, bullpens, and tarping areas. In addition, right beyond the third base bleachers was an indoor hitting/pitching facility. It was interesting for this to be in the dream because, as much as Bobby thought about building houses, building his own ballfield was never something he considered. In his mind, he just played on them, while other people were in charge of building and maintaining. Yet, his love for construction and baseball finally merged together into one brilliant vision. It was one of those dreams that you wish always happened. That is, until its ending. At the conclusion, he suddenly saw JoJo, who was all-the-way naked and pointing a gun at his face (a desert eagle). Before she could pull the trigger, the scene changed. He then saw her sharpening a knife and threatening to assault him with it. Right after that, he visualized her next to his two beloved Nissans, pouring sugar inside of both gas tanks. His last vision of her was inside of the bedroom. And yes, they were having sex with each other. Right after the peak feeling, JoJo quickly pulled out a small kitchen fork from underneath her pillow. She then stabbed him at the side of his neck, instantly causing blood to gush out onto the sheets. Right then and there, the dream was over. Bobby woke up in an intense sweat, breathing very hard. Scared for his life, he looked around his room to make sure that no one was in there with him. He then flipped on his bedroom light's switch and kept it on for the next ten-to-fifteen minutes (just to be on the safe side).

For the next couple of days, Bobby continued to struggle mightily with the breakup. JoJo kept showing up in his dreams. And though he had thrown all of the pictures away, his brain perpetually recreated them. Thoughts of her would not let up, regardless of what he did. It was like an all-day downpour of rain. Just as much as it crushed his heart, it made him angry – much of it being redirected at his own self. He didn't understand how he could still be so in love with a person who did him so dirty. It was a double reality: knowing that JoJo was no good, but at the same time, desiring her more than anything in the world. He knew the girl. She was passionate about romance just as much as he was. Thus, he was aware that JoJo wasn't just redeeming time by going to yoga class or writing a novel. She wasn't taking long walks in the park, listening to wholesome music or podcasts. No, not at all. A *whole* other guy was now in her life, and she was enjoying him to the fullest. Another thing that bothered Bobby was the fact that she chose another baseball player. Terrell was great in his own right. Probably Division I or late-round draft material. But Bobby was, at just sixteen, already good enough to be playing triple-A ball and having a legitimate shot at getting a spring training invite. So yeah, it took a big swing at Bobby's ego. Little did he know, though, that JoJo never meant to keep her thing with Terrell going after that first night. She knew, going into it, that she was going to have fun with him. However, her experience far exceeded her expectations and, therefore, became something she was unwilling to give up. That is why it was so easy for her to let go of Bobby. Cold, but understandable.

On Friday morning, Shelby prepared another breakfast for her and her son. She did not know about his most recent episode, as she had made it back home around midnight, and Bobby had already fallen back asleep. When she asked him how he was doing, he told her that he was good. But she could suspect something in his tone when he said it. Most good moms are never fooled about that sort of thing. They know their children. Even so, she didn't inquire any further, as she was doing her best to trust the natural process of his healing. Anyways, after eating, she prepared his lunch for later and told him he was on his own for dinner. Right before heading out the door, she promptly put 80 bucks in his hand (three 20's and two 10's). She kissed him on the cheek and told him to not spend it all in one day. Bobby then walked her out. Along the way, he thanked her for always having his back and being positive. She told him, "Always, son," and hopped into her Hyundai. As she pulled out of the driveway, he watched her departure while leaning against his car and putting his hands in his pockets. Once she was out of sight, he stayed there for a moment and looked down. He started to think of what to do for the rest of the day. Now that he had wheels, there were so many possibilities. On a *Friday*, in the summertime? It was a high schooler's paradise. Part of Bobby resisted this realization, though. He felt the isolation of his own home drawing him in. Out of nowhere, something in his head began telling him, "You're not good enough. You don't even deserve to breathe. Your own girlfriend left you because you're worthless. No one loves you." In truth, it was an attack to steal his soul away from earth. To his credit, though, he conquered the negativity and went back in the house to get dressed. He threw on a classic white baseball jersey and orange shorts – with grey sneakers. Then, he jumped in his 240 and headed northwest for the mall.

Bobby heard his mom about not spending all his money, but he still had plenty left from his birthday. In tangible cash, there was a total of $390 in his wallet. An additional $200 was on his bank card. Good enough to at least buy a couple of things, right? When he finally made it and went inside, he immediately went to one of the cologne venders on the first floor. He had several scents already but had bought all of those ones to impress *you know who*. So, he journeyed out to get something new. Something fresh. He was never big into the extra-strong fragrances but did not like the weak stuff either. A happy medium was perfect for him, and the lady at the counter helped him find it. She gave him a sample of a toilette named "Knight Life," and he instantly knew it was the one. Despite its clever, yet cringy name, Knight Life was one of the best-selling brands on the market. It rarely ever stayed on shelves for more than a week, as its manufacturing plant was in the great city of Barcelona, Spain. The cool thing about it, though, the owners of the company were originally from Rio de Janeiro, Brazil. Many of the world's top soccer players endorsed the brand, and Bobby had the thought of one day being its first baseball representative. Silly, to many people, but very realistic and achievable in Bobby's head. With that in mind, he purchased the $120 bottle (5.7 oz) that the lady showed him and shook her hand in thanks. After spraying some of it on, he continued touring through the immaculate mall of OKC.

His next stop was the LOVER store, which was packed full of people (per usual). It sold a great range of clothing items, but its top selling category was streetwear. The kids loved it. Gamers. Skateboarders. Dancers. Athletes. Aspiring artists and creatives. LOVER had a team of designers that had cracked the code as to how to create an aesthetic to suit people from all backgrounds and styles. Bobby had not really hopped on the LOVER bandwagon yet but was interested in seeing what all the hype was about. Browsing through the different pieces, he came across this long-sleeved hockey jersey. It was dark green, with white stripes on the sleeves that encircled the forearm area. Across the front of the jersey said *INTENSE*, in a white font that was not so big, but also not small. Just perfect. Stitched above the letters, atop the left pectoral region, was a capital 'C' in bright yellow. This, of course, meant "captain." And on the back, in large white font, was *LOVER(S)* (top) *UNITE* (bottom). The jersey had previously been a top seller, but it was summer season, and people were no longer buying long sleeved items at a prolific rate. To avoid potential overstock issues, the store dropped the price from $135 to $105. This was a deal that Bobby could not refuse. For one, it fit his desired look. Two, he always wanted a jersey that wasn't basketball, football, or baseball. And lastly, he simply wanted to add another bag to his hand to walk around the mall with. Though his last motive was both typical and rather shallow, the kid was enjoying himself. And doing so at a time when everything in him wanted to sulk in unhappiness. Bobby was practicing wellness and did not even know it. A product, perhaps, of great parenting, an active lifestyle, and, above all, God's never-ending love. So, after buying the jersey, he walked out of the LOVER store with his chest out and head high.

Bobby then ran up to the food court to buy himself some lunch. He was thinkin' a turkey sub with guacamole, lettuce, and onions – lightly salted chips on the side. Yet, the popular sandwich shop that had it was also the spot with the longest line of people. He wasn't trying to wait that long, so he looked elsewhere. While doing so, he laid his eyes on the most unpleasant thing he had seen all year (yeah, even worse than his own nightmares). All the way on the opposite side of the food court sat JoJo and Terrell, sharing lunch together at one of high tables. They stuck out like a sore thumb, as many of the people around them were sitting at secluded booths. When Bobby spotted them, he paused right in his tracks and immediately felt his heart skip a beat. Yeah, he had been desperately hoping to run into her, but not like this. No, not with another guy. He accepted the moment for what it was, however. Determined to scope them out, he focused in more closely and could hear JoJo laughing at Terrell. He was telling her about one of the times where he had to, in the middle of the night, help his dad chase down a stallion who had run off with a mare. She was very entertained by the story, especially by the fact of the female horse making the male go crazy in pursuit of her. Perhaps, she was taking notes. With that, though, she was enjoying learning more about Terrell. She was fascinated about him being a country boy at heart, despite growing up in the middle of Edmond. In the past, she often imagined holding a cowboy's arm as he walked her around his ranch for the first time. Now, it was reality for her, and she had a lot to look forward to. JoJo was happy, and Bobby could clearly see it, even from a distance of about 100 feet away. Right near him, at an arm's length, was a column that stretched all the way up the mall's ceiling. He leaned against it and then folded his arms together, bags still in-hand. He kept his sights on JoJo and Terrell, and soon, his mind began plotting different courses of action. By far, the most powerful temptation he had was to walk right up on their table and strike Terrell with a right hook all the way from New York City. Bobby was not giant in stature, but he was very strong. Plus, he often shadowboxed with himself and had become quite skilled at throwing crisp punches. So, yeah, that was one option. Then, he thought about ordering a chocolate shake from the ice cream joint, just so he could rush over there and splash it all over JoJo's chest (she was wearing a white tank, with jean shorts and cowgirl boots). She was due for it, wouldn't you agree? But the last thought turned out to be the best one: leaving the food court and getting lunch from somewhere else. For about a minute, he went back and forth on which one he would choose. Great energy began developing in him, which turned out to be a mix of anger and anxiety. To manage the rush, he started taking deep breaths, just like his mom had taught him. As he inhaled, he closed his eyes and drowned out everything that was in front of him. Now, all that registered in his brain was the smell of Knight Life cologne on his neck and shirt. He held his breath for a full seven seconds. Finally, when he exhaled, he opened his eyes again. Only, he could no longer see JoJo and Terrell at their table. A group of young women, all in pink dresses and brown high heels, was now in the way of them. Bobby waited another thirty seconds just to see if they would move, but they remained still. In truth, all the girls in the group were getting ready for a bachelorette party, figuring out what they were going to eat before they began their eventful evening. They couldn't decide quickly on what to get and who was going to pay for it all. You would assume that the maid of honor was there to take care of everyone, but that's beside the point. Together, they stood there long enough to give Bobby something else to behold. And, consequently, he ended up going with option number three. He pushed himself off the column, pivoted his body around, and walked away. Moments

later, he took the escalator downstairs and exited the mall through its
far west doors. As he got into his car and buckled his seatbelt, his eyes
became filled with tears. They added together for a capacity that was
just shy of the threshold for a solid cry. Bobby looked at his reflection
in the rearview mirror to confirm his own hurt. At the same time, he
also confirmed to himself that he was being a man about it. A strong
man, at that. In his heart, he knew he was doing the right thing. He
understood the potent costs of caving to toxic masculinity, all in the
name of anger. He knew that, at the end of the day, JoJo was not
worth it. It didn't take away the sting, though. But that was *okay*.
The sting was not going to last forever. So, he then pulled himself
together, started up his car, and got the hell out of there.

The clock now read 2:45, and Bobby was going east on the I-44
highway. As he was getting off on the MLK exit, his phone started
to ring. He had upgraded the radio system the week before, so he
now had a control unit with Bluetooth and USB abilities. Through
the screen, he saw Shawn's name and number appear. Pulling up to
the light, which was yellow and about to turn red, he answered the
phone.

"What's up, Shawn? How are you, man?"

"I can't call it! Got off a little early today, so you know I'm all the
way ready to kick it now! How you been, though, my guy?" Shawn
asked.

"I been alright, bro. Out here, ya know, just doin' my best." Bobby replied.

Shawn had no clue of what "doin' my best" really meant, but he
could sense that Bobby was going through something personal. It
almost made him leave the conversation there, but he *really* wanted
to see what he was up to.

"Well, that's all we can do, Bobby. I know you're gonna make it
through. But listen, me, my girl, and a couple of my friends are going
up Celly's later. We already got our spot reserved and paid for. I know

it's a little last minute, but I wanted to extend the invitation to you. Whatcha say, hoss, ya got anything already goin'?"

"Naw, bro. I'm actually super free. I'd love to come." Bobby said.

"Cool. Hey, we'll all try to be there at like 7:30. We're gonna eat good and play a couple games of bowling. They got some arcade games, too, if you like playing those. But bowling is definitely the move. Tonight's like their Midnight Bowl night, so you know it's gonna be lit! You know where it's located?"

"Yeah, on the other side of Bella's, right? Bout six minutes south?"

"Yep, that's the one. Cool, bro, I'll see you tonight." Shawn said.

"See ya, bro." Bobby concluded.

After hanging up, Bobby continued traveling east on 63rd street. On his way, he stopped by Braum's to finally get his meal in. This time, he went more healthy, ordering a grilled chicken sandwich with no fries. But, he *did* have himself chocolate shake (don't reprimand him too bad, he deserved it). On a regular day, he would have gotten it to-go, but he was very hungry. In addition, now that he had a full night ahead of him, which featured another meal, he wanted to eat as early as he could. He ended up eating his food at a booth that was along the windows of the far north side of the place. As he did, he finally processed what had just happened at the mall. He was having such a good time by himself. Then, boom. There she was, once again, ruining everything. Only this time, she was actually physically present. Bobby was beginning to think that she was inescapable. That, no matter what he did, she was forever going to affect the way he lived life. But then he thought about the relief of getting away from the situation. How he had to put forth the energy and effort to flee away from her, both in his mind and in reality. Crunching on his food, he thought about how he wouldn't have been available for Shawn's call if he had gone through with one of his initial plans. He would have either been escorted out by police or ordered, by mall security, to leave and never come back. There was no winning. Yeah, it would have felt good in the moment, but it would have stained his future. Bobby was very proud of himself for executing self-control. Now, instead of going home and being angry all by himself, he was going to be enjoying a night out with friends. A day of victory. After finishing his sandwich and shake, he resumed his eastward journey back home.

At his crib, Bobby made sure that all of the chores were taken care of. He took out the trash, swept and vacuumed the floors, and straightened up the living room and kitchen. Afterwards, he hopped inside of the shower to get freshened up for his big night. This time, no withdrawals. Instead, he thought about what he was going to wear and how cool he was going to look pulling up in his new car. About how he and Shawn were gonna catch up with each other. Meeting new friends and seeing other pretty girls. Things along those lines. He was truly excited and thankful for Shawn reaching out.

Going back into his room, he stared at his bag from LOVER, and then it hit him: he could wear his new hockey jersey. In his dresser, too, were some silver shorts that went well with it. To make his outfit pop, he put on neon blue shoes with white crew socks. Bobby didn't have a haircut at the time, so he pulled on a dark grey dad hat that he had bought from the Happs bookstore. He stared at himself in the mirror to assess whether or not the outfit looked good. Even though the pieces blended together nicely, he decided not to wear them, as he was already getting hot from the thick material of the jersey. So instead, he pulled out another one of his white baseball jerseys. Only, this particular one had dark red pinstripes and no sleeves. Yeah, a cut-off baseball jersey, with *OILERS* on the front and number 42 on the back (in honor of the great Jackie Robinson). It was a jersey Shelby had bought him exactly a year prior, and he had only worn it once. Underneath, though, he wore no undershirt, so that his chiseled arms and broad shoulders could stand out. Bobby also had good, smooth skin, so if anyone could pull this look off, it was him. For bottoms, he picked light brown shorts and running shoes to match. He kept on the Happs golf hat that he originally planned on wearing. This time when he looked in the mirror, he had no doubts that it was the right selection for the night. He smiled at himself, saying, "Well, Bobby, don't *you* look handsome." Shortly after, he grabbed his keys and headed out the door.

Bobby got to Celly's at 6:59. A little early, but he always had the habit of doing so whenever he went out with friends. It was mostly because he was coming from the country, so if he ever forgot something, he could go back to grab it and still have time to spare. He didn't forget anything this time around, however, so he sat inside of his Nissan and waited for the others to arrive. About ten minutes later, Shawn pulled up in his Malibu. Lisa was in there, too, as this was the first time the two of them ever rode together in the same vehicle. Even so, Bobby saw Shawn pull in and was amazed at the allure of his car. The sun was perfectly positioned in the spot that made Shawn's car go back and forth between colors every time the angle changed. Bobby sat in admiration as he watched it consistently go from baby blue to light green. But it just so happened that there was a parking spot right next to Bobby's, and that is exactly where Shawn parked. Seeing Bobby already waiting, he rolled down his window as he pulled next to him.

"What's up, Bobby? I'm glad you made it, bro!" Shawn said to him.

"What's up, bro." Bobby said, before immediately getting to the point. "Your car is insane!"

"Thank you, man. She's my baby." Lisa then made an intentional coughing sound to get Shawn's attention. He looked at her and saw she was giving him the eye. He knew what it meant. "Okay, I'm kidding. *This* is my baby. Her name's Lisa," he said, as he gently touched her chin. He then pointed back to Bobby. "Sweetheart, this is my friend Bobby I been telling you about."

"Nice to meet you, Bobby." Lisa said to him, feeling affirmed.

"Nice to meet you, too." Bobby responded.

Lisa's beauty and femininity shocked Bobby almost as much Shawn's car did, and she had hardly said a sentence to him. He did his best to not make it obvious. At the end of the day, too, he respected Shawn and never wanted to cross him in any way. He wasn't ever planning on pulling a *Terrell*, even if it was just in his imagination. What an act of honor and love for one's neighbor. For him to turn down the thought of trying to perform the same dirty act that was done to him. Not to even say that Lisa would have even considered, for she was completely swept from her feet by her boyfriend. But it is to say, though, that Bobby was growing in courage, self-awareness, and maturity. Those minor victories were paying off and helping him become better, even in the midst of his own trauma. You gotta respect it.

After mingling for a couple of more minutes, the three of them made it inside of Celly's to acquire their reserved seating and bowling lanes. Shawn was wearing the football jersey that his girlfriend had just bought for him. She, on the other hand, wore a yellow crop top, with light blue denim jeans. For shoes, she had on all-white sneakers. Lisa was a geek, for sure, but she had a great sense of style, which was something Shawn always appreciated. Together, the two of them wore colors that were very complementary. In a way, it was a parallel to their energies and personalities. Gosh. The two of them were far from perfect, but they seemed to do everything right. And effortlessly, too. Bobby noticed this from jump, and he admired them. As much as he wanted something similar to what they had going, he looked up to Shawn for having such a quality young lady on his arm. He understood that Shawn had to have great qualities within himself in order to even attract such a person. Qualities like leadership. Accountability. Honor. Wealth. Intellect, both mental and emotional. Though Bobby was not far from these attributes, he often struggled to attain them because of his lack of a male role model. You have to remember that he was in the middle of adolescence, nearing towards its most intense stage. At times, Bobby was an emotional mess because he knew of no practical ways to cope with life's challenges. His solution was the treasury of feminine energy. Though he was not necessarily wrong for having that mechanism, the *way* he went about it was rooted in emptiness. Lust was there, too, which only made his emptiness increase. This is why he marveled at Shawn. Marvin had been a great example for his son, giving him a solid foundation. Shawn grew up knowing the responsibilities of manhood, for, he watched his own father be a man day in and day out. Having Lisa in his life was the evidence of all the wisdom Shawn had, coupled with all of the groundwork he had already put in. He was ready for something substantial because he was *taught* how to attain it. Thus, Bobby looked at him and saw the person he desired to be one day. Without a doubt, Shawn was good company.

Anyway, everyone else arrived to Celly's during the time frame of 7:20-to-7:33. Two of Lisa's friends from the debate team came – their names were Megan and Frankie (Francesca). The other three people that made it were Shawn's teammates: Eddie, Oliver, and Romeo. Once they settled in their reserved area, everyone sat and caught up with each other at the table. For a moment, Bobby felt like the odd man out, given that he was the only one who did not attend Love High (of course, Eddie had just graduated). But Frankie thought him to be handsome. She was a young girl with the blending of Puerto Rican and black. The color of champagne, or very light brown, she stood about 5'4", with the physique of a bodybuilder (she loved training). Her eyes were a green that would make you remember her face forever. All natural, too (no contacts). And lastly, her hair was long, brown, and straight. On this night, she had it in a green camouflage hair wrap. Even so, Frankie proceeded to ask Bobby to tell the group more about himself, and he gladly did. It instantly relieved him and, thus, deleted any questions he had about belonging in the group. After a while, the waiter came up to them to get their orders. Shawn and Lisa wanted to share a pepperoni pizza. The Rodrigo brothers and Eddie ordered a supreme. And Bobby, Frankie, and Megan shared a large Chicago-style all-meat. Celly's was known for having great pizza. It had the rare attribute of having vast variety without losing quality anywhere in the spectrum. What took the place over the top, though, were its entertainment provisions. Celly's had the best bowling alley in the entire metro area, and there was no debate about it. If you were to bowl one game in there, you would never want to go anyplace else. The best bowling balls. The cleanest lanes. Great spacing. Energetic music, ranging from country, hip-hop, R&B, and pop – some rock and roll was in there, too, every once in a while. But its stamp was its Midnight Bowl, which was, basically, glow in the dark bowling. Midnight Bowl was scheduled for every Friday and Saturday, from 10 p.m. to 1:30 in the morning. Shawn, Bobby, and all the others, were in for a great night.

Before their food came, the gang had a couple of warmup games. After everyone completed their meals, though, the games became a little more competitive. On one team was Shawn, Lisa, Megan, and Romeo. The other, of course, was Bobby, Oliver, Eddie, and Frankie. Eddie and Oliver were, by far, the best bowlers of the group. They had the most strikes and spares. Romeo was a solid player, too, as he had learned a from watching his big brother. Bobby and Frankie, on the other hand, were not very great. And Shawn, Lisa, and Megan were decent players. It was funny, though. Each match came down to rolls between Oliver and Romeo. And every time, Romeo rolled seven, and Oliver rolled eight. But despite the intensity of the games, everyone had a blast. There was also a relationship development during that span. While waiting their turns to bowl, Bobby and Frankie got more acquainted with one another. She told him about traveling with the debate team and her experiences in Puerto Rico, and he told her about being a life-long athlete and, check this, a DIY enthusiast. Bobby was *finally* starting to reveal more of himself. Even so, Frankie was emotionally smart and aware. She could sense the brokenness in Bobby and was almost sure that it stemmed from a prior relationship. As a result, she did her best to keep her flirting to a minimum. Very mature. Very necessary. But whenever she *did* flirt with him, he felt its power in fullness. It was like she had direct access to his heart, as Bobby could not help but be vulnerable. Luckily, though, he had come across someone who was willing to carefully cultivate his energy. And at the end of the night, they exchanged their information with each other.

Everyone left Celly's a little bit after 11:45. Most other groups stayed till about one in the morning, but a couple of hours did the crew just fine. When Shawn took Lisa back home, something beautiful happened. Walking her up to her porch, he smoothly put his arm around her. When he did, she wrapped her arms around his waist. Then, they stood still, about six or seven feet away from her front door. Lisa looked up at Shawn, still holding him.

"Thanks for picking me up tonight, Shawn."

"I got you." Shawn replied, smiling and looking into her eyes.

About 30 more seconds passed, as the two of them remained in their embrace. Then, Lisa broke the quiet.

"I'm happy you invited Bobby tonight."

"Oh yeah? Why you say so?" Shawn replied.

"Because he's probably going through a lot. A couple of my friends who go to Happs told me about one of their star baseball players getting done dirty by his girlfriend about a month ago. I got a strong feeling that Bobby is the guy they were talking about. His girl left him for a whole other guy, just out of the blue. *Oh*, and babe, guess who she left him for?" Lisa said.

"Who?"

"Terrell Brooks."

Shawn couldn't believe it.

"Terrell Brooks, the guy from Worth?" He asked.

"Yep, that's him. The one you almost fought at Bella's." Lisa confirmed.

"Wicked! I had no idea."

"Yeah, Shawn. Without knowing it, you helped Bobby tonight. And you did it by just being your *amazing* self. I'm proud of you." Lisa stated.

"Thank you, love."

"Well, sir, I better get inside. It's getting late. Call me sometime tomorrow?"

"Without a doubt. Get you some sleep tonight."

They hugged each other one last time and said their goodbyes. Once again, the two of them departed in purity and good health. When Shawn got into his car, though, he instantly thought about Bobby. He was concerned about him. Before driving off from Lisa's, he sent Bobby a text that read the following:

Hey, my brother, I am happy you tagged along with us tonight. Know that you can roll with us any time we go out and do something. We probably gonna go out to Bella's here in the near future. Either that, or we'll catch a movie at the theater off MLK and 44. I'll make sure to keep you in the loop, though. Looking forward to kickin' it with you again! Much love, bro.

Bobby didn't look at the message right away. He didn't even feel his phone vibrate, as, in that moment, he was walking inside one of the convenient stores downtown. His car's tank was just under the quarter marker, and he had enough money to fill it all the way up. After paying the store clerk 30 bucks and getting his receipt, he headed back to his car, which was on pump number ten. When he uncapped the tank and put the nozzle in, he leaned against his car and looked through his phone. He saw that Shawn had sent the message but still didn't open it. Right above Shawn's notification was a text message from an unknown number. Underneath the digits read "open attachments." At first, Bobby thought it was Frankie texting him so that he could lock her in as one of his contacts. But instead, it was something vastly different. When he clicked on the "open attachment" icon, four pictures opened up in his message thread. At first sight of them, Bobby started to feel as if his heart was failing him. He did not know why he was being haunted. Seconds later, he looked away from his phone and took in the scene of people walking and driving downtown. It was still busy, as everyone was making their rounds to go to night clubs and after-hour restaurants. Had he continued to look on, he would have spotted the same bunch of bridesmaids that he saw earlier at the mall. They were taking pictures by some of the sculptures across the street. Bobby never spotted them, though, nor would he have cared to see them. Soon, he looked back at his device to make sure he was not hallucinating. And he wasn't. Illuminating through his screen were photos of JoJo and Terrell dancing together on the rooftop of a popular spot called Q's. JoJo had on a blue dress and neon green heels, while Terrell wore khaki slacks and a white dress shirt (with a blonde bowtie). The working photographer had taken some close-ups of them. On one photo, they smiled directly into the camera, hugging each other side-by-side. On another, JoJo rested her head on Terrell's chest, as he held her by the waist, looking away to give perception of "off guard." The third shot showed JoJo fixing the rose that was clipped onto Terrell's dress shirt. But the last one was the picture that struck Bobby the hardest. It captured them in a moment of laughter. At first glance, the photo was the literal meaning of picture perfect. But in context, it was a tool for torment. Bobby almost threw his phone down in anger, but he was soon distracted by the clicking sound of the gas pump finishing. So, he then hung the nozzle back into its place and closed his gas cap. Instead of getting into his car, though, he paced back and forth for a solid minute. There was no one on pump eleven, so he had the space to walk as much as twenty feet. Once again, he brainstormed about retaliation. Only now, he had to be extremely more creative with it all since he was not in the same place as them. Q's was downtown, and only minutes away from where Bobby was, but it would have been a waste of energy. The photos were from three days prior, and, in truth, JoJo and Terrell were now cozied up at Terrell's place in Edmond. They were binge watching *Cycles*. But it soon became exhausting for Bobby to have his mind racing so quickly, and, thus, it frustrated him even more. It was a cocktail feeling of scorn, embarrassment, helplessness, and regret. At this point, being the bigger person was out of the window. After taking the high road earlier, he now wished that he would have gone through with plan A or B, instead of C. But he kept pacing. After a while, Bobby became lightheaded from getting so riled up, and to avoid passing out in the middle of a gas station, he ceased walking. He then jumped onto the trunk of his car. For the next five minutes, he sat there, bent over with his face inside of his hands, as his elbows rested on his thighs to hold him up. Who could have even sent him the photos, he thought. The area code was 918, which signified someone from northeastern Oklahoma. Hence, it ruled out both Terrell and JoJo. Well, believe it or not, it was directly from the photographer, who was a man that resided in Tahlequah. When he asked JoJo where to send the pictures, she first put down Terrell's number. But instead of writing hers down as the second, she gave him Bobby's cell number. She wanted to get to her ex in a way that left her fingerprints untraceable. At the end of the day, her goal was to show him how much time and attention her new man was giving her. It's similar to those instances where people send intimate photos, of them and their new lover, to their exes. Yeah, as far as content, this was a little more PG. But still, its intent was just as sickening. Anyhow, Bobby then reached back in his pocket for his phone. He was about to reply to the sender, which was most likely gonna be in the form of a good cussin' out. But before he could do so, something else grabbed his attention.

Spinning around into pump eleven was a classic 1965 car. Yes, it was a Malibu, and yes, it was Shawn. His tank was also low on gas, but he wanted to get Lisa home before filling up. He didn't want to leave her alone in his car that late at night. When Bobby looked up to see it was him, his countenance became a little more stable, and he then placed his phone back inside of his pocket. Shawn got out of his car and saw Bobby sitting there. After closing his door and locking it, he walked over to Bobby and greeted him.

"What's up, bro! Guess our night together ain't over just yet." Shawn said, starting to laugh. They shook hands.

"Hey, Shawn." Bobby replied, grinning but quickly regaining his look of seriousness. Shawn noticed it and put two-and-two together (based on what his girlfriend had just said to him). Still, he eased into it by asking the classic question.

"Is everything alright, man?" Shawn asked him.

Bobby started to break down. Tears filled his eyes, as he could not lie to Shawn and say everything was okay.

"No, bro."

"Well, we can talk about it if you'd like. I got your back, Bobby. I promise everything will stay between you and me."

"Sure. But go ahead and get your gas first. Take care of your business, bro." Bobby told him.

"Okay. After I fill my tank, how bout we pull our cars up to those two parking spots up there?" Shawn pointed at two parking spaces that were right in front of the store's entrance doors.

"That'll work." Bobby replied.

"Bet, see you in a minute." Shawn concluded.

Shawn went inside and paid 40 bucks to fill his car (he had to put more expensive gas in to keep his engine conditioned). When he came back out and started pumping the gas, he studied Bobby, who had jumped back onto his trunk after pulling up to the parking spot. Everything that Lisa had said to Shawn started to become so much clearer. He always knew there was an underlying reason as to why he felt so drawn to Bobby. It was deeper than just baseball. Deeper than just going out and having a good time. No, *this* was about life. Once his gas finished, he ignited his engine and pulled his Chevy right next to Bobby's Nissan. He then turned everything off and walked to the back of his car. Like his friend, he hopped onto his trunk. With few other people around, the two of them sat there in silence. Shawn was just waiting for Bobby to resume the dialogue. The moment was priceless. If you had the vantage point of someone inside of the store, you would immediately be interested as to what they were discussing. Just based on the look they gave each other, you would probably think that they were brothers. Or maybe, cousins. Either way, you would sense that a strong bond was between them. Still, after about a minute, Bobby spoke up.

"It's about my ex."

"That's a good start. Wanna tell me what happened?" Shawn replied.

Bobby then pulled his phone back out. After opening the message thread, he tossed his phone over to Shawn, very much like a think fast. Shawn was startled, as the phone traveled a good five feet in the air. He carefully caught it, though.

"Relax, man! You don't want to break your phone, do you?" Shawn added.

"After tonight, bro, I don't think I'd mind it. Check it out, though." Bobby responded.

Shawn then looked at Bobby's screen. He saw all of the pictures of JoJo and his former nemesis. He looked at each one for about seven-to-ten seconds and then handed the phone back to Bobby.

"I'm sorry, bro. That's messed up."

"It is what it is. I guess I never really had a chance. I ain't rich. I ain't got the best car. Don't got the best looks in the world. All I am is a –"

"A great person!" Shawn interrupted him. Bobby looked as if he was going to keep talking, but he could not find a response. No other male had ever called him great, except when they were talking about his athletic abilities. It affirmed him and counteracted the negative things he was about to say about himself. So, he remained quiet and listened to what else Shawn had to say.

"Bro, I know that dude in the picture. He goes to Worth, but he, himself, ain't *worth* a damn! I got into it with him at the skating rink a couple of months back. He was talking about my dead mother. What kind of person does that? Everyone in the state knows who my mom was, and he had the nerve to talk bad about her just so he could get in my head. Super wack, bro. So what I mean to say is, she downgraded. A big downgrade, too. You're miles and miles more of a better person than Terrell."

"Thanks, Shawn." Bobby said, as he paused in memory recollection. "Wait, was y'all at Bella's that night? This past spring?"

"Yeah, why?"

"Bro, I was there that night! I had just walked in and saw y'all yelling at each other. I thought you looked familiar, but we hadn't met just yet. Plus, didn't you have on a Clear jacket?"

"Yeah, I did. It's my mom's letterman."

"Got you. Unfortunately, I remember Terrell, too. Can't believe he took my girl like he did." Bobby said.

"Well, it's her loss, bro. You really dodged a bullet. I know that's easy for me to say, but for her to do you like that, the best thing you could have done was get outta there. She actually did you a favor."

Everything started to come together for Bobby. Right after Shawn spoke those words, he remembered the times when Shelby tried to get him to reach out to him. She knew that Shawn was a good influence. Now, both of them had their "aha" moments regarding one another.

"Thanks for that, bro. You're a real one." Bobby said.

"I got you, my guy. Keep pushing." Shawn replied.

Shawn and Bobby continued to sit on their cars and talk about life. If they wanted to, they could have done so for two-to-three hours. From behind them, you would have seen Shawn on the left, wearing his orange number 18 jersey. On the right was Bobby, who wore, of course, his white cut-off jersey that had the number 42 on its back. In fact, Shawn was intrigued by the jersey and eventually asked about it.

"I like that top, bro. I see you rockin' 42, is that because of Jackie?"

"You already know it, bro. If not for him, there'd be no *Bobby Bowen*." Bobby responded.

"Absolutely right. There'd be no *Shawn Clement, number one player in America*. He paved the way for us, for sure." Shawn replied.

"For sure, brodie. What about you, though? I see you sportin' 18. Any specific reason?" Bobby asked.

"*Actually*, bro, my girlfriend got this for me. But as far as the number, there definitely is some significance. My mom was only eighteen years old when she gave birth to me. I've worn the number all my life."

"That's pretty cool, man. She would be proud of you. Shoot, I'm proud of you, and I barely been around you for a couple of seconds!" Bobby said, as they started laughing together.

"I appreciate that, man. It means a lot. But I'm down to make it more than a couple of seconds if you are." Shawn then reached out his hand to shake Bobby's.

Bobby smiled. "I'm down with it, bro." He then put his hand out to meet Shawn's. And as of 1:31 in morning, on Saturday, July 14th, Shawn and Bobby formed an alliance that would prove unprecedented. They became best friends. They became *brothers*.

CHAPTER 10: ORIGINS

For the rest of the summer, Bobby and Shawn hung out with each other and got closer. Just as well, Bobby continued his great play in summer ball, and Shawn kept growing in his position at RGM. As far as Bobby's withdrawals, they did not affect him as much as they did at first. It was mostly because he was supplementing his time with his newfound friend. Yeah, he still had his moments where he thought about JoJo, and they usually occurred right when he woke up in the morning time. But he was healing. In truth, a lot of said healing came from watching Shawn and Lisa do their dating. He didn't ever mind being their third-wheel whenever they went out to Bella's, Mocha Time, or any other downtown spot. Like a student, he took down mental notes so that he could use them at a later date. As far as Frankie, he talked to her over the phone a couple of times at the beginning of August. She became a good friend of Bobby's but nothing more. They were both attracted to each other, but Bobby was honest with her about where he was. Still, though, talking to Frankie was healthy and therapeutic. Shelby had still been helping him get through it, too. They did their usual thing and had long talks over a good breakfast meal. So all of a sudden, Bobby had a new shield of protection around him, in the form of Shawn, Lisa, and Frankie. Of course, Shelby was at the center of that shield. And God was the Creator of it all.

Going back to school was a unique experience for the two boys. For Shawn, he had to walk back into the media storm. Everyone couldn't wait to resume pressuring him about whether he was going to play college ball or declare for the draft. No one really had access to him during the summer, as he was either busy working on cars or somewhere on a date with Lisa. But now he had to address all questions, even ones from his peers. Over at Happs, Bobby had to face the music as well. The entire junior and senior classes heard about what JoJo had done to him over summer. It was crazy. The guy almost hit .700 the previous year, but all people wanted to talk about was his ex-girlfriend. JoJo, of course, finished off her steamy summer with Terrell in full stride. She still had zero regrets about it all, and walked around campus like her normal, preppy self. It was about 60-40, as far as the Happs public. The 60 percent that were on Bobby's side looked at JoJo as a monster. Rumored details about what all had happened were pretty accurate. Everyone in this group thought she was disgusting and worthy of being done ten times worse. Yet, the 40 percent that had her side were admiring what she did. In their minds, they were high school students that could never be tied down to any one individual. To them, sex and relationships with another person were just inevitable. In addition, many people from this sample doubted that Bobby had been fully committed to her anyway. After all, he was the best athlete in the school and pretty damn handsome. That's a perfect mix for having *all* the girls, right? Both sides made sense in their reasonings, so you couldn't find too much fault either way. High schoolers will be high schoolers. Even so, only the people who were close to Bobby and JoJo knew the exact context of their situation.

Over time, though, as Bobby continued to be bombarded with all of the questions about his relationship, it became triggering for him. It seemed like someone was asking about JoJo every single day, even though it was just a couple of times each week. In the hallway, someone would come up and ask him, "hey, bro, you good?" Or something like, "Man, Bobby, that's messed up what JoJo did to you." Some people were flat out cruel, though. In fact, one day, in his pre-calculus class, a girl slid him a note on his desk. Exactly, it read, "*you're a worse slut than JoJo.*" The person who did it was one of Veronica Redding's friends. She had told her about the time she stole Bobby's virginity, which was only two years prior. And she was *quite* descriptive. Hence, it exposed Bobby into the light of guilt. So now, he loathed the fact that he had slept with two of the prettiest girls from his school. Because now, his reality was anything *but* pretty. Instead, it was just frustrating. People were being so rude and disrespectful to him. You may be thinking, "but what about the 60-40 split?" Yeah, that remained true. Indeed, more people had his side. But it was the weight of the other forty percent that Bobby struggled with. A lot of it was him realizing that he was the one who got himself into the situation. He was taking accountability for his actions, but who ever said that this was an easy process? Sure, Bobby was having multiple days of victory over the summer, when all he had to do was go play baseball and then come back to take care of home. And in between, he spent a lot of time with Shawn, who added great value and wisdom to his life. Only now, he had to confront the rest of the world, who was accustomed to his former self. It forced him to have a mini-identity crisis. He started thinking, "Do I really deserve better? Was JoJo justified in cheating on me with another person? Is my future *really* bright?" This was just the reality of what was going on. It was tougher than what he expected it to be.

Shawn, on the other hand, dealt with the first month of school just fine. He skillfully found a way to evade all the noise that was aimed at him. One great resource he had available was Lisa. Since they were now seniors, they would go off campus for lunch, and this became one of Shawn's lifelines. It helped him get away from all the pressure and expectations, and allowed him to continue getting to know his girl. Lisa did a phenomenal job in helping Shawn cope with duress of all his responsibilities. She, herself, was experiencing something similar, as people were trying to see where she would end up going to college. Multiple universities had offered her a full academic scholarship. In truth, she was leaning towards going to school in New York to study business. But she communicated to Shawn that she was gonna wait till the second semester to make her decision. Deep down, she hoped that Shawn got a scholarship to a school up there, too. Or if he chose to go the pro route, she wished for his major league team to have minor league affiliates in New York or very close to it. They were getting so close, and she was not yet ready for great physical distance between them. Even so, she knew that it was probable and, thus, *projected* a realistic attitude. In contrast, Shawn had no clue about where he was going to be after graduation. Quite frankly, he did not put much thought into it, either. He trusted in his abilities and remained focused on handling life moment-by-moment. It was this worry-free attitude that was at the core of all of his greatness. He trusted that God would always lead him wherever he was supposed to go. Shawn understood that the time would come where he would have to lock in on all the particulars. He just knew that the time was not now.

Fall practices started in the third week of September. At the very first practice of the year, Bobby addressed his team. Ryan stood next to him in support (he and Bobby were named captains). With all of the Chargers rounded together in a circle, Bobby gave a speech of accountability. He apologized for getting himself benched for the previous season's playoff game. "I carried the weight of it all summer, and then some," he told them. But then he made it clear that it was time to move forward together as one unit. How the team was destined to be even better than it was just five months before. Coach Dillon stood in admiration of him. It wasn't necessarily about him being a good leader, as he always knew Bobby had that quality. It was more so about Bobby no longer having JoJo around to sabotage his future. Coach could tell that his star was genuine. That he was completely focused on the mission to get his team back to the state tournament. Coach Dillon no longer questioned if he did the right thing by benching him. He was proud that he helped contribute to Bobby's character development.

Over at Love, Shawn and the Bulldogs started their redemption campaign, too. They were still bitter about losing to Lawrence. Some of the players even questioned Shawn's leadership and desire, based on the fact that he chose to sit out the summer season. But all of those ideas quickly went away, as from day one, Shawn reestablished that the team belonged to him. No one could detect any flaws in his processes. Every swing, every drill, every step he took on the field: perfection. Everyone else in the group, besides the Rodrigo brothers, had several holes in their game that needed immediate tending to. Coach Titus and his staff were as sharp as they came, but Shawn helped take all the guys to new heights. He had the ability of seeing the game from all three levels: player, coach, and spectator. So whatever the coaches tried to relay to the players, Shawn helped relay that same information in more practical methods. Coach Titus knew this and rarely ever got in Shawn's way. Hence, it was pretty clear that, without Shawn, the Bulldogs were nowhere near a top-five team in the state. If the team was a body, Shawn was its blood flow. Without him, they were dead.

Bobby and Shawn finally met up again on the 22nd day of September. That Saturday morning, they met at Claire's Corner to get some work in. If you were to be behind the cage watching them, you would have had to clean your glasses to make sure that you were seeing correctly. With each round of hitting, Bobby and Shawn hit consecutive line drives. For example, if they were doing a soft toss round of seven, Bobby would crush his seven to the left, and Shawn would strike his up the middle. In an overhand round of ten, Bobby would hit ten crisp line drives, all to the back of the netting. On Shawn's turn, he would hit his ten directly back at the L-screen. And in extended distance BP, both of them would just hit bombs to the upper corners of the cage. The beauty in watching them was seeing them do very similar things from opposite sides of the plate. With that alone, you appreciated the art of hitting a baseball. Without a doubt, Bobby and Shawn were both masters at it.

They had got up to Claire's Corner fairly early – around 8:15 that morning, and their hitting session lasted just an hour. After stretching and doing some arm maintenance, the two of them went over to Mocha Time to grab some breakfast. When they got in and sat at a booth, they ordered their usuals. Once the waiter wrote their items down and departed, Shawn and Bobby started catching up.

"So, man, how everything been going at Happs?" Shawn asked him.

"Oh, it's been alright. It's a little weird because everyone been in my ear about the whole JoJo thing. People love being in other people's business, I swear." Bobby responded.

"I hear that, bro." Shawn said, with a slight grin. "Do you be seein' her a lot?"

"Who, JoJo?" Bobby asked.

"Yeah."

"I mean, I seen her a couple of times going down the hallway between classes." He paused for a moment like he was preparing to admit something. He initially debated on whether to tell Shawn, but he knew that he could be trusted. His advice always came in clutch, and he expected nothing less. Thus, he continued. "Shawn, the girl is *finer* than she was when I was dating her. One day, I had to walk outside into the school's parking lot, or else, I was going to walk right up to her and ask how she was doing. But I didn't even care how she was doing. I knew, for sure, that she been with that dude Terrell. All I wanted to do was look at her up close again. I just wanted to take in how beautiful she is. To take in what used to be mine."

Shawn paused for a moment, himself. He didn't want to make Bobby feel bad for admitting where he was. After all, that type of thing is what led them to becoming best friends. He then figured out was he was going to say.

"Well, bro. First, I'll just say this: *that's tough*. You were with her for a good seven months. Y'all were tight. It's natural to feel that draw when you see her, especially since she is so pretty. But also, man, it's just another form of withdrawal. Think about it. The last time you saw her was that day we went to Celly's, right?"

"Yeah." Bobby responded.

"And you hadn't seen her since. Instead, you was kickin' it with me, Lisa, and the rest of the crew. Playin' ball. Drivin' your new car around the city. You been living, man. But now that you back in school, you're also under the same roof of your ex. That distance is not as far anymore. Therefore, my brother, *you* are being triggered by the fact that you were once close to her. For a long time, there was no boundary of separation. Now, that boundary is larger than you ever imagined. Bro, that's just the way it's gotta be going forward." Shawn said.

"Makes sense. How you get all this wisdom, ain't you only seventeen?"

They both laughed.

"We all live and learn, brother. Ain't that why we here? To learn from each other?" Shawn said to him.

"You're right, man." Bobby said.

Their food was soon brought to their table. After hearing Shawn speak, Bobby felt like the weight of the world was lifted off of his shoulders. He had a lot of buried things that he needed to get off of his chest. About a full month's worth, to be exact. But Shawn was more than happy to help him. Both of them were an only child, which may have been another reason why they were so fascinated with each other's company. Also, they both had great parents in their lives. Whenever Shawn visited Bobby's crib, Shelby made him feel like he was at his second home. He turned out to be an even better person than she expected. She hoped and prayed that Shawn would stay in Bobby's life for a long time. It was like his presence was helping restore time that Bobby had wasted with JoJo. On the flip side, too, whenever Bobby visited Shawn's spot in the Village,

Alicia and Marvin took him in with open arms. Marvin ended up playing a huge role in Bobby's life. He was the very first up-close example he had of a black man masterfully taking care of his family. Bobby had never even been in the presence of a black man who had over 100,000 dollars to his name. Marvin had over *$50 million*. It didn't make sense to Bobby at first, because the Clement home was not a house that just screamed, "a millionaire owns this." Now, it did have the appearance of about $300,000-to-$450,000. Marvin ensured that his family experienced luxury. But it was the way he stewarded it all. Bobby had no clue that a black man could even reach that level of success and stewardship. And when he learned that Alicia was a millionaire painter, he was overwhelmed even more (in a good way). It was like he had walked through the doors of a gate that no one else in the world had access to. He felt fortunate. He felt *blessed*.

About two months later, Shawn invited Bobby over for a dinner at his place. The date was now Friday, November 16th, 2018. Marvin had planned on cooking a big dinner that night, but he got hung up at work later than he wanted to. And Alicia's day was not any easier, either. She had a couple of international agents fly in to view one of her proposals. One of them flew all the way from London. The other, from Rome. Alicia was planning on hosting a great exhibit in Shawnee but needed the experience and leadership of people who were marketing giants. The fact that Alicia was one of the top-grossing artists was not enough to draw thousands of people, especially since other people's art was going to be on display as well. While meeting, they, too, ran long. So yeah, Alicia was hung up as well. Bobby and Shawn both had baseball practice after school. Shawn's lasted a little longer than desired, while Bobby's was shorter than anticipated. It was perfect for Bobby, though, because he now had time to run back home and get cleaned up. His trip to the Village would take about 25 minutes. Shawn was not really worried, either, as all he had to do was go home and prepare for the rest of the night. He also invited Lisa and Brooks Lynn (his buddy from MLK, who was now a freshman center fielder at a college in Guthrie).

On Marvin's way home, he gave Alicia a call. The clock now read 6:45. She had just made it to their house and was in their bedroom undressing. When she saw her phone light up, she quickly answered.

"What's up, honey? You all good?"

"Yeah, baby, I had to run all of these metrics by our legal team today. We got several large investments this week, and we're running on a short deadline. I'm not gonna be able to cook tonight, and I know you're probably tired, yourself." Marvin said.

"Yeah, I'm pretty spent. Those international people were a handful. Both of them were questioning my decision about doing it in Shawnee. To them, OKC is a much better play, but I told them that it will be for the advancement of Shawnee's art community. Babe, there are some really great creatives over there. I just want to increase access. That can't happen if cash flow and event space are both limited to one area! Gosh." Alicia said.

"Hey, I thought *I* was the economist in the relationship?" Marvin said, laughing.

"Oh, shut up!" Alicia said, chuckling. "Anyway, are you gonna get something on the way home? Shawn's got Lisa and two other friends coming, so whatever you get, just make sure you get enough."

"I'm actually still close to Celly's. How bout pizza? I mean, how can you go wrong with a pizza night?"

"That's perfect! Just get a good variety. Not everyone is strictly pepperoni like you, *dear*." She said to her husband.

Marvin laughed. "I hear you, babe. I'm gonna run over there real quick. See you in about thirty minutes?"

"Sounds like a plan, Stan."

"You're so goofy. Love you." He said, both of them laughing.

"Love you too, baby!" Alicia concluded.

Once 7 o'clock hit, Shawn's company started to roll through. Of course, Lisa was the first one to make it, as she was the one who lived the closest. She got there at 7:02. Then, Brooks stepped in at about 7:07. And finally, Bobby walked in at 7:17. Shawn greeted all of them at the front door, while Alicia was still getting cleaned up upstairs. So, if anyone was going to be smelling less than fresh, it was gonna be Marvin. But he had a pass, as he was the one bringin' home dinner. There just wasn't enough time left to go around. Plus, all he did was sit in an office all day, and he barely even had any sweat underneath his armpits. He was going to be okay. Even so, he finally walked through the doors of his home at 7:29. When he did, all the kids were inside of the living room watching Cycles. Bobby was slightly triggered at first, since that was the show JoJo had long been wanting to watch with him. Yet, once the show started, he actually liked its content. It was about a group of teenagers growing up in Detroit, Michigan and was rated number three on the app they were using. But anyway, all their attention went to Marvin after he entered. Alicia was already in the kitchen preparing plates and pulling trays out. Shawn got up to go help her with everything, as he soon brought each of his friends a tray and drinking cups. Then, he sat back down in his spot on the couch.

Marvin brought home a total of six large pizzas: 2 supreme, 2 cheese, and 2 pepperoni. Everyone pretty much had pieces of each one, besides, of course, Marvin. They had a great time socializing together, though. Marvin and Alicia poked a little fun at their son, giving his friends a little glimpse of what he was like at home. Lisa really enjoyed this. Brooks and Bobby made mention of that one day at the Journeymen game when Shawn and Bobby first met, all the way back in April. In addition, they also talked about winter and summer league baseball. And together, Shawn and Lisa talked about their journey so far as a pair and their plans going forward. Excitement and enthusiasm bubbled through the room, and it was a great thing to behold. But somewhere in the middle of all the mingling, Marvin realized that the clock had struck eight. He then told his son to turn on the channel 33 news. When he did, the exact time was 8:04. On the television screen, the news anchors were reporting a story about a fatal event that happened earlier that day, a little after noon o'clock.

"A man is dead today after being thrown off of the ninth floor of a Midwest City hotel. Witnesses say that there was a big altercation in the middle of the hallway, which ultimately continued behind closed doors. Moments later, they heard windows breaking and someone screaming very loudly. And seconds afterwards, they found a man on the ground unconscious. Emergency medics claimed that his heart stopped beating just seconds after they arrived. Several people alleged that the man who killed him immediately fled the scene in a white minivan with black rims. If you see such a vehicle in the area, or have any knowledge on the whereabouts of the suspect, please contact the number on the screen."

Everyone in the Clement living room looked at each other in sheer shock. It was the first time in a while that anyone in Oklahoma had died in such a manner. Shawn immediately switched the channel over to sports, while everyone continued to process the news they just heard. All of them checked their social media sites to make sure that the person was not someone they knew. Yet, they detected zero sad posts with the deceased person tagged in them. The news did not release the man's name because he had no identification cards on him. He didn't even have a wallet in his pocket that would hold such items. Workers at the hotel's lobby told the police which car the man was driving, but it turned out to be stolen. They also gave the information of the name booked under room 932, but it was a false ID. It appeared to be that he was a suspect on the run from law enforcement. Regardless, it was one of the strangest murder cases to ever happen in the area. A true mystery.

No one ever found out, but the real name of the person who died was Jack Foreman. His parents were Henry and LeAnne Foreman, who were originally from the state of Maine. Henry moved down to Oklahoma in 1973 to capitalize on the availability of oil & gas jobs. His wife was a licensed therapist and made the transition smoothly. Just two years after settling in OKC, though, they gave birth to Jack. Growing up as a kid, he was really into science and technology. In elementary school, he proved to be one of the most advanced students in the entire district, and in 1985, when he was supposed to be in fourth grade, his school bumped him up to fifth. Even then, Jack remained at the top of his class. Going into middle school, though, he started to get involved with the wrong crowd. He was used to being bullied by other kids who were considerably less smart than him. But one group of young boys stood up for him and took him in. The group was known as the Active. When you first hear the name, you do not necessarily think about anything negative. Instead, you might be thinking about people going to the gym or putting forth their best efforts in life to achieve health. But "Active" was just a code term. The members, called Activists, were actually a collection of OKC's most dangerous criminals. And yeah, they started off as early as thirteen and fourteen. Jack unintentionally found himself right in the midst of them. They were the first faction that ever accepted him for who he was. He just had no clue that they were about to change him forever. When he got to high school and started maturing into a young man, he became more heavily involved with the gang. He was also becoming more attracted to the feminine and saw that the edge he had as a gang member was something that fueled the imagination of many young girls. So instead of going home after school, he would stick around with his crew, learning how to get away with various crimes. After a while, he started to partake in them. He had a mind that learned very quickly, so it didn't take him long to pick up on things. At the age of fourteen and a half,

Jack had gone from highly respected student, to crafty criminal. In school, his academic performance took a complete 180. It was crazy because he knew how to do all of his work with ease. Only, he didn't feel like applying himself. Instead, he wanted to be in the streets – and at the houses of multiple freshmen girls while their parents were away. Eventually, these desires manifested for him. He started ditching school, staying out late, doing drugs in his own home, and sneaking girls into and out of his room. Not after too long, his parents kicked him out of the house. They were fed up, willing to give him to the cold world before allowing danger to completely infiltrate their home. At that point, Jack was just fifteen and still a freshman. Even so, Jack's partners in the Active provided him with shelter, and, shortly after, he officially dropped out of school. Fast forward ten years, he had become the Active's main leader. And he was very good at the role. Jack had developed a strong capacity to use his natural smarts as a device for selfish and illegal gains. Consequently, he and his crew took their organized crime to a new level. From 1995 to 2003, the Activists went on quite the run. They consistently got away with theft, trespassing, armed robbery, and vandalism. They stole an upwards of 25 million bucks, swiping several of the finest cars and trucks in the process. One time in 1997, Jack stole $10,000 from a casino, right before hot-wiring a guy's red Ferrari that was in the parking lot. He successfully got it to start and then mobbed around the city like a true high-roller. All of his partners were amazed at how he did it, and it was the type of thing that he did consistently. He was the one of craftiest criminals to ever walk on American soil. But all of it came to an end in the early 2000's. A large number of the members were killed, either by police, or by homeowners of the houses they broke into. 23 Activists were murdered in 2001 alone. A lot of the ones that did not die turned clean, as they knew that they had run out of time. Several of them even gave their lives to Christ and became completely new creations. But Jack was the last one who remained steadfast about upholding the Active's infamous image. He was a full-fledged addict of the hustle and never imagined the day when he would give it up. But once 2004 came, he entered into his final dance. In early December of that year, he attempted to rob a convenient store that was about fifteen minutes east of downtown. Only, he never got to the money in the register. He was interrupted by the boldness of a young black girl. Like a true coward, he shot and killed her. Then, he fled the scene. The young lady that he murdered was none other than Claire Hollins-Clement. So now, after fourteen years of running and keeping a low profile, life finally caught up with Jack Foreman. Right on the opposite side of the convenient store, where he killed Claire, was a large hotel that had ten floors. This was the same hotel that he was thrown out of. How ironic. In the same place where he took a life, his life was also taken. And it just so happened that someone released the surveillance footage of his 100-foot fall. The video immediately went viral on the internet for the whole world to see. The title: *"Man thrown off the ninth floor of an Oklahoma hotel."* It gathered 30 million views in the first ten days of publishing. God is an Avenger.

JoJo and Terrell's relationship soon began to come across bumps in the road. Terrell had been pretty busy with fall ball, which meant that he had to decrease his time spent with JoJo. This made her have flashbacks of Bobby and all the times he would be unavailable because of being on the diamond. Yet, to her credit, she developed more of an inner fortitude to deal with it. Plus, the fact that Terrell came from a rich family, and was able to offer her material things, made the process a lot more bearable. For instance, one time he apologized to her by having someone drop off a bouquet of flowers at her doorstep. Along with it was a golden 12-inch necklace. Hanging on the chain was a diamond-plated medallion, with *'JoJo'* carved out in the center. He had also left a note saying that he missed her and was looking forward to their next time together. Needless to say, she was very forgiving.

But in December, Terrell had a severe injury happen to him. While helping his dad feed the horses on their ranch, one of the *geldings*, named TT (Titanium Tent), jumped up near him and kicked out with great force. When he did, he struck Terrell in his right hip, causing him to immediately fall on the ground. But it got worse. TT got more intense after feeling himself hit his owner. Charged up even more, he wildly jumped up in the air, and upon landing, his back left foot crushed Terrell's right femur. His father was still at the water faucet when it happened, but when he heard Terrell scream, he hurried over to where he was. Seeing him hurt, he immediately called the ambulance to rush him to the hospital. Terrell ended up having to have emergency surgery to repair his blood vessels. And of course, he was going to need two more procedures to repair his hip and thigh. This ultimately meant that he was done for the upcoming season, and maybe even the next. And for his new girlfriend, it meant that she was not going to get her quality time in the way she was hoping. Instead, she now had to cater to all of Terrell's needs. You probably already know that this was something that she dreaded. She contemplated leaving him, but that would have crushed any credibility she had left in the eyes of her public. Thus, she stuck by him. But she was miserable. They both were.

When the spring of 2019 came around, Shawn and Bobby repeated the greatness that they had a year prior. Bobby and the Chargers improved to a stellar 21-3, but Shawn and his Bulldogs did them one better. 25-0. The two juggernauts ended up meeting in the state championship game. It was a back-and-forth affair. Bobby and Ryan, like usual, led the way for the Chargers, driving in five of their eight runs. But Shawn and his teammates matched them, using the long ball as a great equalizer: *two* grand slams – one in the bottom of the third and the other in the bottom of the eighth. After that, the game stayed locked at 8-8 and stretched into extra innings. Both teams were silent in the tenth. In the top of the eleventh, though, Bobby hit a solo home run to lead off the inning. Then, Ryan followed him up with a solo shot of his own. Thus, the Chargers' back-to-back homers made the score 10-8. But the next three batters all made outs. In the bottom of the eleventh, the Bulldogs responded by loading the bases with the first three hitters. You'll never guess who was the fourth batter. Okay, you did it again! Shawn was next up. On the first pitch, he took a slider for strike one. Next was a fastball that was outside. Ball one. Then, Happs' pitcher looped a slow curveball in there that caught Shawn completely by surprise. He didn't swing. Strike two. After that, Bobby signaled slider again to his battery mate. When the lefty let go of pitch, he was sure that Shawn was going to swing and miss. Out of the hand, it felt like his best pitch of the day. But Shawn made great contact with it, and the ball must have traveled 390 feet in the air. Except, it was pulled foul. Bobby then signaled slider again to double up. He must have thought that Shawn would be fooled, expecting a fastball instead. But when the pitch was thrown, Shawn swung his bat with perfect timing, hitting the ball in the air to right-center. From behind the plate, Bobby watched the ball soar into the distance. With every half-second, agony and admiration battled for his heart. For his team, he hoped that the ball would stay inside the park so that, at worst, the score would just end up tied. But he knew the look of homers when they came off the bat. And since it was his best friend that hit it, a deeper part of Bobby hoped that it would keep going beyond the boundary. And it did. In fact, when the ball crossed over the outfield fence, it appeared to be still rising. Shortly afterwards, the Bulldogs dugout erupted with energetic joy and rushed to the plate to wait for Shawn's triumphant score. Their guy had done it for them. A walk-off grand slam to win the 2019 state championship.

When the game was over, Shawn made his big announcement to the Oklahoma sports media. He informed everyone that he was declaring for the 2019 big league draft. And a month and a half later, he was drafted number one overall to Pittsburgh. Bobby did big things that summer, too, as he was invited to play a full summer of ball in a highly competitive league in California. He was going to be competing with all of the top high school talent in the country. Many of them were on the draft radar, but no one as much as Bobby. Now that Shawn had graduated and got drafted, baseball analysts now named Bobby Bowen the number one amateur player in the United States.

After his first three weeks in California, Bobby flew back to Oklahoma to celebrate his birthday at home. Shawn also celebrated his birthday, as he brought eighteen in as an official professional ballplayer. Everything had come together for him, and he wanted the same exact thing to happen to his dear friend a year later. Three days before flying up to Pennsylvania, he invited Bobby up to Claire's Corner so that they could get in one last session. It was their longest practice yet, as neither of them wanted to leave each other. Shawn had been such a light for Bobby for the past 340+ days. And on the flip side, Bobby pushed Shawn to be even greater than he already was. There was no envy between them. Just love and respect. After wrapping up in the facility, the two of them went outside to put their ball bags in their cars, which were parked right next to each other. Then, they both got in their respective driver's seats and rolled down the windows. It was time to wish each other well. Bobby started it off.

"I'm gonna miss you, man. You go up there and make some noise. Give them coaches something to think about come next spring." Bobby said.

"I got you, bro. Even though I'm gonna be in PA, never hesitate to hit me up. I got your back for life, and I mean that. Give 'em hell this summer. You only got bigger and better things ahead of you. You're up next." Shawn replied.

"Will do, man. Love you, bro. Take care of yourself up there. I'll be calling you soon."

"Sounds like a plan. Love you too, bro. Stay safe in Cali." Shawn concluded.

They then pulled out of the parking lot of Claire's Corner and went their separate ways. Bobby had a bittersweet feeling on the way home, as he was going to miss being in such a close proximity to Shawn. He wished that he still had one more year of high school, like him. In other words, he was starting to realize that time waited for no one. But he genuinely knew that their bond was unbreakable. He knew that, in due season, they would get together again.

Shawn went back home to finish getting all of his belongings packed for his flight. Marvin joked with him that he could just buy all knew stuff, since he had just signed a multi-million-dollar contract. Nonetheless, he still wanted to ease into that process as slow as possible. He had plans on being a great steward with his newly acquired wealth. Marvin was proud, as he saw Shawn sticking to his teachings. Alicia was very proud of him, too. To show him how much so, she painted a life-size image of him rounding the bases after his walk-off grand slam at state. Man, and wouldn't ya know, it was just like the one she painted of his mother. She entitled the new one *Por la Victoria 2.0*. Marvin had the brilliant idea of sending him off with *both* of the paintings. "He can hang both of them up in his new apartment in Altoona," he said to Alicia. She agreed. Before Shawn made it home, she placed both of the pieces against the headboard of his bed. When he finally arrived and went into his room, he saw them and instantly broke down crying. He then sat down on his bed and stared at them in admiration. Moments later, he looked into the sky and touched his heart, saying, "I love you, Momma." Soon, his parents came into his room, and they all shared a family hug. He thanked Alicia and complimented her work. In addition, he thanked both of them for setting him up to be such a successful young man.

About thirty minutes later, Lisa came over to wish him safe travels. Shawn heard her car pulling up and immediately ran outside to hug her. She had on a Pittsburgh jersey that had number 18 and Clement on the back. As much as Shawn was flattered by her wearing it in support of him, he was more enthralled by her scent. Hugging her, with his nose touching her shoulder, he took in what had to be the deepest inhalation of his entire life. Lisa held him tightly, trying her best not to cry. They separated, grabbed hands, and began a small journey on the nearest neighborhood sidewalk. Soon, Lisa began the conversation by bringing up the positives. She was full of energy.

"Okay, Shawn. The best part about it all is that NYU is only 4 hours away from where you'll be staying. That is *extremely* better than what we first thought, right?"

"Yeah, it is, babe. It worked out perfectly. I'm just happy you chose the school that was best for *you*. I got no doubts that you'll kill it up there."

"Thanks, *darlin'*. But you know I'm gonna be visiting you all the time, right?" Lisa said.

"Oh, no. *I'm* gonna be coming to you! You're gonna be *way* busier throughout the week than I will. Plus, you'll have homework and other stuff you'll wanna do on the weekends. Lisa, I want you to enjoy your college experience. We'll have our time when it's due." Shawn added.

"I guess you're right. How bout this, though? On fall break, I'll come visit you. That way, I'll be completely free, and you'll have no excuses to convince me of doing something different. Is that okay, *sir*?" They both started laughing.

"Yeah. That sounds like a plan."

They then had about twenty seconds of silence, as they continued their romantic, yet bittersweet walk. Then, Shawn spoke again.

"I'm gonna miss you so much. Like, I don't even know how to put it into words." He said.

"Maybe this is what you mean." Lisa responded, as she let go off his hand and stepped directly in front of him, face-to-face. She then inched in closer, and he closed the rest of the distance. Right then and there, Shawn and Lisa shared their very first kiss, and it lasted for a duration of fifteen seconds. While holding it, a small tear rolled down Lisa's cheek. She then pulled away from him and looked into his soul.

"I'm gonna miss you, too." Lisa said.

The couple kept walking around the neighborhood for about another nine minutes or so. When they got back, Lisa hurried in to give hugs to both of Shawn's parents, and right after, hugged Shawn one last time. She then proceeded to head back to her home.

Back in Spencer, Shelby and Bobby sat in the living room of their home, talking about how California had been to him. He told her that it had been fun and that most of the guys were pretty cool. Then, she brought up the inevitable.

"Bobby, you better be staying away from them girls over there. I'm not naïve." Shelby said.

"Ma, I been solo dolo for over a year now. I ain't bout to let no chick get in my way like that again. Trust me, I learned my lesson. Plus, doing something like that would be so dangerous and stupid!"

Bobby said this while feeling slightly convicted, though. About a week before, he met this girl named Carly, who was from SoCal. Same age as Bobby, too, and perhaps, one of the *finest* girls he had ever come across (she was a model). They were at the mall when they met and had a nice fifteen-minute talk right outside of one of the fashion stores. But at the conclusion of the conversation, the girl invited him to leave with her and do, well, you know what. It took everything in Bobby to say no, as her physical appearance inspired every ounce of his existence. To him, she was like a campfire on a very chilly night: he didn't want to depart. But, to his credit, he did just that. When he denied her, she walked away with an attitude, aggravated that Bobby had the nerve to actually reject her. That was something that rarely ever happened to her. But *that day*, she had a piece of humble pie. Anyhow, when Shelby brought this up to him, he also felt it as confirmation to continue to stand his ground when it came to females. They continued talking.

"I just want the best for you, Bobby. Temptation is real. But at the end of the day, I'm proud of you for how far you've come. You are headed for something that is so much bigger than yourself. Bigger than baseball, even. Many people are going to be inspired by you, all because you persevered and kept working in the midst of great adversity."

"Yeah, I hear you. I can feel it, too. Whenever I see those kids looking up to me, I feel the responsibility of not letting them down. With that, too, I know how easy it is to do just that. It's always easy to do things wrong." Bobby replied.

"Absolutely right, son. But just because it's hard, that doesn't mean it's impossible. Always remember this: the best things in life come with hard work, dedication, and the refusal to give up. What's yours will always be yours, as long as you uphold your integrity and do right by God. If you do that, son, there is nothing in the world that you can't achieve. You understand me?"

"Yeah, Ma. I understand you."

After their talk, they enjoyed a homecooked meal together. Shelby had whipped up some chicken and rice casserole, with green beans on the side. The two of them kept talking about life. For the first time, Bobby heard his mother's wisdom in its fullness. It was because he had deleted the sources of toxicity out of his life.

That, in turn, allowed him to embrace all of the things that were for his advancement. He was finally starting to master his rhythm of healthy living. All he needed was a little push from those who saw his potential. Some words of wisdom and acts of kindness. Some shining examples of a dream-like reality that was actually reachable. All he needed was *unconditional love.*

A week later, on Wednesday, July 10th, 2019, Shawn stepped into the box for his first professional plate appearance in Altoona. The first pitch he saw was a blazing fastball, at 97 miles per hour. It was on the inside corner for strike one. Right in that moment, Shawn knew he wasn't in high school anymore. The pitcher saw how startled he was, so he decided to double up with it. Bad mistake. Shawn had already timed up his fastball, and when he saw the second one, he hit it over the fence in left field. An opposite field home run for his first minor league hit. He ended the day going 3-4, with two RBIs.

About two hours later, over in San Diego, California, Bobby stepped in the box for his first at-bat since returning west. He, too, saw a high velocity fastball: 94 miles per hour. Like Shawn, he took it for strike one. Only, the pitcher on the mound wanted to be more traditional in his approach. Instead of going fastball again, he attempted to trick Bobby with a 85-miles-per-hour slider. No one ever saw that ball again. Literally. Bobby sent it into the trees that were directly beyond the left field fence. A leadoff home run. The statistician in the booth estimated that the ball probably traveled a distance of 515 feet. That was the longest ball ever hit in the ballpark's history. Like his friend, he finished the day going 3-4. Only, Bobby drove in four that game and also threw someone out at third base. He felt good to be back in "Cali," as Shawn called it.

One hundred and seventy-seven years earlier

In February of *1842*, a global abolitionist, by the name of Gerald K. Sullen, sat in an inn that was right in the heart of Alabama. He was continuing a westward journey to pass along some hopeful information from up north. Yet, in this moment, Gerald was filled with melancholy. His wife of nine years, Alexandria, lived in New York with their son, Harrison. For years, Gerald perpetually traveled back and forth between the US and London, in efforts of advancing the American abolition movement by working with international men who had the same end-goal. It was a job that always kept him out of the house, and Alexandria often reprimanded him about his constant absence. She argued that he was starting to dishonor his vows to her. In addition, she told him that their son rarely ever had a fatherly voice to guide him. At the time, Harrison was eleven years old, nearing the most crucial point of his boyhood development. Even then, though, he was forming some resentment about his dad. And out of that, he rebelled against his mom. Whenever Gerald would be home for a change, he would allow his son's disrespect to perpetuate, which angered Alexandria even more. She would often tell him that he cared about thousands of Negroes more than he cared about the two people that waited for him at home every night. This struck Gerald's core. But she loved him very much and would often take those words back. And at the end of it all, she couldn't deny Gerald's nobility. He *truly* felt called to helping end the slavery of black people. In fact, he was so committed to it that he was willing to give his life for it. And it almost happened that way, too.

Later on that year, in July, he finally reached his target destination of Mississippi. A couple days within doing so, he came across a group of mean men. They were a collection of plantation owners that were having a gathering at one of the town halls. People had been hearing more rumors about separating from the Union, and they were meeting together to discuss different strategies of slave retention. They had a fear that a new assembly of black people would begin issuing allegiance to the northern military. It was their absolute mission to make sure that none of them came from their properties. Anyhow, about twenty minutes into the meeting, Gerald walked in the room and interrupted them, assuming that his white skin would make him immune to any suspicion. That, somehow, they would assume that he was a slave owner himself. He thought that, since they were in such a deep part of the south, they had no clue of global abolition developments. "Surely, I'm in the clear," he thought. But that was nowhere near the case. All of the men immediately questioned Gerald about where he was from and why he came to where they were. When Gerald tried to lie to them, he did an extremely poor job. His countenance, speech, and look in his eyes did not portray blatant hatred for all people with black and brown skin. Though the men in there were shallow and immature, they were not completely senseless. They could detect someone who was the polar opposite of them. For one thing, Gerald's shoes automatically gave him away. He had on boots that were only manufactured in north Pennsylvania, which was known as one of the free states. The mean men knew that Gerald had not got them from any place that was in the south. Another thing that blew his cover was his verbiage. Gerald spent a lot of time in London and had picked up on their dialect of English. When he tried to simple his American English back down, he actually sounded even smarter. As you can see, he probably wouldn't have done well as a stage actor. Anyway, the men were not fooled. They knew he was from the north. Thus, they jumped him. They beat Gerald up so badly that he was knocked unconscious. After finishing up with him, they tossed him into a nearby cotton field and left him there to die.

Lucky for Gerald, a group of empathetic enslaved persons saw him from a distance. The sun was starting to set, so everything became a bit more dim. From afar, they thought Gerald was one of their own. Yet, as they inched closer, they realized he was a white man that was just darkened up from his own blood. Some of them were fearful that he was a former owner that had been run off by his slave workers. But one man, by the name of Donny, could sense that Gerald was a person of peace. Donny convinced all of the others to take him into one of the outbuildings and give him medical attention. They then laid him on one of the beds. It took them about thirty minutes to get him cleaned up. During that time, Gerald slowly regained his full consciousness. As they kept wrapping him, he began speaking.

"Thank all of you for doing this." Gerald said.

"Don't thank us. Thank God." A lady, by the name of Whitney, said. She was the one giving him herbs and covering his wounds.

"I suppose I have Him to thank as well." Gerald responded, with conviction. He knew that, for seven months, God had been telling him that it would soon be time to go back to New York and tend to his family. But the passion for his cause was very difficult to let go. To him, he existed for no other reason, and that made him ignore a lot of other things – his family being the most significant thing of all. However, God was patient with him and awarded him with one final task. It also helped that many of the men and women of color, that now surrounded him, were very faith-filled themselves. Anyhow, soon, Donny walked up and sat next to him.

"Now that you back to speakin', where you from, fella?" Donny asked.

"I'm from up north. New York, to be exact." Gerald responded.

"Ya don't say? What's your name then?" Donny said.

"My name is Gerald. By trade, I am a blacksmith. Yet, by Providence, I am part of the global abolitionist effort to end the unfair and unnecessary bondage of Negroes. I come in peace."

"Hell, you should've told those men up the way that you came in peace. Maybe you wouldn't have been beat to almost death. What were ya thinkin'?"

"Well, my goal was to reach all of you. I didn't necessarily do it under my desired circumstances, but I did it." Gerald then slowly sat up on the bed, grimacing in the process. He then pulled out a piece of paper from his pocket. It was a drawing of what looked like a triangle with dots at each corner. At the bottom, in the center, was an unfilled circle. Above it were the words "home base," and "hitter." Lastly, in the middle of the drawing was a dot that had the word "thrower" written underneath it. He handed the paper to Donny, who immediately started asking questions. One important thing to note also: Donny was the only other one in there that knew how to read.

"T-hro-wer? Hom-ie, Bas-ie? Fella, what is this here? Is this some escape plan that you boys done drawed up to try to get us out of here? Cause listen to me now, every time any of us had tried to do it, they ended up killin' one of us. None of us here plan on dyin' no time soon. Mister Gerald, you understand me?" Donny said.

Gerald looked Donny in his eyes and saw the passion. Seconds later, he began smiling at him. Donny almost took offense, but his confusion, as to why Gerald was smiling, kept him at bay. Moments later, Gerald explained the paper more in depth.

"That there, friend, is no escape plan. Well, at least, not in the typical sense. What you have in your hand is a diagram of a new game we have begun playing up north. It's called 'base.' Not, bas-ie, as you tried to pronounce it. Base. Ya know, like race?"

They all looked at each other in bewilderment. It caught them by complete surprise, and Donny did not like it one bit. Of the bunch, he had the most pride. He looked at Gerald intensely.

"So you're saying that ya came all the way down from New York just to show us how to play a damn game?"

"I mean, when you say it like that.." Gerald said.

Suddenly filled with great energy, Donny jumped off the bed and threw the paper on the floor. "I WON'T HAVE NONE OF IT. WHAT ABOUT US LIVING IN CHAINS IS ANYTHANG LIKE A GAME? WE'RE REALLY LIVING THIS HERE!"

"Donny, settle down, this man is not here to cause no fuss. You said it ya' self, right?" One of the other men, named Feltman, said to him.

"NAW, FELTMAN. I DON'T LIKE IT, I SAID! I AIN'T GOT TO LIKE IT! YOU LIKE LIVING UNDER A MASSA TELLING YOU HOW YOU 'SPOSED TO BREATHE THE AIR INTO YO' BODY? HOW TO CLEAN UP THE COTTON LEFT OFF HIS FIELD, JUST CAUSE HE LIKE SEEING YA SWEAT? HOW TO TAKE CARE OF HIS KIDS WHEN OUR BABIES IS OUT HERE SLAVIN' THEY LIFE AWAY? NAW, BROTHER, I DON'T GOT TO LIKE A *DAMN* THING. IT AIN'T NO GAME, MISTER GERALD!" Donny yelled.

"Donny, calm down, you gon' get Massa to come out here! You tryin' to get yo' self whipped?" Whitney urged to him.

Finally, Donny stopped his tirade. Still, though, he continued to pace back and forth as he calmed his nerves. After a while, he became aware of the depths of his hurt. He was emotionally intelligent enough to know that Gerald was not the root cause of his anger. No, it was about how his own blood, sweat, and tears were never considered valid. How God had allowed him to be in such a terrible place, all while still claiming His love and leadership over his life. It turned out that Gerald was not the only one taking exception to the Lord's recent doings. A lot of questions burned deep in Donny's heart. But he just didn't know that one of the answers was right in front of his face. Even so, Gerald finally spoke up again.

"I understand that all of you are hurting. As beat up as I am right now, it is not even a scratch in comparison to the hell that these people have put you and your families through. For that, I am truly remorseful. It's not right." Gerald said. Donny heard the sincerity in Gerald's voice, which led him to finally stop pacing. Standing still, with his arms folded, he listened closely. Gerald resumed. "With that in mind, may I now continue to explain our diagram here?"

Everyone in the room looked at Donny. Seeing them all carefully seeking out his approval, he nodded his head for Gerald to keep going.

"Okay. This, here, is a new game called base. You only need two things in the game: a stick and a ball. A stick, you can get from any tree, and a ball, you make outta anything you'd like. Just make sure it's not too hard, so no one gets hurt. Ma'am, could you please hand me back that paper?" Whitney picked the diagram up off the ground and gave it to him. He then pointed at the bottom. "See, here is where one person stands with the stick. He or she is called the *hitter*." Now, he pointed at the middle. "Right in front of this person is the player holding the ball. That person is called the *thrower*. Can anyone guess where the rest of the players are?"

"On those there corners, sir?" Feltman asked, pointing at the paper's edges.

"My dear friend, you are very correct. These players are called the fielders. And those corners you just mentioned are called bases. First, second, and third. The thrower's responsibility is to throw the ball to the hitter. And of course, the hitter, then, has the job of skillfully hitting the ball out into the field. When he or she does so, the next task is to run around the bases in order. The fielders must get the ball back to the thrower in order to keep the runner from advancing and eventually reaching home base. Whenever that happens, the game's first score occurs. Y'all all followin'?"

Gerald then continued explaining the rest of the primitive rules of the great game. In the end, Donny and all of the others were actually intrigued by the idea of it. They now had something else to do out in the field besides work. It was something that they could call their very own and not be bothered about it. Donny apologized to Gerald for getting so revved up, and Gerald received it in full understanding. Shortly after, they finished aiding Gerald's injuries and allowed him to sleep there that night. They promised to guard him, just in case the mean men were still on the hunt for his life. On the following morning, he departed to begin his journey back to New York. When Gerald K. Sullen finally made it back home, his life as an abolitionist was officially over. For the rest of his life, he worked as a blacksmith and devoted the remainder of his time to his family.

Meanwhile, Donny and his companions played the first-ever game of base(ball) in the south. The game proved to be so fun that even their owner participated in it from time to time. Many of them picked up on the game quite well. No one was as skilled as Donny, though. He was a natural. Over time, he became a master at the craft and taught as many people as possible how to successfully perform the game's movements. It made the time go by so much faster. Instead of dreading life, he now looked forward to playing base every single day. And did it for years.

Twenty-three years later, though, when the US issued the decree of freedom, Donny and his family moved up north to a state you'll never guess. Okay, you're right again. You don't have to brag about it now, you've done it throughout the entire story. But yes, he went to New York, and when he arrived, his first goal was to track down Gerald. He sought his information by asking people, "hey, ya know of a blacksmith named Gerald?" Thirty-three people told him no. But the thirty-fourth told him exactly of Gerald's whereabouts. When he found him, Gerald was so surprised to see Donny. They immediately caught up on things. Donny told him of all of the years he spent playing the game of base, while Gerald told him how his family was doing (his wife was a textile worker, and his son was now a dentist). He told Donny that he was going to have to find quality work and offered him a position as a blacksmith's apprentice. But he knew that Donny still had the strong desire to keep playing ball. So, he then gave him leads on some of the local teams that were looking for new players. Donny was 47 at that time but still well-able to play. Thus, he found a spot on a team that was just south of what is now known as Buffalo. The name of the team was the Styles. Whenever Donny was not playing ball, he worked under the leadership of Gerald, learning how to apply his lifelong work ethic into something new. Something that would finally reward him and his family in a substantial way. Donny became a damn good blacksmith, too, even better than Gerald. Around the time of Gerald realizing his apprentice passing him up, he had an even bigger realization: he was still contributing to the deletion of slavery. Though he was no longer knee-deep in the abolitionist realm, he attacked the physical and mental barriers in a different, yet practical way. In turn, Donny freed Gerald from something, too: all of the lingering guilt that was resting in his heart for de-committing from his lifelong pursuits. The enemy had tried to make him think that all his efforts were in vain and that he was especially ineffective by simply being a *family man*. But God used Donny to combat this and help him see the true value of family and leaving a legacy. And for the rest of Gerald's life, Donny was his best friend. Ten years later, though, Gerald passed away from tuberculosis. But as he was nearing death, he made sure to dedicate part of his will to Donny, which ended up being a tremendous help for him and his family. The moment Donny shed tears at Gerald's burial was the very first time he cried as a man who was free. He loved his friend and planned on making the most out of everything that he taught him.

A year after Gerald's passing, Donny got news that had traveled up from the southwest. There were new job opportunities down in Indian Territory. The area was very much so in a developing stage and needed skilled craftsmen in all realms. It was a no-brainer for Donny, especially since he now had the additional resources to make the move actually happen. Hence, in 1877, he migrated southwest to see if he could capitalize. When he finally made it, he found work almost instantly. Life was continuing to come together beautifully for him. And many of those questions in his heart finally received their answers.

Anyway, after working for about seven months in what is now known as Oklahoma, Donny decided to use his own resources to start a ball team. He put out flyers in several towns that attracted many young men who were desiring to play. By this time, base had evolved into *baseball*, and many people around the country had started playing. Many people were playing in Indian Territory, too, but only for the fun of it. There were no official teams, and Donny sought to change that. He was no longer the great player he once was, as he was nearing the age of sixty. In addition, the feeling in his hands was starting to diminish, due to many years of blacksmith tasks (and of course, 40+ years as an enslaved man). As you know, in baseball, once the hands go, it's pretty much over at that point. *But*, Donny knew the ins and outs of the game like no one else, and because of that, he decided to become a manager. Thus, he founded a team that was called the Skillsmen of Indian Territory. He had jerseys made that said *SKILLS* across the chest. No numbers were on the back, of course, as that did not become a thing until the 1920's. Even so, Donny was able to find the very best talent that Indian Territory had to offer. His team was very diverse as well, having men that were of Native American, African American, Asian American, and Mexican American backgrounds. The Skillsmen played teams from all over the region: Texas, Missouri, Kansas, Arkansas. It didn't matter. They rarely ever loss, and when they did, it was not by much.

So, the Skillsmen were the premier team in the area for several years. By 1900, they had begun barnstorming all across the country and often played against major league teams. During the team's very first national campaign, it featured two distinct players: Anthony Hollins and Teddy Bowen. Anthony played center, while Teddy played third base. Both of them were righty throwers and switch-hitters at the plate. Together, they were the most fantastic one-two punch that anyone had ever seen. Crisp, powerful swings. Cannons for arms. Very quick feet and hands. Great baseball IQ. Phenomenal hand-eye coordination. They both were the full package. In today's world, they'd be known as five-tool players. They were so great that, in 1905, they were invited up to Detroit for a major league tryout. Only, the scouts never intended on signing them because of the color of their skin. They just wanted to see if two black men from Oklahoma could really outclass the so-called best players in the entire world. In the workout, they proved that they could do just that and possibly do even greater than anyone ever thought. However, neither of them ever got the chance. Thus, they returned back to Oklahoma and resumed playing for the Skillsmen. No big league team ever got in touch with them again. Even so, the two of them never ceased to play the game with a great attitude and constant effort. They never became bitter about not making it to the majors. Instead, they passed down the love of the game to their children. Fast forward a century and change, their great-great-grandsons, Shawn Clement and Bobby Bowen, continued living out that same love for the beautiful game of baseball. And just like them, they were the *very best* in the land.

www.ingramcontent.com/pod-product-compliance
Lightning Source LLC
Chambersburg PA
CBHW031939240626
47153CB00003B/790